A
Beautiful Blue Death

A Beautiful Blue Death

"A *Beautiful Blue Death* makes for excellent reading with nary a false note, presenting a world fully realized and confidently rendered. It will delight readers who are in for an old-fashioned murder mystery complete with the razor logic of our man Lenox. Homicide by poison—how wonderful is that!"

—Robert Olmstead, author of *Coal Black Horse*

"A delightful throwback to more traditionally bent tales, and I can't wait to see what happens next with nobleman detective Charles Lenox and his lovely sidekick, Lady Jane."

—Sarah Weinman, *Confessions of an Idiosyncratic Mind*

"What a delight this book is! I sat in front of the fireplace and thoroughly enjoyed meeting Charles Lenox and the lovely Lady Jane. Charles Finch brings early Victorian England right into our homes, peppered with cucumber sandwiches and bodies."

—Louise Penny, author of *Still Life*

"The story is pleasantly old-fashioned and diverting . . . with a complicated puzzle to fathom out and a period setting calculated to appeal to fans of that other great Victorian sleuth, Sherlock Holmes."

—*Denver Post*

"Enjoyable from the first page . . . The mystery is a satisfying puzzle and the characters and tone make this book exceedingly pleasant to read, preferably with a cup of tea at hand." —*Mystery Scene* magazine

"Readers who appreciate refinement and elegance will find it very much to their liking." —*The Tampa Tribune*

A

Beautiful Blue Death

———⋅⋈⋅———

Charles Finch

St. Martin's Minotaur 🐂 New York

This is a work of fiction. All of the characters, organizations, and events portrayed in this novel are either products of the author's imagination or are used fictitiously.

www.minotaurbooks.com

Library of Congress Cataloging-in-Publication Data

Finch, Charles (Charles B.)
    A beautiful blue death / Charles Finch
        p. cm. — (First chronicle of Charles Lenox)
    ISBN-13: 978-0-312-38607-8
    ISBN-10: 0-312-38607-9
    1. London (England)—Fiction.   I. Title.

    PS3606.I526 B43 2007
    813'.6—dc22

                            2007011273

10   9   8   7   6   5

To my mother

Acknowledgments

I'm deeply grateful for the help of the following people: Kate Lee, Charles Spicer, Ben Sevier, Jen Crawford, Angela Finch, Charles Finch, Stephen Finch, Sam Truitt, Alex Truitt, Louise Crelly, Harriet Bloomstein, Sam Kusack, Alastair Kusack, Eve Stern, Ben Reiter, Rachel Blitzer, Matt McCarthy, John Phillips, Robin Crawford, Craig Thorn, Frank Turner, and the entire group at Oxford.

And in particular John Hill, Roseanna Hill, Julia Hill, Henry Hill, and Isabelle Hill; my father, who has given me a tremendous amount of support; and my grandmother, who gave me a place to write the book, the confidence to think I could, and the abiding lessons of my life.

A
Beautiful Blue Death

Chapter 1

The fateful note came just as Lenox was settling into his arm-chair after a long, tiresome day in the city. He read it slowly, handed it back to Graham, and told him to throw it away. Its contents gave him a brief moment of preoccupation, but then, with a slight frown, he picked up the evening edition of the *Standard* and asked for his tea.

It was a bitterly cold late afternoon in the winter of 1865, with snow falling softly over the cobblestones of London. The clock had just chimed five o'clock, and darkness was dropping across the city—the gas lights were on, the shops had begun to close, and busy men filled the streets, making their way home.

It was the sort of day when Lenox would have liked to sit in his library, tinkering with a few books, pulling down atlases and maps, napping by the fire, eating good things, writing notes to his friends and correspondents, and perhaps even braving the weather to walk around the block once or twice.

But alas, such a day wasn't meant to be. He had been forced to go down to the Yard, even though he had already given Inspector Exeter what he thought was a tidy narrative of the Isabel Lewes case.

It had been an interesting matter, the widely reported Marl-borough forgery—interesting, but, in the end, relatively simple. The family should never have had to call him in. It was such a characteristic failure for Exeter: lack of imagination. Lenox tried to be kind, but the inspector irritated him beyond all rea-son. What part of the man's mind forbade him from imagining that a woman, even as dignified a woman as Isabel Lewes, could commit a crime? You could be proper or you could investigate. Not both. Exeter was the sort of man who had joined the Yard partly for power and partly because of a sense of duty, but never because it was his true vocation.

Well, well, at least it was done. His bones were chilled straight through, and he had a pile of unanswered letters on his desk, but at least it was done. He scanned the headlines of the newspaper, which drooped precariously over his legs, and absentmindedly warmed his hands and feet by the large bright fire.

What bliss was there to compare to a warm fire, fresh socks, and buttered toast on a cold day! Ah, and here was his tea, and Lenox felt that at last he could banish Exeter, the Yard, and female criminals from his mind forever.

He sat in a long room on the first floor of his house. Nearest the door was a row of windows that looked out over the street he lived on, Hampden Lane. Opposite the windows was a large hearth, and in front of the hearth were a few armchairs, mostly made of red leather, where he was sitting now, and little tables piled high with books and papers. There were also two leather sofas in the middle of the room, and by the window a large oak desk. On the other two walls there were oak bookshelves that held the library he had collected over the years.

Lenox was a man of perhaps forty, with brown hair still un-touched by age. He had been lean in his youth, and now, though he weighed more, he was still a tall thin man who stood erect, though without the uncomfortably ascetic bearing of many tall thin men. He had bright cheeks, a pleasant smile, and a short beard, such as men in Parliament were wont to wear. His eyes were a clear hazel and occasionally betrayed his geniality, for they would sharpen when he was absorbed with an idea or a suspicion.

If at twenty he had been single-minded and occasionally obsessive, at forty he had mellowed and now preferred to sit in front of a warm fire, reading the newspaper with a cup of tea in his hand. He had always loved his friends and his family dearly but took more pleasure in them now. He had always loved his work but allowed himself to be diverted from it more often now. It had simply happened that he had never married, and now he was a thorough bachelor, comfortable company but set in his ways and a good deal more snug at home than in the first ambition of his youth. Lenox hadn't changed, in his own estimation; and yet of course he had, as all men do.

The tea tray sat on a small side table by his chair, next to a stack of books, several of which had fallen to the floor, where he had left them the night before. The servants had learned by now to leave his library as he left it, except for an occasional dusting. He poured a healthy cup of tea, took a large scoop of sugar and a splash of milk, and then turned his attention to the plate of toast. Graham had thoughtfully added a small cake, which was a rare treat. But then, it had been a trying day.

After several cups of tea, a few pieces of toast, and a slice of the cake, he pushed the tray away with a feeling of contentment, dropped his paper on the floor, and picked up a slim leather volume. It was a recently published edition of *The Small House at Allington*, which he was reading slowly in order to savor it. Today he would give himself two chapters: another small reward for coping with both Inspector Exeter and the fearsome weather.

Graham came in after a moment to take away the tray.

"Excuse the interruption, sir," he said, "but will there be a reply to Lady Grey's letter?"

"It's horribly cold outside, Graham."

"Indeed, sir?"

"Really horribly cold. You expect a seal to stroll by you on the street."

"Are you warm now, sir?"

"Yes, a little better. I was only thinking about the cold."

"Sir?"

Lenox sighed. "I suppose I'll have to go next door, though." There was a pause while he looked glumly into the fire.

"To Lady Grey's, sir?" said Graham.

Lenox didn't respond. He continued to look glum. Finally he said, "Yes, to Lady Grey's. I hate to do it, though."

"I'm sorry to hear that, sir," said Graham.

"It's beastly cold outside."

"It is, sir."

Lenox looked more and more glum. "Can't be helped, I expect," he said.

"No, sir."

Lenox sighed. "Will you get my things, then?"

"Of course, sir," said Graham. "Does this mean that you don't wish to reply—"

"No, no, no. That's why I'm going over."

"Very good, sir."

As the butler left, Lenox stood up and walked over to the window behind his desk. He had been looking forward to a night in by the fire, but he was being foolish, he thought. It was only a house away. He should put his boots on—they were tossed under his desk, next to an open copy of *Much Ado*—and get ready to go. They would be just about dry, he hoped. And in truth he looked forward to seeing her.

Lady Jane Grey was a childless widow of just past thirty, who lived in the next house over. She was one of his closest friends in the world. This had been the case ever since they were children in Sussex. Sir Edmund, Charles's older brother, had once been in love with Lady Jane, but that was when they were all much younger, when Charles was just out of Harrow and on his way to Oxford.

Lenox and Lady Jane were neighbors on Hampden Lane, living next to each other in a row of gray stone houses on a little slip of an alley just off of St. James's Park in the neighborhood of May-fair. As it had been for some time, Mayfair was the most presti-gious address in London—and yet he had decided to live there because it was so near St. James's, where Lenox had gone with his father when he was a child.

The park was surrounded by palaces: Buckingham Palace to the left, St. James's Palace to the right, and Westminster Palace, more commonly known as Parliament, straight ahead. Like so many parks in London it had begun life as a place for Henry VIII to shoot deer, but Charles II, whom Lenox had always been fond of as a schoolboy, had opened it to the public and had of-ten fed the ducks there himself, where he could talk with his subjects. Only thirty years ago they had changed all the canals into lakes, bred swans on the lakes, and planted beautiful willow trees. People skated there in the winter and walked through the brilliant green fields in the summer, and no matter what season it was, Lenox took a walk through it most nights—at least when he didn't have a case.

As he looked through the window of his library, Lenox could see the chimneys on Hampden Lane giving off black wisps of smoke, as his own did, and he could see that all of the houses were brightly lighted, and inside all of them tea was either on the table or had just been finished.

He stepped back from his window and told himself that he would see about the note in a few minutes. Perhaps Jane would have another cup of tea for him, at any rate. For now, he picked up the evening paper again and read with great interest, while Graham arranged his things, about the parries that Disraeli and Russell were trading back and forth; for Parliament was just back in session.

⇗ Chapter 2 ⇖

Even his meager boots, which had failed him all day long, were able to carry Lenox a distance as short as next door without his feet getting too wet. He tapped on the door, cheerfully calling out "Lady Jane!" through a side window.

Among the qualities that made Lenox perhaps the premier amateur investigator of his era was his memory. He could call up in his mind without any trouble crime scenes, people's faces, and, most easily, notes from his friends. Lady Jane's note had said:

Dearest,
Would you come over before supper, perhaps at a little past six
o'clock? Something has happened. Do come, Charles.

> *Yours, faithfully, &c.*
> *Jane*

After a moment's worry, Lenox had decided not to be alarmed. Close friends can write such notes to each other over small matters. He grew gradually more certain that it was something usual—one of her nieces was in love with the wrong man, one of her nephews had gambling debts—the sort of thing she always consulted Lenox about.

Lady Jane's butler was an enormously fat man named Kirk. He had gone into her service when Graham had gone into Lenox's, and the two butlers had been friends ever since, though Graham gave the impression that he slightly disapproved of Kirk's gluttony. At Lenox's knock, Kirk opened the door, looking graver than usual, and led him into the drawing room where Lady Jane sat, waiting alone.

She was a very pretty woman, almost pale, with dark hair, red cheeks, and red lips. Her eyes were gray and often seemed amused, but they were never cynical, and her intelligence shone out of them. She wore her usual white frock top with a gray skirt.

Her husband had been Captain Lord James Grey, Earl of Deere, and they had married when they were both twenty. Almost instantly he had died in a skirmish along the Indian border, and since then she had lived alone in London, though she paid frequent visits to her family, who lived near the Lenoxes in Sussex.

She had never remarried and was considered one of the high rulers of the best part of society. Such was the general respect for her that nobody ever so much as breathed a question about her friendship with Lenox, which was long and very close— perhaps the closest in either of their lives—but admittedly somewhat odd, given the general restrictions that governed the interaction between men and women. Lenox counted on her as the brightest and the kindest person he knew.

The drawing room was Lady Jane's equivalent of Lenox's library, and he knew its contents by heart. It was a rather wide room and also looked out over the street. The wall on the right side was covered with paintings of the countryside, and on the far end was a fireplace that reached nearly to the ceiling, with a bronze sculpture of the Duke of Wellington standing on the mantel, to the left of which there was a desk. In the middle of the room was a group of sofas, one of which, a rose-colored one, being where Lady Jane always sat.

And there she was when Lenox came in.

"Oh, Charles!" she said, standing and rushing toward him.

There was no deviant nephew, he saw immediately. Something had gone seriously wrong. He took both of her hands and led her back to the couch.

"Have you had your tea?" Lenox said.

"No, I'd forgotten," she said. "Kirk—"

She stopped speaking and looked to Charles, still gripping his hands.

"Kirk," he said, to the butler still standing at the door. "Bring us two glasses of warm brandy. Have someone come in to fix the fire, as well. And then bring us tea, with a bit of food."

"Very good, sir."

Lenox looked at Lady Jane and smiled. "It will be all right, old friend," he said.

"Oh, Charles," she said again, despairingly.

A footman came in and gave them each a small silver-handled glass. Lady Jane drank her brandy, and then drank Lenox's when he handed it to her, while the footman prodded the fire back into shape. Then she began to speak.

"It's ridiculous, I know," she said, "but I feel a bit as though I'm in shock."

"What happened, my dear?" asked Lenox.

"Do you remember a girl named Prudence Smith, Charles, a maid I used to have? We called her Prue."

He paused to think. "No, I don't," he said.

"She left about three months ago to work for George Barnard, because her fiancé is a footman in his house."

"And what's the matter with her?"

"She's dead," said Lady Jane, and took the last sip of brandy in her glass to steady her nerves.

"I'm so sorry," he said.

"I know," she said. "It's too, too awful."

"Do you have any idea of how she died?"

"Poison, I think. That's what the housemaid here says. It was she who heard the news."

"Murder?"

"Or suicide. I don't know."

"How appalling!"

"It's too much to ask—"

"Never."

"I was hoping—"

"Of course," he said.

He looked outside. He would have to begin right away. The snow was falling even harder, and it was almost dark, but he turned back to her, smiled cheerfully, and said, "I'd better go over while the trail is fresh."

She smiled through her tears, and said, "Oh, Charles, it's too good of you. Especially on a day when it's so cold."

He sat with her a few minutes longer, making small talk, trying to comfort her, and then asked Kirk for his hat. Lady Jane walked him to the door and waved goodbye as he stepped into a hansom cab and directed the driver to Bond Street.

George Barnard would dislike this, thought Lenox as he rode along. He was a man of immense personal pride, which extended equally to his finest paintings and his lowest pots and pans. A death by poison in his house would offend both his own impervious sense of order and his certainty that most of the world ran by his clock.

He was a politician—once a Member of Parliament, though more recently he had been appointed to a variety of more permanent government roles. He and Lenox were friends, or, more accurately, acquaintances who came into frequent contact. Lenox had too little personal ambition to be counted among Barnard's truest friends. And had begun with too much money.

Barnard, by contrast, had grown up in impoverished

middle-class gentility, somewhere slightly south of Manchester—a far cry from Whitehall. How he had made his money was considered a great mystery, and London society was constantly speculating about it. Some said he had made his first fortune playing on the Exchange, or even as a merchant, but if either was true he had long since thrown it off. He had arrived in London as a conservative MP but had quickly left elective government for unelected posts.

He was currently the director of the Royal Mint, a position once held by Sir Isaac Newton, which explained why he had begun to buy the physicist's possessions at recent auctions. He had done well as the mint's director, a job in which he worked hard—apparently, according to most people, because he so loved the material of his labor: namely, money.

George Barnard's single quirk was the orchid. Atop his house was a glassed-in greenroom, to which he admitted very few people and in which he tenderly cultivated his flowers, splicing their delicate hues in search of a perfect subtle shade, closely guarding the amount of water and sun each plant received. He traveled far and wide, in his rare holidays, to collect species of a commensurate rareness. The destination didn't matter to him, unless you could call some genus of orchid a destination.

Lenox could say this of him: He did not stint in his generosity in the field of his chosen passion. Whenever he went to a party, he took the lady of the house a flower of exceeding beauty and rareness, one perfectly chosen to match her temperament and sense of style. There was no lady of his own house. Barnard was a bachelor.

It was thus said that you could monitor George Barnard's social schedule by following his blossoms from address to address. Depending on whom you asked, this habit was either charming òr cloying. Lenox was neutral on the issue; though if Barnard had not been so proper, so trustworthy, so unblemished, he would have seemed to Lenox to be sinister.

～ Chapter 3 ～

By the time the cab drew to a stop, Lenox's watch had nearly ticked to seven o'clock. He had stopped at Bond Street to pick up his friend Thomas McConnell, which had put him a good deal out of his way.

As he had guessed correctly, Barnard's first decision had been to bring in a high-ranking officer from the Yard. From the other carriage in front of the house, it looked as if it might be Jenkins, a young detective. His presence wouldn't be a bad thing usually, but Lenox guessed, again correctly, that the owner of the house had told Jenkins to come alone. It was all a struggle between Barnard's impulse to keep things quiet and his impulse to exercise his authority. If Barnard had his way, there would be no doctor, no routine examination of the premises, only an imperious dictate to resolve matters, and quickly.

So it had been necessary for Lenox to bring Thomas, who was a doctor.

The house was a very large yellow one, of the kind that was sometimes called a mansion. It had a garish coat of arms over the door, which made Lenox wince every time he saw it, and each of its dozens of windows showed some light. Barnard always had a

surfeit of guests. He also threw parties by the dozen and had a famous annual ball, which wasn't far off.

Lenox stepped gingerly from the brougham, avoiding a well
of slush by the curb. He had had, just a little while before, the
happy anticipation of supper and a night in his library ahead of
him, but that loss couldn't still the tiny hum of excitement in
his mind—who knew what was inside this house, where it would
lead him, how it would end? He loved his work.

Barnard was standing on his stoop, engaged in a solemn conversation with the young detective, when he spotted Lenox and
Thomas approaching.

"Charles!" he said.

"George, how are you?" said Lenox. "I'm sorry about this
business."

"Terrible matter. Under my own roof. No end of embarrassment, you know."

"Did the girl serve upstairs?"

"Indeed she did! Only for two weeks or so, of course, or I
would have been able to spot it before it happened."

"Of course," Lenox said. Barnard was already fibbing. Hadn't
Lady Jane said that it had been three months? "I'm here because
Jane asked me to come lend a hand."

"Not necessary," Barnard said. There was a pause. "How is
Jane?"

"Well enough, I think."

"Still, not necessary. Not at all. We've got Jenkins here. Good
man." He spoke as if Jenkins weren't present.

"Have you met Thomas McConnell, George?"

"I haven't had the honor. George Barnard," he said, reaching
out his hand.

"A pleasure," said Thomas, who had met Barnard dozens of
times.

There was a brief pause; then Lenox spoke again. "Still,

George," he said, "you won't mind us having a quick look inside? To put Jane's mind at rest?"

Barnard was evidently troubled by this request and paused before he answered. He was weighing his desire to please Lady Jane, whose good graces he wanted to be in, against his annoyance with Lenox for coming. At last he said, "For Jane, yes, I suppose. But Jenkins has seen to everything already. Says we need a doctor, but I don't see why. Clear case of suicide."

"Suicide?" said Thomas.

"Suicide," Barnard said emphatically. "There's a note, plain as day. Still, go in if you wish."

"Thank you, George."

He walked into the house with Thomas and Jenkins at his side, while Barnard walked toward the grand front staircase, seemingly dismissing them from his mind. Lenox had seen this front hallway many times, at the beginnings and ends of parties, but now, for the first time, he concentrated on the small gilt door to the side, which was guaranteed to be of cheap wood on the reverse and stood beneath a vast mirror, one of the dozens of doors concealed all over the house that led downstairs to the servants' quarters.

He opened the door, and the smell of the kitchen drifted up. Barnard always served good food; you could say that for him.

When they reached the bottom of the stairs, Lenox waited for Jenkins to take the lead. But apparently he wanted first to have a word.

"It's an honor to meet you, Mr. Lenox. We've never been formally introduced."

"It's an honor for me too," Lenox said to the inspector.

Thomas stepped to the left and took a sip from a flask, while Jenkins hurried after him.

"It's down here," he said.

"I know," said Thomas. "In houses of this design the servants' bedrooms are always to the left, and the kitchen is always to the right."

Lenox smiled to himself and followed the two men.

They were walking along a clean well-lit hallway, slightly wider than Lenox had expected, with small drawings of flowers in between each set of doors. Some of the doors had small personal details—an embroidery that said SARAH, a garland pinned against a hinge. The noise from the kitchen receded behind them, but they could still hear the business of the house being conducted.

At the end of the hall, a door was slightly ajar. Thomas stopped and asked Jenkins if it was the correct room, and Jenkins answered that it was. Both men stepped back for the first time, and allowed Lenox to come forward. He put a leather glove on his right hand and opened the door.

"Why do you wear a glove?" Jenkins asked.

McConnell answered for his friend. "There's a new technology emerging—fingerprinting. Have you heard of it?"

"No."

"A chap named Herschel, magistrate in India, started to put prisoners' handprints next to their signatures. At first he did it just to scare them into being honest. But then he noticed the individuality of the fingers and decided he would focus on them rather than on the entire hand. Ingenious, really. Still rather hit-and-miss, the whole thing, but Lenox and I agree there's potential in it."

Jenkins looked at the back of his hand. "The prints from your fingers?"

"Turn your hand over," McConnell said with a smile.

"Oh," Jenkins said. "I think I see what you mean."

Lenox had by this time scanned the scene and was ready to take a closer look. In front of the three men was a modest room—altogether unremarkable, if you had seen servants' quarters before, save the fact that the body of a dead human being lay on the bed.

But first, thought Lenox, the room. He usually left the body for last, because the clues surrounding it were so much more likely to vanish in a short amount of time.

The room measured out as a perfect square, no doubt identical in shape and size to most of the other bedrooms on the hall. On the right, fitted snugly against the wall, was a narrow bed. On the left, barely leaving space to walk through the room, were a desk, a bureau, and a small seamstress's table. High on the left of the back wall there was a window of middling size.

The room was, if anything, more tidy than the house upstairs, which was strewn with the expensive debris of Barnard's life. The desk was bare except for four objects, which he would examine in a moment; the bureau was bare, though he would have to look in the drawers; the seamstress's table had a few bits of thread on it, but even those were tucked together neatly.

What did the room say about the victim? Either that she was most fastidious or that she had few possessions—more likely the latter. She was not without some personal sense of taste, however. A picture of Hyde Park was tacked above her bed, which perhaps she had bought on her half day or received from a beau. And Lenox saw, as he opened the drawers of her bureau with his handkerchief, that she maintained her clothes as well as she could. Beyond personal taste, he thought, perhaps she took some pride in herself.

Thomas and Jenkins were both standing in the doorway, and even when Lenox went to the far left corner of the room, they only peered in slightly more intently.

"Big enough for a thin man," said Jenkins, and Lenox nodded without turning.

He was referring to the medium-sized window that Lenox was inspecting, which looked out at a view of the feet walking by on the street, in an almost direct path to the wheels of his own carriage. It was, as Jenkins said, big enough to admit a man or, just as likely, to let a woman out. It was flung open. And on such a cold day.

"Probably too trampled outside to show anything. Scuff marks on the windowsill, which we should bear in mind. Don't know why they're there. It's slick and so is the floor under it, but they probably would be anyway, just from the melting snow. Jenkins," Lenox said, "have any of the servants been in here?"

"No," the young inspector said. "Mr. Barnard posted the housekeeper at the door as soon as the body was discovered. And apparently the housekeeper is something of an iron maiden."

"Do you know what an iron maiden is, sir?" Thomas asked.

Jenkins blushed and didn't answer; he addressed Lenox. "None of the servants, no, sir."

"And did Mr. Barnard tell you if he himself touched anything?"

"He said he hadn't. Only picked up the note, there, on the desk."

"I see," said Lenox.

The open window puzzled him, but no doubt it would all come clear. He stepped back into the center of the room and got on his hands and knees. There was nothing on the floors—not even dust, to speak of—under the desk or the bureau, or under the small table, or in plain sight. Except for one thing. In the middle of the room, on the floor just next to the desk, were three or four drops of something. He scratched at one with his fingernail: wax.

He thought about this for a moment, filed it away, and then thoroughly examined the space under the bed, trailing his fingers along the underside of the mattress and shining a candle against every dark corner.

So! he thought. We have only the desk and the body. He stood up and walked toward the desk.

It was a thin piece of deal, without drawers but with sturdy legs. On top of it were an empty glass, with the stain of some drink on its lip; a new candle, which had never been lighted; a small brown unmarked bottle made of glass, with a rubber stopper; and a smooth piece of paper, the suicide note.

"A suicide, on the face of it," said Jenkins.

Lenox thought for a moment. He would mention what he had seen (or rather, seen the absence of) in a few moments. He wanted to be unencumbered by Jenkins's awe or embarrassment (who could predict which) while he looked at the desk.

"Indeed," he muttered. "Indeed. . . ."

He leaned over the desk on his fists and read the note.

It is too much. Sorry, James, I am sorry.

The note was unsigned.

"Is James her fiancé?" Lenox said.

"Yes."

"He's in service here?"

"Yes."

Lenox thought for a moment and nodded. He would take the glass and the bottle home to examine.

But before anything else, he thought wearily, it was time to disillusion the young detective.

"Jenkins," he said, "you think this is a suicide?"

"It seems clear enough, sir."

"I need you to fetch James for us. But don't bring him into this room. Find a table somewhere."

"Yes, sir."

"And Jenkins—had it occurred to you that there should be a pen on this desk? Something that crossed my mind."

The inspector frowned. "A pen?" he said.

"To write the note."

"Perhaps it's in a pocket?"

"Maids' uniforms don't have pockets, a relic of the time when their omission was thought to make stealing more difficult."

Jenkins looked at the body. "And nowhere in the room?"

"No," said Lenox, trying to make his voice kind.

"But she could easily have carried the note around with her."

"I don't think so," Lenox said. "If you look at it, the paper is uncreased and unwrinkled."

Jenkins stared at the desk. "Well, perhaps she took the pen and then replaced it," he said.

"In the grip of suicide? Unlikely. There's a chance, but I'd lay odds that we find it's a murder. Someone wrote this with their own pen and left it here. Notice the small squiggly letters— probably somebody trying to hide their handwriting. Forger's tremor."

Jenkins sighed. "Yes, you're right, I imagine." Then he looked up and said, "I'll find the fiancé."

Lenox nodded. Then, thinking, he looked at the desk and the doorway until he was satisfied and turned to the bed.

"Thomas," he said. "The body."

Chapter 4

Thomas McConnell had moved to London from Scotland, where he had grown up, shortly after the conclusion of his formal medical education. He was a doctor. He opened a practice on Harley Street within six months of his arrival, advertised as a specialist in surgery, and set about making his name. This he had done quickly and impressively; he was open to new techniques, and his skill with a scalpel was surpassing. By the time he was thirty, he had one of the leading practices in all of London.

And then, when he was thirty-one, he married. More specifically, he married up—to Lady Victoria Phillips, who was nineteen at the time. McConnell was handsome, had a fair amount of money, and came from a good family. But in each of these respects, the civilized world agreed, he was infinitely inferior to Toto Phillips, who had beauty, fortune, and a name by any standard you cared to choose.

She married Thomas McConnell in the year she came out, because, her friends knew, he was different from the men of her milieu and generation. Those men had been her friends from birth, and they would always be her friends. But she could never have married any of them. Thomas was manlier, less dandy, less corrupted by money, and he had ideas: about books, about plays, about the cities of the Continent, about beauty, about her beauty, about her. Their wedding was a celebrated one, because while he had married up, he hadn't married so far up as to disqualify him from benefit. The Prime Minister— Toto's father's friend from public school—had come, along with half of Debrett's.

For the first three years, Thomas and Toto were happy. It was during this time that Lenox first met McConnell. Lady Jane was, after a fashion, Toto's mentor—they were first cousins but treated each other as aunt and niece, Toto's mother having succumbed to a fever when her daughter was only eleven. So Lenox was thrown together with the young couple a good deal. Thomas had reduced his practice, and he and his wife went out most evenings and traveled widely together. He accepted with goodwill her social schedule, and she accepted with equal goodwill their yearly visits to his family in Scotland.

But the first three years had ended, and the halcyon days of their marriage had ended with them. Thomas had all but abandoned his practice by then, and he began to drink too much. Toto had taken to spending six months of the year at Longwell, her father's estate in Kent, just outside of London, while her husband remained in the city.

There had been a further deterioration, to the point, after five years of marriage, that the couple rarely appeared in public and were said not to be on speaking terms. But something had relented—either they had given up or they had resolved to make the best of things—and they were now, aged thirty-six and twenty-four, settling into the long view of life. It could end in two ways, Lenox had always thought: either in cold politeness, or in a new, quieter kind of love. Toto was so young, and McConnell so idealistic. But perhaps they would learn to compromise. At any rate, they had seemed kinder to each other the last few times he had seen them together. Lady Jane thought so too, and she was reliable about things like that.

But there had been a casualty of the past six years. Toto was still one of the most important women in London's highest social circles, but Thomas was no longer as brilliant as he had been, in any sense of the word. He no longer performed surgery, and, perhaps more sadly, he no longer possessed the golden shine of a handsome young man with ideas and ambition. He had been through the worst of the drinking, but he still drank far too much to wield a scalpel. There had been so much money after he married Toto that he no longer needed the practice, so it had eventually been sold for a song to a young Phillips cousin. All that work, building the practice up, his own place—that, too, absorbed by his wife's family.

He now studied all sorts of minor subjects in his spare time, from chemicals to psychology. For a while now marine life had been predominant among these interests—McConnell collected samples of rare cold-weather fish and mammals, the prize of his collection being a perfect Eastern Dolphin. Every few years he took trips, sometimes dangerous ones, off the coasts of Greenland and the fjords. Upon returning he would present his findings to the Royal Academy (he was a member) and contribute his lecture to their journal.

But it wasn't medical work. The only work he did of that sort was the kind that had brought him face-to-face with the corpse of Prudence Smith. For the pleasure of it, he helped Lenox when he was asked and, though he tried not to betray it, felt an inkling of that old pleasure again, of real work, the excitement of the human mind examining the human body.

He was of middling height and weight, with curly blond hair, a face that was at the moment unshaven, and which told of his drinking. His eyes were lidded but occasionally sharp. He had been putting a golf ball across the cavernous ballroom in his house to a waiting footman when Lenox arrived to pick him up.

Now, when Lenox beckoned him toward Prue Smith's body, he roused himself out of observation and stepped in the room toward the bed.

She was, Lenox saw, almost a beautiful girl, with dark hair. He put her age at around twenty-five, a good age to marry.

McConnell leaned over her and then, before he touched her, said, "Do I need to worry about fingerprints?"

"I don't think so," Lenox said. "The process doesn't work well on bodies yet; it's too new. In fact, I think fingerprinting will be lost here—too many prints all over the place. Except for the glass, which was wiped clean. Interesting, that."

Thomas stood up.

"Do you assume, then, that the poison was what really killed her?"

Lenox thought for a moment. "If it was suicide, which I gravely doubt, it was undoubtedly poison. If it was murder, the murderer would be stupid to masquerade the death as suicide by poisoning and then kill her in another way. There wouldn't be any benefit to it."

"Unless he thought that the bottle of poison would go unquestioned."

"That's why I brought you. But I imagine you'll find it's poison."

"So do I," said Thomas. "Even so."

He pulled a pair of gloves from his breast pocket and put them on. The first part of the body that he examined was the face, which was drained of color.

"We can rule out a few of the common poisons," he said. "They would have left her blood close to the skin. She would have been flushed."

Lenox didn't respond.

Thomas unbuttoned her shirt as low as he decently could, to verify that the chest wasn't flushed either. He then lifted her shirt and prodded her stomach, without any visible effect. Next he pulled her shirt back down, licked his thumb, and drew it across her neck and her lips.

"No makeup on the neck," he said. "Or lividity—that is, bruising. She wasn't strangled. And the lips look normal."

"Would you like me to step out for a moment?" Lenox asked.

"No," McConnell said. "Not unless you feel you need to."

He then pulled her clothes off entirely, so that her body was naked except for her underclothes. He ran his hands over her ribs and looked up and down each leg. He lifted each leg to a 45-degree angle and ran his hand across the underside of her knees. Then he rolled her onto her side and examined her back.

"Puzzling," he said. "Most poisons—"

"Yes?" said Lenox.

"Never mind. I've got it."

McConnell lifted both of her arms and examined the vein at each inner elbow.

"As I thought!" he said. "Red!"

Lenox knew better than to answer. McConnell probed her body thoroughly, tested each limb for stiffness, and checked the back of her neck. Then he stood up, lifted her clothes back over her body, and removed his gloves.

"What would you like to know first, Charles?"

At this moment Jenkins reappeared in the doorway. "I've got the fiancé, James, in the kitchen. Mr. Barnard was none too pleased to have him pulled away, but I—what did you find out?" he said. "About the body?"

McConnell looked pointedly at Lenox.

"What killed her, Thomas?"

"She was neither stabbed nor strangled nor shot. She was, in fact, poisoned. She ingested the poison between twelve and one this afternoon, because she died at around two, based on the stiffness of her body, and the poison used takes a little over an hour to kill. Between one-forty-five and two, I think. She fell asleep, I believe, which would follow logic, as the poison I suspect has a pronounced sedative effect. Her body has not been moved since her death, and she was not active in the hour between ingestion of the poison and death. Otherwise, her ankles would look puffy and red."

"I see," Lenox said.

"There is one further point. She was killed by a relatively rare poison: *bella indigo*, the beautiful blue. The name is ironic: the veins in the victim's extremities, depending on their size, turn red. The idea is that to have blue veins is *bella*, or beautiful, because the fact that they haven't turned red means you'll live."

"Is it a common poison?" Lenox asked.

"On the contrary, the murderer probably used it because it's so much harder to trace than something like arsenic or strychnine. And in fact, if you will permit me a moment of theater, I have a suspicion."

Thomas pulled one of his gloves back on and walked to the desk. From his jacket pocket he extracted a miniature glass bowl and a packet of granules. It was a characteristic of McConnell's that he always had useful kits or medicines in his pockets. He placed the bowl on the desk, tapped a few grains of the powder into it, and picked up the unmarked glass bottle from the desk.

"I believe this is the poison we're meant to think killed the girl."

Lenox nodded.

"Look for the color purple. That will be *bella indigo*," he said, and tapped a drop of the liquid into the small bowl. For a moment nothing happened, and then suddenly the entire bowl was yellow.

"Just what I thought," he said. He looked at Lenox. "This is a bottle of poison. Probably arsenic or, if not, some related substance. Worth trying to trace, as you can occasionally find who bought it from the ledgers that apothecaries keep, especially if it was bought in London. But this much is certainly true: The contents of the bottle I am holding did not kill the girl on the bed."

❦ Chapter 5 ❦

I t's murder, isn't it?" said Jenkins.

"Yes," said Lenox. He walked slowly back down the hall toward the kitchen, feeling tired. It was past eight by now and he had a good deal left to do. At the least, he had to talk to the fiancé and then to Barnard. Tomorrow he would begin in earnest. This moment was never altogether pleasant: when murder was confirmed and a case truly began.

The kitchen was a very hot square room with a low wooden ceiling. It smelled heavily of starch and meat, but it was clean. On one side of the room there was a large open fire, whose flames were just beginning to die into embers. Hanging from pegs above it were cured ham, sides of beef, and baskets of onions and garlic, and other food was piled high in open cupboards all around the room. In the middle of the floor was a long wooden table, crudely made, where the food was prepared, with steam still rising from it because the maids had rinsed it with boiling water at the end of the day. Evidently Barnard was eating out. And sitting by it was a short lean man with his head in his hands, making muffled noises every now and then. Lenox stood by the table, while McConnell and Jenkins stood behind him.

"James?" said Lenox.

The man looked up with bloodshot eyes and said, "Yes, sir?"

"I'm Charles Lenox."

"Yes, sir."

"I'm very sorry for you, James. I truly am." It wasn't quite proper to shake hands, but Lenox did it anyway.

"Thank you, sir."

"Time is the only friend you have, I'm afraid."

"Yes, sir."

"I know you've had a difficult afternoon—beyond difficult, I daresay—but I'd like to ask you just a few more questions. For her sake."

"Yes, sir."

"Very well. Do you know of any reason why Miss Smith might have been unhappy recently? Had you two been quarreling?"

"Gracious, no, sir. I was with her most of the morning, sir, and she was as happy as she could be."

The footman put his head in his hands again, and Lenox sat down next to him at the table.

"Thomas," Lenox said, "may I use your flask?"

McConnell pulled a tall flask from his waistcoat.

"Have some of this, James," Lenox said.

"Sir?"

"It's gin, I believe."

James took a quick sip and then a longer sip. "Thank you, sir."

"James," said Lenox, "I will tell you the truth. There is a strong chance that Miss Smith died by someone's hand."

"Not suicide?"

"No, not suicide. In fact, between us, I'm sorry to say that it's nearly certain."

"That she was murdered?"

"Yes."

The young man bent forward over the table, and a lock of his hair fell across his forehead and into his eyes. He made fists of his hands but didn't slam them down.

"James?" said Lenox.

"Yes?"

"Can you think of any reason why this might have happened?"

The young man was still looking at the table. His black hair had tumbled out of its shape and looked wild. He had interlaced his fingers and he was twisting his thumbs.

"No," he said.

"Or anyone who might have done it?"

"No," he said.

"How long had you been engaged?"

"For four months, or near it. She came into service here to be—oh, damn it all. . . ."

Lenox paused and then offered him another sip of gin. The young man took a deep sip this time and held on to the flask.

"Who were her friends here?"

"Just me," James said. "She hated it here. Enough so she wanted to go back to Lady Grey's employment. Her friends was there."

"She disliked the other members of the staff?"

"Oh, hated 'em!"

"James, which members of the staff in particular did she have quarrels—"

"Charles," McConnell said, "if I may interject?"

"Yes," Lenox said.

"An ounce of *bella indigo* would be had cheaply at forty pounds."

James looked up at the mention of the sum. "What's forty pounds?"

"It's no matter," Lenox said. "Thank you, Thomas."

It was clear, when he looked up, that James had started crying during this interchange. He had tried to keep his head down but failed.

"You loved Miss Smith, James?" Lenox asked.

"Of course I—"

"I did not intend to question it. I'm sorry to have been indelicate."

James looked at him and began to cry again.

"Keep it together, man. Here, have another sip of gin," Lenox said, and James did as he was told. Lenox sighed. "We can always speak again later."

He placed a hand on James's shoulder and turned to go upstairs. Thomas approached the table and put two crowns in the young man's hand.

"Take a friend to the pub," he said. "A doctor's opinion." He smiled, picked up his flask, and followed Lenox upstairs.

"Forty pounds?" Lenox asked as they climbed the stairs.

"If not more."

"It would be clever of a servant to use every halfpenny he could find to buy it, I suppose, but you're probably right."

"I probably am." Thomas took the last sip of gin in the flask. "Will you drop me a note when anything happens?"

"Of course," Lenox said. "Come to dinner this week, and we'll talk it over."

"Just as you say."

They had reached the top of the stairwell, and the doctor stepped outdoors. He had forgotten his coat and came back in to retrieve it from the housekeeper. "Good luck!" he said, and went to the curb to find a cab.

Jenkins and Lenox stood in the hallway. It was a vast corridor, with the myth of Bacchus painted around its walls, and a silver punch bowl on the center table that Barnard used only at parties, insisting it had belonged to Henry V.

"Are you taking this case, sir?" said Jenkins.

"I think I shall. For an old friend."

"I hope we can work together, then. The Yard must be involved."

"It must, I suppose."

"Yes."

"But all the same, it is fortunate for the dead that you did not leave here with Barnard's verdict. I have no desire to reprimand—"

"Of course, of course, you're right," Jenkins said hastily. "But I shan't miss another trick, you may count on that."

Lenox smiled. "Then we'll have it out yet."

He was lucky to have had Jenkins on the job this evening. High-ranking but young; one of the few people from the Yard who had anything approaching a good opinion of him. No doubt it would all change tomorrow.

Barnard strolled into the front hall.

"George," said Lenox.

"Have you reached a conclusion?"

"Not quite yet. Shall we have a talk tomorrow morning?"

"Lenox, I'm a busy man, you know—"

"It is entirely necessary."

Barnard sighed in a martyred way. "Very well," he said. "Shall we have breakfast here at eight o'clock?" He looked as if Lenox were asking him to chat with Daniel while the lions built up an appetite.

"At eight," Lenox said. "And before I leave, may I have a word with your housekeeper?"

Lenox could see that Barnard was being pushed to the end of his tether, but Barnard walked over to the bell rope and pulled it. In less than a minute, a fat woman with an austere face and short gray hair, wearing a brown dress, came into the hallway.

"Mr. Barnard?" she said.

"This is Charles Lenox, and this is a man from the police. Answer their questions."

"Yes, sir."

"I'm going to my club for supper. I'm tired of this. Girl committed suicide."

"Good night, sir."

"Good night, George," Lenox said; Barnard walked out. "May I ask your name, ma'am?"

"Miss Harrison, sir."

"Very good. Miss Harrison, can you tell me who the current occupants of the house are?"

"Mr. Barnard, myself, two footmen, two upper maids, one of whom was Prudence Smith, two lower maids, a cook, a chauffeur, and a boy. In addition, Mr. Barnard has five guests this week."

"Five? Goodness. I'll leave them for later, but can you tell me if they were all here between ten and two today?"

"All five, yes. They were all in the drawing room and then at lunch during those hours, including Mr. Barnard."

"And the staff?"

"Everyone except the boy, who was running errands, was either downstairs preparing food or upstairs serving it."

"And were there any milkmen or salesmen or anybody of the kind who came to the door, either the upstairs door or the servants' door?"

"None. I answer the door myself. Mr. Barnard prefers a housekeeper to a butler."

"I have your word on that? None?"

"Yes."

"You no doubt hired Miss Smith, is that correct?"

"I am responsible for all hiring."

"And supervised her too?"

"Yes, sir."

"Was there anything peculiar about her these last few months?"

Miss Harrison looked as if it would physically hurt her to speak, but after a tense moment, she said, "No, sir. And now I really must be off to finish the evening's chores."

⟳ Chapter 6 ⟳

The thin, winding path of Hampden Lane was trapped in shadows, but two lights gleamed shallowly into the darkness. Graham was still awake in Lenox's own house, and Lady Jane was awake too, hoping for his visit. Tired though he was, he had the cab stop at her door, which looked so much like his: a white door to a gray house.

"Jane!" he whispered through the side window.

There was a flurry of quiet steps, and the door opened a crack.

"Charles! Quiet, quiet, we mustn't wake Kirk, he'll be so cross!"

But she had, perhaps, underestimated her butler, who was in his own way as dependable as Graham, for when they sneaked into the dimly lit drawing room, he was standing there with a tray of spirits and sandwiches.

"With your permission, my lady," he said, "may I—"

"Oh, Kirk, you darling man, yes, go to bed. Thank you so much."

She smiled at him and then sat down on the edge of her rose-colored sofa, in the middle of the room, to pour them drinks. Lenox saw a down-turned book alongside a chair near the window, and it was clear to him that she had been waiting there, where she could see when he returned. Lenox wandered toward her desk. She had a far more splendid one in the morning room on the second floor, where she wrote to her friends, looked out over the garden, and had her breakfast, but she used the desk in her drawing room for a thousand smaller things, and it was cluttered, like his own, with all the artifacts of a happy life—unread papers, silver trinkets, old books, pencils, and pens. It made Lenox feel as if he had come home to see it.

"Charles," she said, "I knew you would come. It doesn't mean you aren't good to do it, but still, I knew you would."

She finished pouring their drinks: a scotch and warm soda for him, blended to the color of amber, and a glass of sherry for her. They each took a sip and then, for some reason, perhaps the strain of the evening, perhaps their relief that it was over at last, looked at each other and laughed. She gave him a plate with several sandwiches on it and took one for herself.

"Will you tell me what you learned?" she said.

"As you can imagine," said Lenox, leaning back, "Barnard was none too pleased with the whole matter."

"Of course not, the beast."

"He had enlisted a man from the Yard named Jenkins, which was a blessing, actually, because Jenkins let McConnell and me have a look at everything. There aren't three other men on the force who would have."

"Thank goodness that man wasn't there, the one—oh, I always forget his name. . . ."

"Exeter."

"Yes!"

"Exactly what I thought, my lady," he said, and laughed.

"Well, and what happened?"

"George stomped around a bit and insisted that there was nothing at all mysterious about any of it, which raised my eyebrows right away. He asked about you, of course."

"Did he? What do you mean by *of course?*"

Lenox laughed. "It's no secret that he's set his cap at you."

She blushed. "That's not true," she said, with a slight stammer.

"Toto told me she thinks it's better than Mr. Collins in *Pride and Prejudice*. She also said you ought to marry him just for our private amusement. It would pass the time."

"That's wicked of Toto. I'll say something stern about it next time I see her." But she couldn't help laughing a little bit.

"But look here—about the case. Is there anything, Charles?"

"Is there anything what?"

"Anything mysterious? I know you well enough to see when you're stalling."

He put his hand on her shoulder. "I don't like to tell you this, but she was murdered."

Lady Jane froze with a sandwich nearly on her lips and then, roused by Lenox's offering her the sherry, smiled strangely.

"I knew it in a way."

"How could you have?"

"You don't remember her at all?"

"Not at all, I'm afraid."

"She was a sweet enough girl, you know, but she was—how shall I put it?—she was provocative."

"Do you mean with men?"

"With men, yes, and with her friends. She was lively and cheerful, but she was also in low spirits now and then—all of those things to such an extreme that I recognized them, when usually the servants are as utter a mystery to me as I try to be to them."

"In low spirits—do you think suicidal?"

"Not that sort of low spirits, no. I only mean that she had two sides to her. As we all do, I expect."

There was a long pause before Lenox spoke.

"Well, I'm glad you told me. That may help."

"I hope."

"But you know, I only just spoke with her fiancé."

"Nevertheless," she said.

On Lady Jane's face was a peculiar mixture of emotions: sorrow, unhappiness, reluctance—but also determination.

"I think, Charles," she said, "that if you mean to take the case, you should hear what I'm telling you."

"All right," he said, nodding.

"Now, will you tell me what you learned?"

"When we arrived, there was a note, a glass, and a bottle of poison on the desk."

"Nothing else?"

"Oh, yes—and a fresh candle."

"Not a pen?"

"Good for you," he said. "You would make a better inspector than Jenkins."

"The police's uniforms are so ugly, though."

"Not quite the thing, you're right."

"And what did the note say?" she asked.

"It said, *It is too much. Sorry, James. I am sorry.* Unsigned."

"Rather strange."

"I would tend to agree, but that remains to be seen. She may have written the note herself, after all, either because she intended to commit suicide and somebody hurried her along or on another matter entirely."

"Then how do you know that it's murder?"

"I'm nearly sure, and that because of McConnell. It was the bottle of poison on her desk, you see."

"What killed her?"

"A rare, expensive poison called *bella indigo.*"

"Well, and won't that serve as easily as another poison, if you want to die?"

"There are two things. First, it is a truly expensive poison; it costs more than her yearly salary for an ounce."

"She could have stolen it from Barnard."

"That occurred to me. But more importantly, the poison on her desk wasn't the poison that had killed her."

She raised her eyebrows.

"And there was no pen, but the note was uncreased, which most likely means that she hadn't carried it around, or it would be folded. One generally doesn't write a suicide note and then return a borrowed pen. After the note, the actual suicide is usually next."

"You know the thing you mentioned earlier, Charles? About George Barnard?"

"Which part?"

"You know, about . . . ?"

"Oh, about his liking for you?"

"Well, yes. I was thinking, perhaps I could use that—well, those feelings, though mind you I don't think they're actually there—but at least use our acquaintance to spend some time with him and see what I can see. If that makes sense."

Lenox whitened. "Absolutely not."

"But Charles—"

"Absolutely not! I won't have you doing that. For one thing it might be dangerous."

She was about to speak when they both heard footsteps across the great hall.

"What was that?" Lenox asked.

"I have no idea."

"Stay here."

He went to the door, wheeled around, and went quickly into the hallway. He found a small young woman in a nightdress. She looked vaguely familiar.

"Will you follow me, please?" Lenox said.

She nodded, and they walked into the drawing room.

"Excuse me, Lady Grey," said the woman, "I only—"

"Lucy! Why are you awake at this hour?"

"I only wanted to 'ear a word over Prue, m'lady."

There was a pause, but then Jane looked at her sympathetically. "You poor thing," she said. "Charles, this is Lucy, one of our maids. She was Prudence Smith's close friend. Sit down, dear."

Lucy looked embarrassed at the thought of sitting down.

"How do you do?" said Lenox.

"Lucy," said Lady Jane, "we know nothing for certain yet—whatever you may have heard in the hallway—but you will know when we do. And now you should really get some rest. We've all had a trying day."

"Yes, m'lady."

But Lenox held up a hand; both women waited expectantly. He walked to the desk, found a pen, and quickly scratched a few words across a piece of paper. Then he walked to Lucy and handed the paper to her.

"Does anything strike you as strange about this?"

"Lucy," Lady Jane said, "you must *not* divulge what you are reading to—"

But for once, Lucy didn't listen. She read the note twice, Lenox could tell, because her lips moved with the words. Then she looked up.

"Two things, sir."

"Two things?"

"Yes, sir."

"What are they, Lucy?"

"The first is she would never call 'im *James*, formal-like."

"What did she call him?"

"Jem, always Jem. Or Jemmie, if she was in a mood."

"But she may have felt formal, if she was going to commit suicide."

"Maybe, sir. But there's the second thing."

"What's that?" said Lenox.

"Prue couldn't read nor write."

∽ Chapter 7 ∾

"Graham, cancel my trip to Villefranche," Lenox said, when at long last he reached home.

"Sir?" said Graham. He was sitting in small chair in the hallway, still dressed as he had been earlier that evening, reading the late penny paper. When Lenox came in, he folded it and placed it in his jacket pocket.

"Villefranche, Graham, on the Riviera. I must have told you."

"No, sir. Although I did notice several maps of France on the desk in your library, sir."

Lenox sighed. "That's the second trip canceled this year, you know."

"Yes, sir."

"Paris in the autumn, before the damned forgery, and now Villefranche. There are many interesting archaeological mysteries in Villefranche." One of Lenox's passions was the Roman Empire, about which he read endlessly. From time to time he visited spots where the empire had left its mark, large or small.

"Sir?"

"And beaches, Graham. Warm beaches."

"I'm sorry, sir."

"Paris, and now the coast."

"I'm sorry that the trips have been delayed, sir."

"Doesn't seem quite fair."

"It does not, sir. Your nightcap, sir?"

They walked together into the library, and as Lenox sat down Graham gave him a glass of hot wine.

"That's the ticket," said Lenox, taking a sip. He sighed. "I was planning a trip of two weeks. I had the mapmaker order a map of the region."

"I believe it came this afternoon, sir. There was no opportunity to give it to you before you went to Lady Grey's."

"Can you lay your hands on it, Graham?"

"Certainly, sir."

He left and came back a moment later with a long tube in his hand. Lenox took it from him and cleared off a section of his desk, knocking some books to the floor.

"Ah!" he said, as he unrolled it.

It was a beautiful map of the Côte d'Azur, a beautiful map being one of his favorite things in the world. He had always wanted to be a traveler in his heart, and while he had made it pretty far— Russia, Rome, Iceland—he had never lost that childhood vision of himself, dusty and tired but triumphant, finding something completely new out on the edge of the world.

"Look, Graham," he said, pointing to the thin edge of the coast. "That's where we were going to go."

"Beautiful land, sir."

"Beautiful."

Both men lingered over the drawing, and then, with a sigh, Lenox rolled it up and placed it in an umbrella rack, which he had taken from his family's house as a place to keep his favorite maps. His father had used it for the Japanese scrolls he liked to collect. They were a family of collectors, as the marble busts of ancient Romans in the back corner of the bookshelf attested.

"Graham," he said, "we shall get there one day, you know."

"There is no doubt in my mind, sir."

Lenox smiled and then sighed one last sigh. "Are you too tired for a quick word?"

"Of course not, sir."

"We had better sit down, then."

The two men moved toward the armchairs by the fireplace and both sat down, although, while Lenox leaned back into a pillow and took a sip of his wine, Graham perched upright on the edge of the cushion.

Briefly, Lenox related what had happened over the course of the evening: the note, the poison, the fiancé, the wax on the floor, the examination, the window, the unused candle. Graham seemed to absorb it all fairly steadily.

"So you see," Lenox finished, "I must do it, if only for Lady Jane."

"If I may express my opinion, sir, I agree entirely." Graham was a fierce partisan of Lady Jane's.

"Did you know the girl at all?"

"Miss Smith, sir?"

"Yes."

"I knew her to nod hello to in the streets, sir. Mr. Kirk disapproved of her."

"Kirk did?"

"Yes, sir. And he is more lenient than some men in our profession."

Lenox laughed. "I see," he said.

"At the same time, sir, she was popular with the girls of this house and in Lady Grey's."

"They were disappointed when she left?"

"Extremely, sir. They thought of her as slightly exotic, I believe."

"Graham, I need you to do something for me."

"Of course, sir."

"I need you to find out who the five people staying with George Barnard are."

Graham nodded.

"No doubt you've already concluded that they are our best suspects. The open window concerns me, of course. But Barnard's horrid housekeeper insists that all five guests were in the house the entire time, and that no milkman or anyone of the sort came along in the relevant hours."

"A claim with definite liabilities, sir. Any house can be penetrated."

"Yes. But still, I think that they must be our best lead. And I think as well that you could find out about them more easily than I could. There are questions I cannot ask. And you know how much I trust you."

"Thank you, sir."

Lenox and Graham had an unusual bond, often formal, sometimes bordering on camaraderie, much of it unspoken. This bond went back a great many years and was seared into both men's memories because of certain rather dark events that had taken place. This matter of asking Graham for help on a case was part of that unusual bond—a result of trust in Graham as a man, first of all, and in his competence too. In the end, each man relied on their deep mutual loyalty, which would be hard for anyone to test. Lenox found Graham to be almost perfect in this unique role: honest, respectful but never toadying, willing to make a point that might disagree with his employer's—always, in short, his own man. Of all the men he knew, he thought Graham among the finest.

"Will that be all right, then?" Lenox asked.

"Yes, sir. If I may suggest something else, sir?"

"Go on."

"I think I might also have an easier time than you in finding out more about Miss Smith, sir."

"The same sort of task, only here on Hampden Lane?"

"Exactly, sir."

"Dashed good idea, that. Wish I'd thought of it. Jane says she was provocative, and you say she was exotic. What does that mean?"

"I shall try to find out, sir."

"Ask the girls in both houses—at any rate, it was your idea and you'll know how to handle it."

"Hopefully, sir."

"Good work. All right then, take the day off tomorrow to do those things. Oh," he said. "Here are a few pounds to do them with."

"Thank you, sir."

"Good night, Graham."

"Good night, sir."

He sighed. "Villefranche, Graham."

"Yes, sir," he said.

The butler walked out of the room, though Lenox knew that he would sit in the hallway until Lenox himself had gone to bed. Which would be wonderfully soon, he thought.

The fire was dying but warm, and once again he took off his boots and his socks and warmed his feet, which were again wet and cold, by the embers. He picked up *The Small House at Allington* and read a chapter, sipping the last of his warm wine while he did. What a long day it had been!

And oh, how he had been looking forward to the seaside! Well, well, he thought. It will all turn out right. He dropped the book to his side, placed his hands on the top of his stomach, and stared, for a few moments, into the fire. Poor Jane, he thought. *Bella indigo*, whatever that was. He would have to visit a chemist on his own. . . .

His eyes began to close, and he knew it was time to wander up to his bedroom and put on his nightcap. He heaved his body from the chair and said, as he walked into the hallway, "Oh, and

Graham? You had better cancel the trip with Mr. Kerr in the morning."

Graham was, of course, seated in the hall, reading his newspaper and eating an oat cake. "Yes, sir," he said.

"And you'd better give him fifty pounds as good-faith money for the next trip." Lenox yawned. "He'll be terribly cross, you know. I keep canceling."

"Yes, sir."

"Now really, Graham, go to bed. I'm only going to have a bath and fall asleep."

The butler stood up, and Lenox smiled at him.

"Good night," he said. "And good luck tomorrow."

Graham nodded. "Good night, sir," he said, and sat down again in his chair, pulling the newspaper from his pocket.

~ Chapter 8 ~

Lenox's stationery was plain white, with his address printed at the top in dark blue. When he woke up the next morning, he took a piece of it from his bedside table, wrote in a quick hand, *Prudence Smith could neither read nor write*, and put it in an envelope without signing it. On the envelope he printed the name MCCONNELL and then rang a bell to fetch a servant, whom he asked to take the letter to his friend's house on Bond Street.

That done, he lay back in bed, rubbed his eyes, and looked at the time: seven-thirty. He would have to hurry to make breakfast with Barnard.

He thought as he dressed about the shocking moment when Jane's maid had discredited the suicide note entirely. The idea of murder had clicked from probability to truth. At the same time, he thought, there was a closed household to deal with. Five guests; even more servants. Although there was the open window. And the unused candle, which troubled him. How often were candles changed? He should ask Graham. Or better yet, ask Graham to find out from one of the servants at Barnard's house.

It was funny, he thought; his first case had revolved around a candle, too. He had been only twenty-two and had gone to visit a family friend, Lady Deborah Marbury, to pay his respects after her son's violent murder. John Marbury had been discovered shot, slumped over the table at his club, and Deborah had been sure it was his friend Hawkins, whom she thought rather a bad influence.

The details from the paper, mixed with the sorrow of his father's friend, had rankled Lenox. Slowly he had begun to nibble around the edges of the case, going to the club where it had happened (and where he was a member), asking around a bit about Hawkins. The deeper he went the more perplexing it got. Hawkins appeared to be innocent. For one thing, Hawkins had been facing young John Marbury across the card table, but the wound indicated that the bullet had come from the roof across the street.

He solved the case by looking through the card room at the club, where he found, tucked beneath a curtain, three half-used candles and an only slightly used fourth one. One detail that policemen had found puzzling was that Hawkins had had three candles. He had explained he needed them to read his cards by, but it was a well-lighted room. Then he had added a fourth candle, and almost immediately Marbury had been shot. The fourth candle was the signal. A single candle wouldn't have done, because the brightness wouldn't have shown across the street. There had turned out to be gambling debts. If the game had gone the right way, the fourth candle would have stayed underneath the table.

Lenox had anonymously given his findings in a sheath of papers to the police at Scotland Yard. The case had been instantly settled, and since then Lenox had been fascinated by detective work. People reached him only by word of mouth. He was an amateur—and because he worked for free, not needing to do otherwise, he attracted many poor clients. On the other hand, because he was from one of the oldest and most respected families in England, he also attracted the rich and the noble, who expected him to have the discretion of a friend.

What had made him think of all this? The candle. . . .

At ten minutes before eight, he stepped into his carriage. Graham ran out to catch him and handed him a note that had just arrived. It was from McConnell:

Only one apothecary in London sells bella indigo. *Nos. 4 and 9. Penny Farthing Place. Fellow named Jeremiah Jones.*

Lenox thought this over and put the note in his pocket, then asked the driver to go.

It was a bright sunny morning, but cold, and the snow still crunched underfoot. He arrived at Barnard's house a few minutes after the hour and greeted the housekeeper amiably, though he received little reward for it.

In the hallway was a young man, perhaps recently down from university or still there. He had on glasses and wore his hair slightly longer than most men of his age. But he was dressed well, in a blue morning suit with a carnation in the buttonhole, and clearly felt at home in the house.

"How do you do?" said the young man.

"Very well, thank you."

"I'm Claude. I'm staying here with my uncle, you know."

"It's a pleasure to meet you, Claude. I'm Charles Lenox."

They shook hands.

"It seems impossibly early to me," said Claude.

"It's already past eight," said Lenox.

"I like how you say *already*, as if eight were a particularly late hour."

"It's not early for me, I must say."

"It damn well is for me."

"You're younger."

"And may it stay forever so. Still, I must see a man about a thing. Good to have met you," he said, and bounded down the steps to the street.

"You too," said Lenox, and followed the impatient house-keeper into the breakfast room, adjacent to the formal dining salon. It was a small octagonal room looking out over the back garden, with a circular table at its center, where George Barnard sat with a nearly empty cup of tea at his elbow, studying a pale blue orchid.

"Charles, sit down," he said, without looking up.

"Thank you," said Lenox.

"This is a beautiful flower, don't you think?"

"Indeed I do."

"I mean to give it to Lord Russell's wife this evening."

"Are you dining with the Prime Minister?"

"I am," Barnard said. He looked up and smiled. "But break-ing my fast with no less a friend."

It was an odd thing to say. Barnard went back to his flower. There was a pot of tea, and Lenox, in the absence of an offer, poured himself a cup.

The window by which they sat overlooked a small garden, full of banks and rows of flowers less fantastically unusual than Barnard's orchids but beautiful nevertheless, and Lenox stared into it until his host saw fit to speak. The moment came at last, after eggs and bacon had been served and Lenox had eaten a good deal of them.

"I'm getting a new man in here," Barnard said, to open their conversation.

"Are you?"

"To replace Jenkins."

Lenox's heart fell. "Why?" he said.

"Incompetent. Getting a man named Exeter. Jenkins insisted that it was murder. Nonsense, I told him. The girl was probably jilted. Happens all the time."

"It was murder, George."

Barnard paused and looked him in the face. "I disagree."

"Do you feel no responsibility to the girl?"

"I do. But I think your facts are wrong. You're only an amateur, Charles."

"That's true," Lenox said.

"And Exeter seems to be leaning toward my theory on the matter."

"Exeter." Lenox sighed.

"I want the plain facts, Charles, and I don't think you've got them. Due respect. Bringing Toto's failure of a husband in as a witness. No jury would believe a drunk. And Exeter's a good man. Jane has no need to worry. Tell her it will be solved. Or, better yet, I'll stop by."

"No, I can tell her."

"As you please."

Lenox stood up. "All the same, George, you won't mind if I look into a few of my ideas?"

"Not at all. But in the end, we'll see what the Yard thinks of it."

"Of course."

"Have you had enough to eat?"

Lenox took a last sip of tea. "Delicious, as always," he said. They drifted out into the main hallway, where he saw a familiar face.

"Mr. Lenox, sir, how do you do?"

"Very well, Inspector Exeter"—for it was the sergeant himself—"though this matter weighs on my mind. We must do our best for her."

"Aye, well said, Mr. Lenox."

Barnard said, "You know this man, then?" Lenox nodded. "Look here," Barnard went on, addressing Exeter, "you'll figure this out straightaway, won't you? I've no doubt you're as incompetent as the rest of them."

"No, sir," Exeter said. He glanced at Lenox with a sort of uneasiness.

"Sure you are. But on this one you suspend your usual stupidity, all right?"

"Yes, sir. It's in good hands, sir. You can trust me." He smiled weakly.

Barnard turned his attention to Lenox. "I hope you're coming to the ball next week?"

"Of course." The ball was an annual event at Barnard's. Of the winter balls it was the best known, and while during the season there would usually be several such affairs on a single night, nobody dared to throw one opposite his.

"Farewell, then," said Barnard. He looked intently at the flower even as he said it, and Lenox was left with the inspector from Scotland Yard.

Exeter was a large man, with black bushy eyebrows, a matching mustache, and thick pink features. He wore a full uniform wherever he went, and his helmet drooped over his eyes. He swung a blackjack around by its leather hoop seemingly without cessation, excluding the times when he put it to other use, most often when he dealt with what he called the lower orders.

London's police force was barely thirty-five years old. Sir Robert Peel had organized the first Metropolitan Police Force in 1829, when Lenox was a lad, and as a result the men who joined were called either peelers or, more likely, bobbies. Its powers were new and uncertain, and Exeter represented both the good and the bad in the institution: the better chance of public order, and the risk of the abuse of the power needed to maintain it.

When he entered the force, Exeter had recently retired from the military and had chosen to become a beat man, walking the streets at night and taking the word *beat* for each of its several meanings. A quick series of retirements and deaths within the Yard had seen him promoted beyond his ability, and hard work had allowed him to rise even higher. He was now one of the half dozen most prominent detectives on the force, and also among the least naturally talented or intuitive of his rank.

There was no point, for Lenox, in trying to tell himself that he did not dislike Exeter. The man was a snob toward those beneath him, and a cloying sycophant to those above, unless they happened to come under his power, when he dropped all pretense of respect and became merciless. And yet, thought Lenox, I don't envy him, having to deal with a man like Barnard. That beastly talking-down to. He thought guiltily that he was glad he could afford—literally—not to put up with a man like Barnard. If only Exeter had been slightly more intelligent. . . . But then, he thought, if wishes were horses, beggars would ride.

The housekeeper brought Lenox his hat and his coat, and as he put them on he said a final word to Exeter.

"If I may give you one piece of information, Inspector—the girl was murdered."

"That sounds like an opinion to me, Mr. Lenox."

"It is not, Inspector. Good day."

And he walked out through the heavy doors, trying to imagine a way in which he could solve Prue Smith's murder without access to any of the suspects, for he knew he had probably entered the house in a professional capacity for the last time during this case.

~ Chapter 9 ~

London on a winter midday held few pleasures for Lenox. There was smoke in the air, which made his eyes tear, and there were too many people along the sidewalks, fighting for the thin path of cobblestone without snow piled atop it. And yet he felt more determined today than he had yesterday evening. In part because Exeter was involved.

He had set himself just one task for the day, or at least until Graham told him what he had discovered, and that was to see if he could trace the *bella indigo* that had killed the young maid. In the meanwhile, he was walking toward the Houses of Parliament, after having run a morning's worth of overdue errands, to have lunch with his older brother, Edmund.

His brother held the seat of Markethouse, the town attached to their family's estate, Lenox House, and while he was not active in the Parliament, exactly, he attended when he could and could be counted to vote along party lines. He was, like Lenox, a liberal, and he approved of the reforms of the last thirty years, but he was also a baronet and held a good deal of land, which made him generally well-liked on both sides of the aisle—or at least accepted as a known quantity.

His full name was Sir Edmund Chichester Lenox, and he lived with his wife, Emily, a pretty, plump, motherly woman whom everyone called Molly, and his two sons, in the house where he and his brother had both grown up. He had two distinct personalities, Lenox always felt: his more businesslike demeanor, in the city, and his truer self, the man who resided at home and felt most comfortable in old clothes, out for a day of shooting or riding or gardening. He was two years older than Charles and, while they looked alike, Lady Jane always said they were instantly recognizable as themselves. Edmund was the same weight and height, but he looked softer, and his manner, while equally polite, was somewhat more eccentric, a trait no doubt cultivated by the solitude of Lenox House in comparison with London.

The two brothers were immensely fond of each other. Each envied the other his pursuit—Lenox followed politics passionately and longed, from time to time, to stand for Parliament himself, while Edmund adored the city and often felt, rather romantically, that to crisscross it wildly, searching for clues and people, must be next to bliss. Occasionally he tried to solve the local crimes at Markethouse from his armchair, but the newspaper rarely yielded up anything more spectacular than a stolen policeman's helmet or a missing sheep: poor fodder, he felt, for a budding detective. As a result, the first thing he always asked his brother was whether he was on a case.

Lenox walked through St. James's Park and then went a short distance along the Thames to Westminster.

He loved going to the Houses of Parliament. He and his brother had gone with their father as children, and he still remembered eating lunch there and watching the debates from the visitors' galleries. These days, he often visited his brother or one of his several friends there.

The buildings had burned down in 1834, when he was a boy, and had been rebuilt over the next few years. And then they had added the tall clock, called Big Ben, only five or six years previously—was it 1859? For Lenox's money, Parliament was one of the two or three most beautiful buildings in London, in that yellowish stone unique to England, with its high towers and intricately carved walls. Its vastness alone was comforting, as if generations could rise and fall but these eight acres, these halls and rooms, would keep England safe. Nobody, on the other hand, would ever care about Big Ben.

The public, when it visited, entered at Westminster Gate, but Lenox went to a small door on the other side of the building, facing the river, and there, waiting in the hall, was Edmund. This was the members' entrance—straight ahead, up a staircase, were the chambers of government. To the left and the right were the members' rooms, which were closed to the public. If you took a right, you went to the dining rooms and smoking rooms of the House of Lords and the Queen Empress; to the left and you were in the branch dedicated to the House of Commons. The two brothers turned left, to Bellamy's.

Bellamy's was a large spacious restaurant looking over the river. Dickens had written about it—the butler Nicholas and the provocative waitress Jane—in *Sketches by Boz*, and their father had always told them that William Pitt's dying words were, "Oh, for one of Bellamy's veal pies!" It had old dark mahogany tables and smelled of cigar smoke and the waiters' pomade. A lot of grizzled old men sat around talking grumpily, sticking as close to the fires as possible, and a lot of animated younger men took drinks at the bar.

Lenox and his brother sat at a table next to a window, under a portrait of Fox, and Edmund, staying true to form, immediately said, "Well, dear brother, and what are you working on?"

Lenox smiled. "Lovely to see you too, as always. Are young Edmund and William well? And Emily?"

"Don't be that way, Charles, what have you got? Why, only the other day in the country we had a silver thief."

"A silver thief! In mild Markethouse! And was he caught?"

"Well, it was not so much that there was a silver thief as that there was a matter of misplaced silver."

"Who could have misplaced so much silver? Did you think of insurance fraud?"

"It was a fork, to be precise."

Lenox raised his eyebrows. "One fork, you say?"

"But a serving fork, you know, so it was really quite large. And of good silver. Very well made. And old. An heirloom, really."

"How many men were assigned to the case? Did you break up the silver ring?"

"It had fallen under a chair, you see. But I only read that the next day."

"So it was touch and go for a turn of the sun?"

Edmund smiled. "Have your laugh."

Lenox did laugh, and then put his hand on his brother's arm. "Shall we order?" he said.

"Yes, yes."

They each decided that they would have the same thing, the only thing the chef did decently: roasted mutton with new potatoes and buttered peas under, and a flood of gravy over the entire thing.

"And a bottle of claret?" said Edmund.

"Unless you have the business of the people to attend to, this afternoon?"

"No, we're in committee."

"Then yes."

"Now really," said Edmund, "stop delaying, and tell me what happened with the forgery. The Yard has refused to leak it to the press."

"It was Isabel Lewes."

Edmund gasped. "It couldn't have been!"

"It was indeed."

"She was out of London!"

"No, she wasn't."

"And how are you so sure?"

"There was a sapphire necklace involved."

"Really?"

"Yes."

"Well, please, go on!"

"Another time."

Edmund groaned.

"At the moment, I am at work on another matter."

"What is that?"

"You're certain you want to hear?"

"Of course, of course!"

Just then the mutton came, and as they poured the wine and cut the meat, Lenox briefly relayed to his brother the events of the previous night and of that morning. He omitted only the name of the poison, because he didn't want to risk being overheard.

Edmund was a little overexcited by the new case and for some reason kept saying that he was "as good as a vault" and would be happy to stay in the city to "ferret out the truth, however dark it might be."

"It is a perplexing matter," Lenox concluded, "because the motive of any murder is most likely to originate from one of the victim's daily acquaintances, but none of her daily acquaintances would be likely to use such a means of murder."

"Mightn't the murderer have stumbled upon the poison? In Barnard's house or elsewhere? A servant could easily do that."

"I thought of that," Lenox said. "McConnell sent a note over this morning, saying that only one apothecary in London sells the poison, so I mean to ask there. But I think it unlikely. It would be so easily traced to whatever house it came from."

"But perhaps the murderer thought the fake suicide would never let the police get so far."

"Perhaps. At any rate, I shall see the chemist this afternoon, and he can settle it. If so, the case will be solved."

"Yes," said Edmund. But he looked uneasy.

"Is anything the matter?" Lenox asked.

"I'm in the midst of what you might call a moral dilemma."

Lenox looked at his brother, who was in his tweed jacket and had a spot of gravy on the old Harrow tie they both happened to be wearing that day, and at his furrowed brow, and felt an enormous surge of fondness for him.

"Tell me what it is, if you like."

"The dilemma is whether or not I ought to."

Lenox suddenly looked very serious. "It is related to this case?"

"It is."

"Then you must, Edmund."

"One man can have several loyalties to consider at once, dear brother."

"To whom must we be loyal beyond the dead? Surely none of the family is at all involved."

"I am loyal to my family and, as you say, to this young girl—but also to my country."

They had finished eating. The waiter cleared the plates away in the long pause that ensued. Both men leaned back and lit cigarettes, and Lenox drank a sip of wine.

"A matter of state?" he said at last.

"Yes."

"Then it is your choice. But you shall have my discretion as a detective and as a brother, should you choose to tell me."

Edmund smiled. "I know that," he said. He sighed. "I may as well."

The two men leaned close to each other, and Edmund said, "Barnard is storing this year's gold in his house."

"What do you mean?"

"The coinage."

"The mint's gold? To go into circulation next month?"

"Yes."

Lenox sat back and whistled softly.

The mint was located in a very secure building in Little Tower Hill, near the Tower of London. It was a yellowing stone building that sat behind a tall iron fence. Its front was pillared and wide, though it was only very rarely that somebody went in or out. In a busy street, it was silent. Whenever Lenox passed it he felt the million jealous eyes that had stared at it in the past. Inside, delicate machinery converted bars of pure gold into exact-weight coins, which were then distributed to the nation.

Barnard ran this operation with great care. For instance, it had once been very common to see nicked coins, with little pieces cut out of the sides, not enough to render them worthless, but enough that if the nicks were in a pile they were worth something. Barnard was the first director of the mint to recall nicked coins and melt them back down into gold ingots. This was the sort of care he took.

"Impossible," Lenox said.

"I'm afraid it's true," said Edmund.

"That changes things a bit."

Edmund laughed. "A pile of gold is slightly more important than Mrs. Shattuck's serving fork."

Lenox couldn't help but laugh, too. "But why?" he said.

"The mint was no longer secure. There had been attacks."

"Who attacked it?"

"We don't know. There's an ongoing investigation. A very threadbare rumor says the Hammer Gang, who run by the docks and control a good deal of the prostitution and robbery over there along Canary Wharf, but that may be false. Probably is."

"But then why not a bank? Or the Parliament?"

"Neither is safe. Neither has half the precautions of the mint, and they're both too public."

"But Barnard's house?"

"The attacks on the mint were persistent and very careful. Whoever did them would get past several guards, giving them a sleeping pill or too much gin or a blow to the head, and then retreat when it became too dangerous. But they had penetrated farther and farther at each attack, and by the end they were close to the gold, no matter how many guards we put out."

"I see," said Lenox.

"Yes. We had to throw them far off the trail. Barnard also had a perfect room for it—difficult to get to, with only one access point, easily guarded. He *is* the director of the mint, Charles, and it is a closely guarded secret."

"That's true."

"And Barnard cares too much for his position, and his reputation, to let anyone near the gold. He has men around it all the time who don't even know what they're guarding. He probably told them they were looking after a rare orchid."

"True too, I suppose."

"Perhaps that's why he wanted the murder to be a suicide so much," said Edmund. "Scared of an attempt on the gold."

"You may be right."

"At any rate, the gold will be there for the next two weeks, nearly two million pounds. Anyone who stole it would immediately become one of the richest people in the British Empire."

"Where in the house?"

"In a secret room beneath his greenhouse."

Lenox whistled again, more loudly this time.

"Well," he said. "This is an entirely new case."

"It is, I think," said Edmund. "But I hope you appreciate the utter secrecy which I must ask of you. For the next two weeks, that means the cost may rise as high as delaying the murderer's arrest."

"I know," said Lenox. "But you were right to tell me."

"You understand, needless to say, that the board of trade is having difficulties, and that our economy *must* hum along with regularity for the next year, for Lord Russell's government to accomplish anything whatsoever."

"I understand. Though I am unused to hearing you speak so strongly about the government."

"We were both raised to serve, Charles."

They looked at each other.

"Well," said Lenox, "shall we have the trifle for dessert."

∽ Chapter 10 ∽

Edmund's revelation about the mint's gold had rendered the source of the *bella indigo* no less important, and as soon as he left Parliament Lenox took a cab to Jensen's. It had begun to snow again, and Lenox looked forward to five o'clock, when he could have his tea. It was more the pleasure of the ceremony and the comfort of his fireside that he looked forward to, for of course he was still full from lunch.

Jensen's was not the chemist whose name Thomas McConnell had given him—the sole apothecary in the city of London who sold *bella indigo*, to his knowledge—but Willie Jensen was a man Lenox knew and trusted and one with whom he had consulted before. His apothecary was on a corner somewhat close to Hampden Lane, in Brook Street, and Lenox often passed it when, as was his custom, he took long walks after supper. The shop had a bright lantern hanging in front of it above a large chalkboard advertising its goods.

He arrived at a little past two and pushed open Jensen's door. The space inside was small but tidy and smelled of cinnamon and soap. There were rows of creams, hairbrushes, and powders on plain wooden shelves along the walls, and rows of small, apparently unmarked bottles behind the counter. Jensen himself was an old man, who smoked without cease throughout the day and spoke in a thick brogue. He had tufts of white hair in his ears, none on his head, and white whiskers on his cheeks.

A customer was already at the counter. He appeared to be a footman, and he was, Lenox overheard, seeking a respite from the gout for his employer, one Lord Robinson of Bruton Street. Jensen told the footman that his master would need to see a doctor—to which the servant responded with a horrified shake of his head, betraying, no doubt, Lord Robinson's own prejudice—and gave him a small bottle of medicine.

"Twice a day," he said, "and tell Lord Robinson to eat lightly."

This suggestion met with a reaction even more violent than the one to seek out a doctor, and by the time the footman hurried through the door, Lenox had begun to picture this lord as grotesquely fat and singularly averse to medical treatment and fewer than seven courses for dinner. Too fat to attend the House of Lords, or his name would have been familiar.

"Mr. Jensen," he said, approaching the counter, "I fear I shall be no easier a customer than that young man."

"What ails you, Mr. Lenox, sir?" said Jensen, in a strong Irish accent.

"Something called *bella indigo*, I'm afraid."

"Wait a moment, sir, while I get my spectacles." The old man reached beneath the counter for his glasses and put them on. "Ah," he said, squinting through them.

"What demands such close inspection?" asked Lenox.

"You're the first ghost I've gazed upon, sir."

Both men laughed, the detective with his head thrown back and the chemist in a thick, rasping voice.

"Mr. Jensen," said Lenox, still laughing, "I believe that's the first joke I've ever heard you tell."

"I was savin' her up, sir."

"It was worth the wait."

Lenox chuckled again, and Jensen lit a short cigarette, which fit snugly in his hand.

"Now, sir, how've you come across a thing as nasty as *bella indigo*, if I might ask?"

"In a case for Lady Jane Grey."

"Must be ugly business, Mr. Lenox."

"Uglier by the moment, Mr. Jensen."

"Tell me how I can help you, sir."

Lenox pulled McConnell's piece of paper from his pocket. "Have you heard of a man named Jeremiah Jones? Another chemist?" he asked.

"How did you get that name?"

"My friend Thomas, the doctor you once met."

"Ah, Mr. McConnell. Knows a far sight more than many of the trade about their work. Yes, he would know of Jerry Jones."

"Is this Jones a man to deal with?"

"He is," Jensen said. "A peculiar man, Mr. Lenox, but honest."

"And not likely to bridle if I ask him whether he has sold a vial of poison recently and to whom?"

"He might be, sir, he might be. Wait a moment, though."

Jensen turned around and wrote something on a piece of paper. Then he folded it twice and handed it to Lenox.

"Give him this note and two pounds, Mr. Lenox, and be careful you don't read the note."

"As you say, Mr. Jensen. Thank you, as always."

"A pleasure, sir."

"One of these days I'll buy something, perhaps."

"Well, sir, I've seen a ghost now, so my days of nonbelieving are over. But anything for Lady Grey."

Both men laughed again, and Lenox waved goodbye as he went out the door. He came back into the store a moment later.

"It may be today after all," he said, reaching into his pocket. He found the small brown-stoppered bottle of poison from

Prue Smith's desk and set it before Jensen. "Any chance of tracing this to its owner?"

Jensen picked it up and looked carefully at the crest on the stopper, where a row of numbers were printed into the glass. "I could try," he said. "Arsenic, is it?"

"I think so. How did you know?"

"Common, this sort of bottle. Let me keep it."

The old man put it into his pocket, and Lenox said goodbye again and went outside to a waiting cab, having foolishly elected to send his carriage home after the morning errands. He gave the cabbie the address McConnell had written for him and set-tled back in his seat.

"Are you sure?" the driver asked. "Penny Farthing Place, sir?"

Lenox looked at the paper. "That's right," he said, so the man shrugged and lifted the reins.

They rode through Grosvenor Square and through the streets inhabited by those of Lenox's friends who lived in large, freshly painted houses, with activity within and without; then, gradu-ally, there was a subtle change and they were riding through streets slightly less well-founded, where perhaps the paint was a few years older; then, after those, through streets Lenox had never seen; and, at last, into the fringe of the Seven Dials.

When people thought of London, they generally thought of the West End as aristocratic and East London as poor, and while this was generally true, the poorest part of London, the Dials, was in the West End, just a ten- or fifteen-minute drive from Lenox's house.

The neighborhood had gotten its name from a meeting of its seven largest avenues; it was the sort of place where the streets were so narrow that the sky looked dark, and the cobblestones were cracked and broken. There were dozens of pubs, called the Queen's Arms or the Prince and Peasant, all badly lit, with pints of penny gin. Dogs ran in the streets, and scavengers trav-eled along the sewers, some of them children, looking for the glint of a spare coin, a pack of cigarettes, even a length of rope, anything to sell. Nobody had enough room to live.

But the Dials wasn't the worst part of London in Lenox's opinion; that was the Rookery, by Bainbridge Street in East London. The vices here were drink and cruelty. The vices there were theft and prostitution. The Rookery was the home of the Hammer Gang, which Edmund had told him might have been involved in the attempts on the mint.

The cab stopped in front of a tiny brick house with broken windows and no shingle declaring its business.

"Will you wait?" Lenox asked.

"Not likely, sir."

"This ride has cost a shilling, correct? Here's a shilling. And now here's another," he said, pulling it from his pocket and showing it. "It's yours if you wait for ten minutes. After ten minutes, you may leave."

The man looked at him warily and said, "Fine."

Lenox nodded and slid into the street. He looked at his pocket watch, said, "Ten minutes, beginning now!" and knocked on the door.

Jeremiah Jones spent forty-five of Lenox's precious seconds coming to the door, and another fifteen asking him what his business was. He was a thin stooped man, with wild white hair sticking up, an uneven collar, and spectacles on the tip of his nose. When the detective handed over the piece of paper and the money, the man looked at the paper, smiled thinly, pocketed the money, and walked inside, leaving the door open, which was, Lenox presumed, an invitation to go in.

The room he entered was perhaps six feet high, so low that both men had to stoop. There was one table in the middle of it, and one chair. On the back wall was a door, which must have led to the living quarters and the storeroom. The potions were nowhere to be seen, but there was a large ledger on the table and a gilt silver pen on top of it. Other than the table, the chair, the book, the pen, and a small kerosene lamp, the room had only one distinguishing feature: an enormous boy of fifteen, strong, fat, and tall, who appeared to be eating an entire black sausage—or at least he had eaten half a foot of it and looked by no means ready to slow down. He was sitting on a stool.

"Yes?" said Jeremiah Jones.

"I need to know about *bella indigo*."

Jones took a snuffbox from his pocket, pinched a large amount of snuff, and stared at it, rolling it reverently between his fingers. Lenox felt his ten minutes melting away. But at last the chemist placed the snuff in his nostril and snorted it in. Then, mystifyingly to Lenox, who still had one eye on the boy and his food, Jones simply left the room through the door in the back wall.

Lenox counted to sixty before he asked the boy, as politely as he knew how to, where the man had gone. The boy looked up slowly and said, "He gone through that door."

This could have been more helpful. "What's in there?" Lenox asked.

"D'you 'ave summing to eat?"

In the best society such an abrupt change of subject was unusual, but Lenox searched in his pocket and produced a piece of candy. The boy looked at it the way a lion might look at a bony old antelope, half hungry and half disappointed, as if he had been hoping that Lenox might produce a twelve-pound roasted chicken.

"Another room," he said, reaching for the candy. "That's what's in there."

Lenox gave up, and the two resumed their rather gloomy silence. After another half minute, though, Jones came out again, carrying a small turquoise bottle.

"Fifty pounds," he said. "But it's nearly eleven months old."

"Why does that matter?"

Jones looked up. "Because *bella indigo* only lasts for a year after it's brewed."

"Where do you get more?"

"Oxford."

"The university?"

"The only place in England that grows it. Or in Europe, for that matter. It's a famous poison, in my trade, from Asia, but only Oxford dares to grow it."

"And sells it?"

"Oh, no—never. They wouldn't sell it. Very closely restricted."

"Then how did you get it?" Lenox asked.

"Well, not never. See now, would you like to buy it?"

"Can you tell me when the last bottle of *bella indigo* was bought and by whom?"

"Do you have two more pounds?"

Lenox handed over the money, and Jones pulled open his book, which seemed to be cross-referenced, in a remarkably Byzantine way, by the potion's source.

"Four years ago," Jones said.

"So the bottle you sold would no longer be effective?"

"No."

"And you're the only person in London, or in England, who sells it."

"Yes."

"Except for the person who gives it to you from Oxford?"

Jones slammed the book shut and carefully capped the pen and placed it back on top of the ledger. "Good day, sir," he said.

Lenox stepped forward. "Please, one more question. Here's another pound."

He handed Jones the money.

"One more."

"Why do they make it? At Oxford or anywhere?"

"Why do they make any poison, sir?"

"No other reason?"

"Well," Jones said, "it has one other use."

"What's that?"

"The chemistry dons sometimes mulch their flower beds with it," he said. "It's particularly good for roses and orchids." And then he walked through the door again, without so much as looking back.

Lenox said thank you as quickly as he could and ran outside to catch the cab before it left. When he stepped onto the curb, though, he saw that it was several blocks away already and looked ready to turn. A shilling didn't buy what it had when he was a boy.

"No!" he said, and waved his arm, and in his haste stepped into the road. But he was unaccustomed to the broken cobblestones of the neighborhood, and his foot plunged halfway up his calf into an icy pool of water beside the gutter.

Lenox swore only rarely, but he did so now. The chill ran through him, and as he began to walk the wind battered his leg. But he made haste, and soon he was out of the Dials; perhaps there would be a cab, and then, he thought hopefully, it would be no time until he was in his library, sitting by the fire and eating something good.

✑ Chapter 11 ✑

The man who walked up the stoop of 11 Hampden Lane that afternoon, just before four o'clock, was not, his friends would agree, Charles Lenox at his best. He had been forced to walk the better part of the way home, and a fringe of snow covered his coat, the brim of his hat, and his scarf. One of his feet, he was convinced, would fall off soon, and the other one, though near-perfect by comparison, felt as if it was stepping barefoot on the street as he walked.

Add to that his perplexity about Prudence Smith's murder, his eagerness to solve the case for his dear friend, and the fact that he was worn out and hungry from his walk, and one might begin to understand his circumstances.

But when an upper maid opened the front door to him, he said hello as cheerfully as though he had been out for a lazy walk in late spring. She took his coat, his hat, and his scarf and asked if she ought to bring tea to the library, to which he assented. Only when he had walked through the hallway, turned right, and shut the doors of his sanctuary behind him did he sigh and wince and gingerly remove his mutinous boots.

Things soon began to improve. The fire was warm, and he

had changed into a spare set of hunting clothes—a houndstooth suit—that he kept in a drawer in the back of the room. And when the tea came, he felt warm enough, and cozy in his high-backed chair, watching the snow fall outside, with a paper in his hand that he might choose to read or not, as the mood took him, and a happy heaviness in his eyes, as of contentment.

He asked the girl for his slippers, and she fetched them, and in the space of fifteen minutes, happiness had returned to his face, and before he had even had a chance to read the headlines the newspaper had fallen from his hands and he had dozed off pleasantly into sleep.

He awoke thirty minutes later, first half-sleeping and then gently opening his eyes. As he gazed into the whitened street, he thought drowsily that it had been a perfect nap—the sort a man runs into now and again by chance, when he has had a difficult day but comes back to his hearth to find a brief moment of peace and rest, the sort that leaves him renewed, still sleepy, and at ease with the world.

There was a knock on the door, and he heard the maid walking briskly across the hallway to answer it. It occurred to him then that Graham must not have returned yet from the two tasks he had set out to do.

The maid tapped on the door to the library, and Lenox said, "Come in." She swung the double doors open, and Lady Jane, who was on the threshold, said to her, "Bring the tea now if you would, my dear."

Lenox stood up and smiled.

"I've only just woken up," he said, "from the loveliest nap."

"What a lucky thing!" Lady Jane said, pulling off her gloves and leaning back, with an exhale, into the red sofa. She was wearing a pale blue dress that brought out the flush in her cheeks.

"Oh, it was very nice."

"Such a horrid day, too. I saw you coming back home from my window, Charles, and I saw your poor leg was drenched, and I thought I would give you an hour to rest, but it's only been forty-five minutes and here I am already. I hope you don't mind."

"Never," he said. "Or, if ever, I would have minded forty-five minutes ago, when I first came in. But at the moment nothing could bring me more pleasure. Now, have you had your tea?"

"I haven't."

"Neither have I."

"I know," she said. She smiled. "Your maid told me that she brought it in, but you were asleep. She's bringing a fresh pot now."

"I thought I heard you say something to her."

"It will only be a moment, I think."

"It seems ages since lunch. Though the company was good; I was with my brother."

"Edmund!"

"I enjoyed seeing him, of course, but it was hours and hours ago. You're lucky you didn't find me fainted dead away on the sidewalk."

"Did you have a trying day, otherwise?"

He smiled. "Of course not," he said.

"Oh, I know you did, you fibber. Was it too terrible?"

"I'll only admit I was cross with the city when I came home, but it passed within a moment and I no longer have any idea of moving to the American prairie."

"Thank goodness. We should have seen much less of each other."

"Not a fashionable enough neighborhood, my lady?"

"Not by half," she said, and they both laughed.

The tea came a moment later, and Jane, as she always did, served it.

"Two pieces of toast?" she asked.

"How about four?"

"Four!"

"Yes."

"A bear couldn't eat four pieces of toast!"

"A bear who had walked through London all day, and stepped in a puddle, and been betrayed by a cabdriver, very well might eat four pieces of toast."

She laughed and handed him his tea and his toast and began to talk about a ball that her friend the Duchess Marchmain was giving next month. They fell into a conversation about old friends, and soon he realized, with a pang of gratitude, and love, that though she had rushed here to speak about the murder, she had seen his weariness and sacrificed her own anxiety to put his mind at rest.

He let her talk a little while longer about the Duchess and her sons—who were known to be as vain as women—and whom they might marry. But when the conversation turned, he told her that he had spent all day on the case.

He recounted what he had done: about *bella indigo*, about his breakfast with Barnard, and about Graham, who was out working on a few basic leads Lenox hoped would reveal something he suspected. And last he told her that he had discovered something else, something potentially important, but had been sworn to secrecy over it at lunch.

It wasn't much of a bounty to give her, but she seemed comforted, by the time he stopped talking, and said only that she hoped she would be able to do something herself.

"I'll get to the bottom of it," Lenox said.

"I know you will." Her face betrayed a moment of worry, but then she took a last sip of tea and began to put on her gloves again. She stood up to leave and they said goodbye, agreeing that they would have tea again the next day, just to check in.

After she left, Lenox thought about what he knew so far. It had been slightly less than a day, and he had learned a great deal: that Prue Smith had definitely been murdered; by what instrument; the clues at the scene of the murder; the probable origins of the poison; the definite motive of the mint's gold; the restricted group among whom the murderer might reside.

But all the same he felt as if he knew nothing. Who were George Barnard's houseguests other than Claude, the young man he had met? Had any of them discovered the gold? How had the murderer's path crossed the housemaid's; had they had some relationship? Was he dismissing too quickly the possibility that a friend or a lover had done it because he was focused on the cost and obscurity of the poison and the presence in the house of the mint's money?

Many murders, he knew, are solved within twenty-four hours. The rest, from his experience, were never solved or took weeks. But at least, he thought with grim satisfaction, he was ahead of Exeter, who was still twisting his whiskers and thinking the girl had destroyed herself while his underlings stroked his ego.

There were *too many* pieces to the puzzle, if anything. The factors that usually determine a murderer's identity had been thrown into doubt immediately.

He pondered the case for half an hour—and then remembered something that Jeremiah Jones had said, thought curiously about it for a moment, and decided he would wait until Graham had come home to think about Prue Smith again. He searched through the books on his desk, found his old copy of *Tom Brown's Schooldays*, and opened it in the middle.

He read quite contentedly until eight, when he had to dress for supper with his friend Lord Cabot, who shared with him a sportsman's interest in politics, and a few friends, at their club, the Travelers. He had put on his dinner jacket and combed his hair when, just as he was nearly ready to leave, he heard the servants' door open and close and knew from the buzz of voices that Graham was home.

He went down to the hallway and at the same time heard footsteps on the stairs below, and a moment later his butler came in, looking worse for the day's wear, much as Lenox him-

self must have looked when he had come home that evening—
cold and unhappy.

"Graham!" he said.

"Sir."

"Lovely day out, isn't it?"

"No, sir, if I may contradict you."

Lenox laughed. "Why are you up here, anyway?"

"I thought you might want to discuss the matter we spoke
about yesterday evening right away, sir."

"No, no," said Lenox, "go to your room, have a fire, change
your clothes, and doze off. If only to please me. And have some
tea."

"Yes, sir."

"We can talk later this evening or tomorrow morning."

"Very well, sir. Good evening."

Graham began to walk back down the stairs tiredly. Lenox
stood and listened, heard a door shut beneath, and turned to
the housekeeper.

"Will you take him the tea yourself?"

"Oh, yes, sir," she said.

"It's my fault he had to go out at all."

"I will indeed, sir."

"Excellent." He turned and began to walk toward the front
door but stopped and turned around. Then he paused and
didn't say anything.

After a moment, the housekeeper said, "Sir?"

"Mary," he said, "will you also take one of those little chocolate cakes I like so well, when you take him his tea? He might en-
joy that."

"Of course, sir."

"That'll do," he said to himself, and opened the front door
to leave.

∽ Chapter 12 ∽

Most of the gentlemen's clubs of London were on Pall Mall and St. James's Street, near Hampden Lane, and Lenox belonged to several of them. Every group of people had a club—the Gresham for merchants, the Hogarth for artists, the Army and Navy, called Rag and Famish by its members, for veterans—but Lenox's clubs were of a higher caste, being clubs dedicated not to a pursuit, by and large, but to the aristocracy.

They mostly resembled one another, being wide white town-houses, usually in the Italianate style, and four or five stories high. Each of them served a different mood or clique.

For instance, he had first joined the Athenæum Club, on Pall Mall, and still spent several evenings a month there. It had the best club library in England and excellent food, and most of his friends from school and university belonged there.

He also went to the Savile Club, which was less politics and more art and science, to the Devonshire Club, which was for members of a liberal bent, and to the Eton and Harrow, on Pall Mall East, for graduates of those two public schools. He belonged to the Oriental Club and the Marlborough Club, the latter of which was considered perhaps the most prestigious in

London. And then there was the Oxford and Cambridge Club, at 71 Pall Mall, which was shortly to play a role in the case.

They were almost all in limestone buildings, and they were all very comfortable inside, particularly the Athenæum and the Devonshire. They all had central halls, where ceremonies and large dinners were held, and where you checked for your friends in thick chairs next to warm fireplaces. Beyond the large halls were a series of smaller rooms for smaller groups: billiard rooms, card rooms, grand old libraries where members dozed off with *The Times* on their laps, chess rooms, tearooms, and, of course, places to eat.

The reason these clubs flourished, Lenox felt, was that this was an age of unusually rigid separation between men and women. He and Lady Jane ignored that separation, but most men spoke very little with women except at parties, and were most comfortable playing a hand of cards or smoking a cigar with their friends, a kind of solidarity encouraged in grammar school, public school, and university, all of which excluded women.

Lenox also belonged to the Travelers Club, on St. James's Street, and there, in the long lounge that evening, the last two members by the fire were Lord Cabot and Charles Lenox—both of whom, it could be presumed, had at least once traveled 500 miles in a straight line from the center of London, which was the very minimum requirement of that club. Lenox wished he had gone farther than Russia—he wished he had gone to the Cape of Good Hope, like Stanley Foster, another member—but he enjoyed the club's company nonetheless. Its members were the most interesting and idiosyncratic of the aristocratic class, from every field and every pursuit, with an emphasis on scholarship. Lenox's father had helped found it, because his own clubs were too full of bores; everybody in the Travelers was an expert on something—ancient Welsh agriculture or Persian illuminated manuscripts or Shakespeare's problem comedies, or imperial Rome, like Lenox—even those with other careers. The building itself was an old stone one, comfortable inside, with a sizable library and a good dining room. Lenox often went there to read at night and perhaps run into a friend who also loved to travel.

But now they were in the lounge, which was a long hall with a painted ceiling and heavy armchairs. Each man had a drink in his hand, and Cabot held the poker and constantly shifted the dying embers in the hearth. He was a fat man with white hair, tidily dressed, and with a quick smile.

The fire was warm, but outside the sounds of a blizzard shuffled against the windows, the fiercer wind that rises when the streets are abandoned at night, the swirls of wet snow against the ground, and the boots of the last men out hurrying along the pavement toward home.

They were talking about the Commons, as they always did when they had supper. Their other friends had melted away by now.

"Your brother," said Lord Cabot. "There's an example."

"Of what?"

"A man with no more idea of leadership than of becoming a chimney sweep! Great fella, you know, and votes well, when he comes to town, but my question is, Who, when he sits in his seat, tells him what to do? Leadership!"

"You may underestimate my brother. He surprised me today."

"But you do see my *point*, Lenox!"

"You think we have no man the equal of Disraeli on the liberal side."

The political situation of the moment was complex. Disraeli had initiated tremendous social reform, but he was a Conservative, and the Liberals were trying to find a match for him. Lord Russell was the Prime Minister and a Liberal, but by common consent he was no Disraeli.

"I should say not."

"Gladstone?"

"Perhaps in time, my young friend," Cabot said. "But Disraeli—"

"He will go down in history as a liberal."

Both men laughed.

"And here we are again. It always signals the time to sip our last sips, when we reach this subject."

Cabot smiled happily and set the poker against the hearth. Both men rose and began to walk across the great hall. Lenox corrected himself; they were not the last members present. An old white-haired man slept on a chair in the corner, his drink still in his hand. The stewards would leave him alone all night, if he slept. Particularly in a blizzard.

"A ride?" said Lenox.

"No, thank you, dear friend, my carriage should be along any moment."

Soon both men were on their way home, having promised each other to have supper again soon. Lenox, stepping into his carriage, sighed and leaned back in his seat. Nearly midnight, he thought, looking at his watch. The streets had a ghostly feel. Who walks among us, he asked himself, with a young maid's death on their hands?

When he reached Hampden Lane, he saw that Graham was still awake; the light in the hallway shone through the front windows. He climbed the steps, opened the door, and saw his butler reading over a set of handwritten notes, in his usual seat along the front hallway.

"Graham," said Lenox. "How are you?"

"Well, sir, and you?"

"Excellent. Just what I needed to get my mind off the case for an hour or two."

"I am gratified to hear it, sir."

"Do you feel more human, Graham?"

"Yes, sir."

"Had a rotten day?"

"Far from it, sir. I admit I was fatigued by the end of my investigations, sir, but as you kindly suggested a cup of tea and a moment by the fire put me right again."

"Always does the trick for me."

"Yes, sir. A good English remedy."

While they spoke, Graham had removed Lenox's coat and quickly brushed his hat, while Lenox hung his cane on a hook to the right of the door, by a small table with a silver bowl on it. He dropped his keys in the silver bowl, and they rang out briefly.

"In my library, Graham?"

"Yes, sir."

"Is there a fire?"

"Yes, sir."

They walked into the library, but instead of sitting in his armchair, Lenox went to his desk and sat down. He motioned Graham toward another chair, by the side of the desk, and then unlocked the top left drawer with a small brass key he removed from his waistcoat pocket. From the drawer he took out a pad of paper and a pencil. Then he locked the drawer again and put the key back in his waistcoat. He cleared a space on the desk, knocking a few books to the ground by accident, and waving Graham off when he tried to pick them up.

"I'll get them later," he said.

As a final preparation, he searched through the papers on his desk and at last lit on what he was looking for, a short mahogany pipe with a silver mouthpiece and, next to it, a leather pouch. He painstakingly prepared the pipe, which he only smoked in the evenings, during his quietest hours, lighted it, and then sat back and looked at Graham.

"What did you find out?" he said.

Graham began to speak.

"I will not have the full results of my inquiry into Miss Smith's character until tomorrow afternoon, sir, if you would be so good as to release me for two or three hours at that time, but

I have a full report of the inmates of Mr. Barnard's house and have confirmed that all of them were present and for the most part in the dining room together, eating lunch, or in the drawing room, playing cards, between eleven and one, the period when Miss Smith ingested the poison."

"McConnell said twelve and one."

"Yes, sir, but to be cautious I extended the window, in the remote case that it was ingested earlier than Mr. McConnell determined. It could not have been later, of course, sir, because she died."

"Go on."

"As you are no doubt aware, sir, Mr. Barnard will hold his annual ball in four days' time. The preparations for the event began long ago, and several of the houseguests arrived in the past few days, to stay until the ball ends.

"Except for Claude Barnard, who seems to live with his uncle, the guest who has resided with Mr. Barnard for the longest time is his other nephew, Eustace Bramwell, who is Mr. Barnard's sister's son. He is a young man of perhaps twenty-two, sir, who has just come down from Cambridge, where he was in Caius College and studied botany."

"Botany?"

"Yes, sir. He has been in his uncle's house for more than a month now and doesn't work during the day. But he has an active social life, I believe, and is a member of the Jumpers Club, which caters, from what I understand, to the younger members of the aristocracy."

"Lady Jane's nephew is a member. Gives her fits. They drink all the time."

"I believe that to be an accurate picture of life at the Jumpers, sir. Eustace Bramwell spends some of his time there. But he is very proper, according to the servants, and, with the exception of his almost constant lectures on class responsibilities, he is quiet and not troublesome."

"I see."

"He was unlikely to come into contact with Miss Smith at great length, sir, and when at home almost never ventured from his room except for meals."

"But he was in the drawing room after lunch yesterday? December twelfth?"

"Yes, sir. He was painting a picture and conversing with Mr. Barnard's newest guest, Jack Soames."

"Soames?"

"Yes, sir, he arrived three days ago. As you know, I'm sure, he is a member of the House of Commons. He had come to stay with Barnard while the two men discussed issues of the mint, I believe, and also because they are close friends in the circles in which they move."

"Anything peculiar? I know him, more or less."

"One thing, sir. This may or may not be related to the case, but Mr. Soames, according to the latest reports, is in dire financial straits."

"Soames! But he's a bachelor with a fair property, I believe. The House doesn't pay him, of course, but his constituency must."

"I fear not, sir. And I hear his property is mortgaged."

Lenox frowned. He had known Jack Soames for two decades, perhaps longer: a large fair-haired man and former athlete who was well-liked, if not entirely respected, by his acquaintances.

"There was also," Graham said, "one more political figure in the house, sir."

"Who is it? Disraeli, I suppose you'll say, and he owes his tailor two shillings."

"No, sir, Newton Duff."

Lenox frowned again. "Duff? Really? Seems so unlikely."

"He has been there a week. As you know, sir, he is not well-liked, even by members of his own party, but he has been, from what I understand, an effective politician—"

"An understatement. He carried the India bill by sheer will."

"He may have some political business with Mr. Barnard, sir."

"He may. Is he meant to stay until the ball?"

"Yes, sir. Although he has his own lodgings, too, from what I understand."

"I see."

Newton Duff was, like Soames, a large man, but the resemblance ended there. Soames was fair, Duff was dark; one was friendly, the other gruff; one was ineffective, the other was furiously effective; one was known to drink and dissipate, the other was of an iron constitution. Soames and Duff under one roof?

"And is he impoverished, Graham?"

"On the contrary, sir, he grew immensely richer this week because of the positive turn in the stock market."

"He trades?"

"Heavily, I understand, sir. I believe his largest holdings are the Star Company and the Pacific Trust, two companies that deal in speculation on overseas goods. In fact, I think both Mr. Duff and Mr. Soames have some relationship to the Pacific company; it might bear looking into."

"No, I think the answer is probably closer to home. It doesn't sound like much of a time, between Soames, who's always drunk, and Duff, who growls if you look at him, and this lad Eustace Bramwell, who's no doubt covered with spots and wears thick glasses. Did Barnard seek out any better company?"

"There is the other nephew, sir."

"The other?"

"Yes, sir."

"Lady Jane always says that nephews are a plague, sent to humble us before God, Graham."

"No doubt she is correct, sir."

"What's this one called?"

"Claude Barnard, sir. He is the son of Mr. Barnard's younger brother, Stephen."

"I met him."

"Sir?"

"This morning. He swore in front of me and said it was early, even though it was eight o'clock."

"The younger generation, sir, is notoriously lax."

"Is this other nephew bookish, as well?"

"On the contrary, sir, he frequents the Jumpers at all hours, and it was he who paved his cousin's way into the club. Otherwise Eustace Bramwell might have been blackballed, from what I learned, sir. Cambridge men are unpopular there."

"Claude is popular, then?"

"Yes, sir. He is twenty-five and still studies at Oxford, but comes down to London to stay whenever the feeling takes him, or so it seems to the members of the household."

"What does he study?"

"First he studied to enter the clergy, sir, then he changed to history and then to the study of literature."

"Not botany?"

"No, sir."

"It's a shame. Unless—are he and his cousin close?"

"Not at all, sir. Beyond the effort of paving his way into the Jumpers, they barely know each other."

"Curious."

"Yes, sir. I understand there is some question of rivalry between Mr. Barnard's younger sister and his younger brother, though both are on good terms with Mr. Barnard himself for self-evident reasons."

"Rich as Croesus, twice as old."

"Precisely, sir."

"Although really he's only sixty or so."

"Yes, sir."

"Ten years ago he was only fifty. And fifty is quite young."

"Quite, sir."

"And who is the last guest, Graham?"

"A surprising one, sir: Colonel Roderick Potts."

"Ah," said Lenox. Potts. That complicated things. He was a steel manufacturer, and the richest untitled man in the whole of the British Isles.

~ Chapter 13 ~

The first two days of the case had been cruelly cold, but when Lenox woke on the third morning the winter sun was shining through his windows and the sky was blue, crisp, and cloudless. The fire in his bedroom's grate had died down, but he felt warm beneath his covers.

He lay still for a few moments, unwilling to begin the day. But at last he roused himself with the prospect of eggs and kippers—and perhaps a pot of coffee—and descended the stairs to the dining room in his robe and slippers.

Ellie, the cook, had not stinted with breakfast. Placed along the wide table, which was covered with a plain blue tablecloth, were the foods that had inspired him to get out of bed, along with toast, butter, marmalade, and a bowl of plums. Lenox happily ate his eggs, which he liked scrambled, and even took a second helping of kippers, which were, as befit Ellie's own bias, slightly burnt.

Only when he leaned back in his chair, with a second cup of milky coffee in his right hand, did he think about the case. He ignored the morning paper, which was tucked beneath the tray of toast, and he ignored the letters that sat on the side table, knowing they would find their way to his desk that afternoon if he had not yet read them.

What did he know? A great deal and very little, it seemed to him. If he was going to speak to the residents of Barnard's house he would have to ambush them, which was not a prospect he relished. It might be all right for Soames, and even for the gaggle of nephews, but not, probably, for Duff, although they were acquaintances. Potts was a trickier matter altogether. He might talk, and then again, as the mood took him, he might not. And clearly, Lenox had already received all the help he would get from Barnard.

And yet he knew more than Exeter, to be certain, and if he had had a few days in Barnard's house he felt he could have solved the case. He knew the means of the murder, and he knew the source of the poison, which was, in all likelihood, Oxford. But did that point to Claude, the wild young student? Or to Eustace, who was a botanist and might have visited his cousin at university? Or to Soames, who lived not far away, in Dulwich, and was well-known for his enthusiastic gardening? Or indeed to Barnard himself, who might have visited his nephew at Oxford and obtained *bella indigo* to feed some particular orchid? All these questions he could only answer by interviewing the houseguests.

He would have to approach the case from the other side, at least in part, he supposed, until he could catch the suspects off guard. That is, he would have to analyze the motive of the case, rather than the means and the possible murderers.

What did he have as motive? He walked around to the side of the table, picked up an apple, and sat back thoughtfully against the sideboard. There was, of course, the money. Who would have known about it? Barnard, to be sure. Perhaps one of his guests had learned it was in the house. Perhaps Prue Smith had stumbled on it.

And then there was the possibility that she had had an affair with one of the men. Or that she had made enemies. He would know more when Graham gave his second report, perhaps—he had learned to trust Graham's findings unquestioningly, without wasting time by asking how he got them—but what did it mean to say that she was exotic? That she was mysterious?

And, of course, the possibility that it was something unknown—revenge, psychosis, unrequited love, another matter of money, anything under the sun.

He decided that he would have to talk to each of the men, no matter how Barnard and Exeter reacted. He would continue to follow the trail from the back end as he had been, but he would have to seek out the suspects too.

"Graham?" he called out, and took a bite of the apple.

His butler came noiselessly through a side door. "Sir?"

"When you find out what Miss Smith was like, Graham, be sure to find out whether she was exotic or mysterious or anything like that. And what those words mean."

"I shall try to do so, sir. I would be able to gather more information if I began right away, however."

"Take the morning, too, then. Do you need more money?"

"If I am forced to bribe anybody, sir, I will tell you after the event."

"No, no, just take the money on my dresser before you go out."

"As you say, sir."

"Good hunting, Graham."

"The same to you, sir."

Lenox smiled and then wandered up the stairs, still eating his apple. He decided that he would run over to McConnell's first to see about the glass from Prue Smith's desk. Upstairs he bathed and dressed, and then asked one of the maids to call for his carriage.

He had taken the glass with him from Prue Smith's room two nights ago and given it to McConnell, although even as he did it he knew that he oughtn't to have. Still, there was only a brief window of time in which he could have acted. Exeter was no doubt still interviewing the servants one by one, while upstairs the murderer played a rubber of whist and dressed for dinner at his club. Within that context, Lenox didn't mind the dishonesty of taking the glass.

A somber servant named Shreve, if he remembered correctly, escorted Lenox into McConnell's vast dining room when he arrived at the house on Bond Street, which was so massive that it seemed to take up an entire block. McConnell himself was nowhere in evidence, but Toto sat at the end of the long dining table, eating a piece of toast that looked enormous in her delicate hand and reading a volume prettily bound in gold.

"Charles!" she said when she saw him. She put down everything wherever her hands happened to be—the book on her plate, the toast on a nearby chair—and ran toward him. "Dear Charles!"

"How are you, Toto?"

"How is darling Aunt Jane? Why hasn't she been to see me? I called two days ago, and still she hasn't come! Oh, and how are you, Charles? I know you have a case. Thomas has been playing with some silly glass noon and night and talking excitedly about suspects and things, which is why he's asleep and I'm forced to eat breakfast all alone at this huge table, like a princess locked in a tower."

She was like something fragile, small, and beautiful that you might find in a forest, living in perfect radiance no matter how torrential the monsoons or fierce the predators. No tempest touched her beauty. Lenox had known her since she was born. He was friends with her father from school—and even before that, now that he thought of it. Their own fathers had served in Parliament together, well before Toto was born.

"Perhaps," he said, "I can make the table seem less huge, my dear, by sitting with you for a moment."

"Oh, do! And Shreve, wake up Thomas and tell him to come downstairs as quickly as he can, or quicker, and bring out another plate and forks and things for Mr. Lenox, would you?" She whispered, as Shreve left, "It *is* a burden, Charles, to be stuck with the grumpiest butler in all of London, and to have him stare at one like a witless ogre, but Thomas says we must keep him, for some reason. My father gave him to us."

"And complains about it every time he gets a chance, my dear. He told me the other day he was damned if he'd do it over again."

"Well, he can have him back, then." Toto picked up her toast from the chair and laid her book aside while she poured Lenox a cup of tea. "There will be coffee when Thomas comes down, but I only drink tea. He says it's lower class not to like coffee, but I don't, so there, don't you think?"

"I can't stand coffee. We shall be lower class together, Toto."

"You liar, all you drink is coffee and I know it, but I agree to your offer nevertheless. Eggs?"

"I only just had breakfast."

"Posh. Shreve, or whoever makes the eggs, does do that well."

They ate and chatted, and after fifteen minutes McConnell came in, up early, for him, and wearing a suit. He said hello, kissed his wife more tenderly than Lenox had known he did any longer, and then buttered a piece of toast and took a bite, all the while standing up.

"Shall I show you?" he said to Lenox.

"Of course."

"Oh, you beasts," Toto said, "sit down and eat!"

"We can't," said McConnell, "we have—"

"I know, your rotten case. Well, goodbye, then."

She stood up and flung her arms around Charles and then picked up her book, which was lying on a stray sausage, and began to read again. Lenox felt that lift of his spirits that he always did when he was with her, as he and McConnell left the room and went across a hall and up a short flight of stairs to the study.

As McConnell unlocked the door, he said, "Amazing, about her being illiterate."

"You got the note?" said Lenox.

"I did."

"It *is* amazing."

"What does it show, do you think?" McConnell asked.

Lenox thought for a moment. "Either that the murderer didn't know her, or that he didn't know her as well as he thought."

⮜ Chapter 14 ⮞

McConnell's study was, like every other room in the house, slightly larger than one could conceive of a room's ever being. The ceiling rose twenty-five feet in the air, and all four sides were paneled in dark red wood. On the far end of the room was McConnell's laboratory, spread out over several tables, one of which was covered with chemicals and another of which had squids in jars and samples of algae and other things of that sort on it. To the left was a high stone hearth, surrounded by leather armchairs and ottomans, and a single couch, on which McConnell, in his darkest days, had dozed through the night, waking to drink or to stare into the fire. On the right, overlooking the street, was his desk.

The room's most distinctive feature was a thin spiral staircase made out of marble, with cherubim carved into it. The staircase led up to a balcony, which encircled the room on all four sides. A thin railing closed it off, but there were chairs and tables overlooking the lower level. Behind them were rows of cases, filled with McConnell's books. Collecting first editions of early English and Latin scientific texts was his hobby, and he had managed to fill many of the shelves, so that standing in the middle of the lower level one could see an entire universe up the small staircase. It was where McConnell had his guests to tea, but he offered nothing to his guest this morning, rightly suspecting that Lenox had eaten with Toto.

The doctor liked to say that this was the sole place in the house upon which Toto had never left her imprint, and while Lenox would never for a second have thought to comment on their marriage to either of them, he had noticed, recently, that in a small way Toto *had* begun to leave her imprint on the study. She had had the late rosemary sent in, Lenox guessed, the flower of remembrance—he couldn't see McConnell putting it there himself—and there were a few new paintings on the walls. They were of wild horses in the Scottish dales, McConnell's home country. Scotland had always divided the two, but she had had them commissioned, Lenox knew, which was just the sort of peace offering she was likely to make.

They walked toward the laboratory at the end of the room.

"The glass," said McConnell, "was trickier than I suspected it would be."

"How do you mean?"

Both men stood by a large black table covered with beakers full of chemicals and solutions, of which the centerpiece was the object in question, enclosed in a case, almost exactly as Lenox had last seen it.

"Well, there was no doubt in my mind that *bella indigo* killed Miss Smith. Poisons, as you know, are one of my hobbies."

"Partly why I asked you to come," Lenox said.

"Of course. As I say, there was no doubt in my mind. I came back that evening and searched through my sources"—he gestured toward a stack of books in disarray by his desk—"and confirmed my first reaction. In conjunction with the small clues that you gathered, I assumed that the glass would yield up no more than what I had suspected. Murder. But there was a bump in the road."

"What was it?"

"When I tested the glass, I found that the resin on its lip was not, in fact, *bella indigo.*"

"Then what was it?"

"It was identical to the contents of the bottle of poison it stood next to on the desk. Arsenic. Mixed with a dash of water, I expect, for it was fractionally weakened."

"That makes my work significantly harder," Lenox said. "If arsenic killed her. Or significantly easier, if Jensen comes up with a name from his research into the bottle."

"Ah. Perhaps if you had sought another man. But I delved deeper."

"And found what?"

McConnell pointed at the bottom of the glass. "Do you see anything?"

"It looks clean, I should say."

"It does. But there were a few specks of poison at the bottom. There usually are—sometimes enough for a small sample if you do it cleverly, though my colleagues would declare that heresy. My own opinion is that one day even a single speck of something will tell us everything about it."

"Doesn't seem quite right, that," said Lenox dubiously.

McConnell chuckled. "Anyway, I checked, and those dregs, unlike the poison that so dramatically turned yellow in the victim's room, turned purple. The glass had been used—filled with *bella indigo,* that is—*then* washed, *then* filled with water and arsenic, and finally drained again into a sink."

"Fascinating."

"A double deception. To confirm what I had found, I looked around the rim of the glass."

"Yes?"

"While there was arsenic on the lip of the glass, there was no longer any sign that any human being had drunk from the glass. No partial print, even. And glass is notoriously easy to find fingerprints on, even with our inadequate system. The glass was washed *after* Prue Smith ingested the *bella indigo* and *before* it reached me, or her fingerprints would be all over it."

"All of it is crafty," said Lenox, "but only to the point that the murderer assumed that the police would conclude that the girl had destroyed herself."

"Exactly. Though the murderer wanted to conceal as well the use of the rare drug."

"Which may mean he knew the poison was so rare it would lead to him, perhaps. That's very helpful. But why not just use the arsenic?"

McConnell looked at him keenly. "That crossed my mind," he said. "I think there are two reasons. The first is that the murderer thinks himself very clever—a doctor, perhaps. The second is that arsenic is less definitely deadly than *bella indigo*, which always kills. Arsenic is hard to dose. It can make people very sick rather than kill them, for instance. And it's easier to trace. The arsenic on the table must have been an afterthought. . . ."

Both men walked toward the armchairs by the fire. A window was open, as it was in every season, and a chill blew through the room.

"Can I offer you a glass of something?"

"This early?"

"It's nearly ten, you know." McConnell studiously avoided Lenox's eyes as he poured himself a drink and took the first sip. "Anything else new?"

Lenox shrugged. "Yes and no. I know who Barnard's guests are, now."

"Who?"

"Two nephews. Neither of them seems the sort. And two politicians. Neither of them seems the sort either."

"Which ones?"

"Soames and Duff."

"Newton Duff?"

Lenox nodded.

"I wouldn't like to have him in my house, for what it's worth," said McConnell, and took another sip.

"Nor would I," Lenox answered. "That doesn't convict him, unfortunately."

"Who's the last?"

"Roderick Potts."

"The fellow with all the money?"

"Yes."

"Toto won't let us see him. She says he's a beast, whatever that means. Perhaps even a perfect beast, which from my experience is a title that she reserves for few people. Shreve, on occasion her father, on occasion . . . well, myself, I suppose." McConnell laughed uneasily and took a long sip of his drink.

"So you don't know him at all?" said Lenox quickly.

"Not at all."

"Toto may be right about him. Jane, insofar as she controls my social life, would never let me see him either."

"Lower class, or a brute?" asked McConnell.

"Both, perhaps. From what I know he has few social aspirations, which sets him apart from most of these enormously rich men who come to London."

"Sets him apart from Barnard."

"You're right," said Lenox, "absolutely right. I would say that the only force strong enough to draw each to the other is a large amount of money. And as it happens, though I can't mention details, there is a large amount of money on the periphery of the case."

"Perhaps at the center."

"It had crossed my mind."

"How did this chap make all his money? Robbing graves, or something?"

"He's from the north, actually, near Newcastle. He manages industrial plants there. Steel, that sort of thing. The end of the country farmer, the beginning of the modern age. Actually, I know very little about him." He would have to think of a way to change that.

"Why did he come to London, then?"

"You've got me there. He lives in grand style quite near here. It may be that he manages his plants from afar and gambles on the Exchange."

"That sounds like Barnard's cup of tea," McConnell said.

"Indeed it does. But you were right to say that Barnard would usually be too proud to have a man like Potts in his house—you know, salt of the earth."

"Curious."

"Yes. Although from what Graham says I believe there may be another possible reason." Lenox frowned. "Apparently Potts has a daughter who has come of age. She's pretty, I gather, and extremely well educated, and she'll have a dowry and a half, should it come to marriage."

"An impoverished older house, you think?"

"Something along those lines, I expect. Potts, as I say, has a grand house in London himself, but he would have gone to Barnard's in any case if he had an ounce of social ambition."

"Of course," McConnell said. "Do you think Potts means to tie the girl to one of the nephews?"

"I doubt it. I imagine he thinks too lowly of them and too highly of his daughter. But if Potts could broker a deal with an older house, one of the Duchess Marchmain's sons, for instance, he might have entrée to a world outside politics and money. Our world, Thomas."

"We see enough of Barnard."

"That's true. But he has more acquaintances than friends."

"What does this man Potts look like?" McConnell asked.

"I don't know, really. A twinkle in his eye, good posture, exercises daily, cold baths, all that, I daresay. The self-made man. Intelligent, whatever you think of him."

"Toto thinks quite highly of the self-made man, of course."

"I do too, if it comes to it," said Lenox.

"As do I."

Lenox stood up. They shook hands and agreed to check in with each other soon, and McConnell saw his friend out of the room.

Chapter 15

It was midmorning when Lenox left McConnell's house, and while the air was brisk it wasn't biting, and he walked along the busy sidewalks in a cheerful mood. The streets nearby were open and sunny, and he felt glad to be outside. His destination was the Jumpers, which when he found it seemed to be a building much like that of any other club: four or five stories, white stone, with comfortable rooms behind the windows. He was soon dissuaded of this impression of normalcy, however, when a shoe hurtled through the front window.

He had chosen to come here because it was the haunt, according to Graham, of Claude Barnard, the young man whom Lenox had briefly met in the hallway at the lad's uncle's house. Graham had said he could be found here at all hours of the day, and indeed, when Lenox asked the porter if he was in residence, the porter, who looked as harassed as Job on a middling day, merely pointed straight ahead to the dining room.

The shoe had evidently had its origin here, for there was a young man, apparently called Pinky, hopping angrily toward the door on one foot.

Claude was seated at the far end of the table, next to someone

Lenox thought might be one of Lord Williams's sons. He stood up without seeing the detective and began to walk out of the room, to calls of disappointment from his companions.

"Got to see to business!" he kept saying.

Lenox waylaid him by the door. "If I could have a moment of your time, young man?" he said.

Claude seemed to be clearly against the proposition. "What for?"

"You may remember that we met yesterday morning."

"The chap in the hallway?"

"Yes."

"Oh! Well, friend of Uncle's, friend of mine. What can I do for you?"

"Answer a few questions. I'd be pleased to take you to wherever you're conducting your business, and we can speak along the way."

Claude looked at him doubtfully. "If you wish, I suppose."

"Thank you," said Lenox.

They stepped into Lenox's brougham, and Claude gave the driver an address on Marmalade Lane, a bad part of East London. Not the usual haunt of young and carefree Oxford students. Soon they had crossed London into a poorer neighborhood.

"Did you know a girl named Prudence Smith?"

"The murdered girl? To look at, nothing more."

"To look at?"

"She was a maid. I saw her. I daresay she saw me, too." Claude smiled jauntily.

"Did you form any impression of her?"

"None. Well, she was rather pretty, I suppose. But no, not otherwise."

"How long have you been staying at your uncle's house, Claude?"

"Not long. A week, perhaps."

"You are on good terms with him?"

"Lovely terms. I'm like the son he never had."

"Did you kill Prudence Smith?"

If Claude was taken aback, he refused to show it. "No. Couldn't have done, I'm afraid."

"What do you mean?"

"Word gets around. I don't know about poison or any of that rot, for one."

"Surely it's the work of a moment to research any poison in the world?"

"Ah, but I have an alibi as well, dear old chum."

Lenox betrayed no exasperation. "An alibi? You seem to have assumed that blame would land on your doorstep."

"My uncle's doorstep, you mean? Well, I can count. Only a few people were about, you know."

"What is your alibi?"

"I was in the drawing room."

"So was everybody else."

"In that case I suppose none of us did it."

"You didn't leave the drawing room?"

"Not really. May have nipped upstairs to the washroom."

"During which time you might have poisoned the young girl."

"I went *up*stairs, old chap."

"Can anybody confirm that?"

"Anyone you like. Messes of people. Maids and things. Footmen by the dozen. And the other guests. The man called Potts was in the room most of the time, reading a paper, and when he flitted out someone else was always there."

"You seem to have thought this through."

"Only the facts, you know."

"Do you have any reason to believe that any of the other guests, or any of the servants, committed the crime?"

Claude frowned. "No, not really. Oh, but perhaps it was Eustace," he said brightly.

"Your cousin?"

"Old Barnard wouldn't like that," said Claude, talking as much to himself as to Lenox. "The bad apple. Might turn him against his sister, mightn't it?"

"You don't like Eustace?"

"Can't stand him. Grim chap. Horrid company. Always reading, you know. Just reads. I chalk it up to bad early influences. The child is the father of the man, I always say. Heartbroken parents, all that sort of thing."

"In that case why did you submit his name for the Jumpers?"

"You don't miss a trick, do you? I did it because Uncle asked me to. No doubt saw the boy's defects and wanted to place him among good sorts."

"You want to please your uncle?"

"Always obliging. Strong family connection. Jumpers through a few hoops." Claude laughed uproariously at the pun.

A few moments later, the carriage had drawn to a halt on a thin dirty street, where the fresh snow was already covered by a layer of dust and children were running about. A few of them ran up to Lenox and Claude, and the elder man gave them each a coin and asked them to watch his carriage.

Claude led his questioner into a dingy wooden storefront with the name THE PAINTED DUCK on a weatherbeaten sign hanging above the door. It appeared to Lenox that they had come to a coffeehouse.

Inside it was dark, even with daylight outdoors, and smelled strongly of dark coffee and tobacco. There was wood paneling on the walls and a great Rumsford fireplace in the center of the room, with horsehair chairs and low tables all around it. Above the bar were bookshelves with souvenir cups on them, and horseshoes hung on the walls. There were dozens of men sitting around sipping coffee, not so much because they liked it as to rent space in the shop, and only one woman, a redhead with furious freckles who sat at the bar and talked to the proprietor. Most of the men were wearing out-of-fashion clothes, mended several times over, and they all talked in low voices, as if they didn't want to be overheard.

The heyday of the coffeehouse had been a century ago, and they no longer drew many of the literary crowd, but they still received support from Parliament. They were thought to provide an alternative to drinking in pubs.

"Your treat, my friend?" asked Claude, finding a table.

"Of course."

Claude ordered them both coffee, and then had for himself some toast with black-currant jam and a hard-boiled egg. Lenox declined food and neglected the coffee after his tentative first sip.

"You have business here, I believe?"

"Of a sort. After all, this is business, too," said Claude merrily.

"I suppose."

"And I have a meeting in a few minutes."

"Then I shall try to be brief. What do you know of your uncle's work at the Royal Mint?"

"Virtually nothing."

"That seems odd."

"It is his private mint which interests me most."

"Does he confide in you?"

"No. You don't think my uncle did it, do you? He's a decent enough chap, I should say. Not the type. Bit flinty, bit imperious, but a leader of men."

"I do not suspect him, no. What do you know of your other guests?"

"Well, there's Eustace, who's a tick. Of the first order. He's probably your man. And there's Soames, who's nice enough. Duff is a hard sort but full of moral fiber. Not likely to murder a girl unless she blasphemed in his presence or something. Potts— well, as vulgar as the day is long, my old man, but I don't see that there was any money in the business."

Lenox had his own opinion of people's vulgarity, but the boy was accurate enough.

"All told, not a very criminal lot," Claude went on. "I should guess that a man slipped in from the street. The papers always have things like that, you know. I saw only the other day about a man who tried to rob a bank by kidnapping the manager's daughter. When he couldn't find her, he took the manager's dog instead! Sorry to say he failed. Gives one hope when a chap can kidnap a dog and get a thousand pounds out of it."

"And the servants?"

"Does one notice servants? There's no butler, which is queer. I wouldn't bet against the housekeeper in a fight with an angry tiger. One of the footmen was engaged to the girl. She herself was the only pretty one."

Lenox rose. "I'll leave you to your business, then."

Upon hearing this, the freckled girl at the counter stood up.

"Good to see you," said Claude.

As he neared the door, Lenox turned around. "Don't tell anyone that we met, Claude?"

"Why on earth not?"

"Because, I hope, you desire the capture of this girl's murderer."

Claude sighed. "As you say. I shan't."

"Thank you."

"Though perhaps I'll tell Eustace that the Yard is closing in on him."

"Please don't."

Claude sighed again. "It's a hard world, when an honest young man can't have a bit of fun after the daily grind."

"Nevertheless."

"Very well."

Lenox walked out toward the sidewalk, where the young boys were watching the carriage intently, as they had been paid to do, and discussing what they would spend their newfound riches on. He looked up and down the street. If only there were some way to fix this, he thought, these children with their worn-through shoes and dirty caps; the women reusing tea leaves until they were nearly white; the men spending their pay on gin, not food; the beggars, often no more than children, playing what they called hookem-snivey: pretending to be badly ill to encourage sympathy. A way to change all that.

Perhaps he would stand for Parliament someday. Somebody there needed to make their primary concern the debtors' prisons, the Rookery, the Dials, the children looking in the gutters for something to sell. The Board of Trade and the India Commission and the Irish question were all very well, but here were human beings in their own city, suffering too.

As he stepped into his carriage he looked back to the coffeehouse and saw the girl sitting on Claude's lap, kissing him on the cheek, and money quickly exchanging hands, and while he considered himself a progressive, he felt again disheartened.

⤳ Chapter 16 ⤳

Eustace would be more difficult to track down than Claude, who seemed to use the Jumpers as a daily office, but he would be easier to catch than any of the other guests. According to Graham, whose research was impeccable, he usually ate lunch either at Barnard's house or at the Oxford and Cambridge Club, which was somewhat subdued in comparison with the Jumpers and thus, in all probability, more attractive to the lad.

The Oxford and Cambridge was on Pall Mall, near Lenox's house, and he arrived in front of it just in time for lunch. The streets were snowy and cold, and as he went through the heavy wood doors he sighed with relief at the warmth.

And here he struck it lucky, saving himself the unpleasant task of lurking about Clarges Street, waiting for the boy to leave his uncle's house: Eustace was in the dining room.

Lenox sat down for a bit of food himself, a bubbling steak and kidney pie with lovely plump pieces of egg hidden inside it. His table was under a portrait of Henry VI where he could keep an eye on Eustace, who was across the hall eating a leg of lamb and reading what Lenox guessed was a scientific periodical. He was a thin lad with dark hair and a pinched, unpleasant face, small dark eyes and a sharp chin, without any sense of lightness about him.

Lenox ate only a little and, as a result, finished before his counterpart. He sat and sipped a glass of Madeira while he waited for Eustace to leave, enjoying, at least, the minor increase of civility that the club presented after Claude's coffeehouse. Although, to be sure, the coffeehouse presented prettier company. Most of the men in the dining room were half asleep and all of them would have fared poorly if judged solely for beauty by a jury of their female peers. The youngest might have been sixty-five, but for Lenox and Eustace. Strange company for a boy up from university.

He followed Eustace downstairs and into the small smoking room, after another ten minutes, and sat quite near him, in an armchair by the window. The young man's clothes were old-fashioned. He had a leaf and several sprigs of some bush peeking out from his pocket, and while he read he touched them absent-mindedly. Clearly, Lenox thought, he was passionate about his subject. Perhaps he had been in a garden just that morning.

Lenox had barely had a chance to speak when Eustace said to him, "What do you think of these horrid liberals, sir?"

Lenox sighed inwardly, but smiled. "I am afraid I count myself in their ranks, though they're not so horrid when you've eaten supper with them once or twice."

The boy frowned. "You've got it all wrong," he said.

Lenox realized that he had run into the worst sort of young man, the one who hangs about clubs for older men, imitating their gentle lives, talking gravely about politics, and always learning the club rules to the letter. On the very lower cusp of the upper class himself, but absolutely firm about maintaining clear rules for the servants. No doubt he sat on the house committee and argued strenuously against the admission of scholarship boys. Lenox would have preferred even Claude.

"I daresay I do have it wrong. But youth is to correct the aged, as they say."

"Well, some of the aged have the right opinion. At this club in particular, you know."

"What political issues do you feel especially strongly about?" Lenox couldn't help but ask.

Eustace perked up at this. "Well, for instance, there's the matter of feudal responsibility. This country was founded on a model of master and man. It's why the sun never sets on our empire, you know: feudal responsibility. And now they're trying to give every man the vote—give *women* the vote, for goodness' sake. What was wrong with the old system?"

"Surely the reform acts make England more democratic, fairer to all its citizens?"

"Read Plato on democracy. Just the mob's appetite running wild. What you want is an oligarchy of the elite. Rotten boroughs are absolutely sound, you know. The Duke of Albany knows better who should be in Parliament than the man who digs his vegetables."

Lenox pegged him as a young man on the lower fringe of the landed gentry, clinging hard to some idea of gentility. It gave him some sympathy for Eustace Bramwell.

"How about imperial reform?"

"Don't get me started: the Indians, the Africans—they need us. Don't you see that? Look at the way we've brought Christian spirit to Burma and rudimentary education to Bengal."

Lenox decided to turn the conversation. "Don't you frequent the Jumpers as well as this club?"

Eustace seemed surprised. "I did, of course, but it was the mistake of a man who is first coming to London, and I fell in with the bad company of my cousin, who forced me to drink, and all sorts—just a moment, sir. Was that a general question, or do you know me?"

"I confess that I know you. I am a friend of your uncle's."

Eustace looked at him suspiciously. "My uncle is no liberal."

"As we get older, there is common ground between us aside from politics."

"I suppose."

"To confess fully, I am here to ask you about the servant who died."

"Are you from the Yard? How did you get in here?"

"No, no, I am an amateur. Charles Lenox."

"Surely not the great expert on Roman life?"

"If you please."

"Why, what an honor, liberal or otherwise! Do you know, I often find myself consulting that book you wrote—that *was* you, I take it?"

"It was," said Lenox. A monograph on daily life from beggar to soldier to emperor, during Hadrian's reign.

"I have to say, that was an ingenious book."

"Thank you."

"And then, you know, the article you published last month in the Academy's journal, about the historical life of Bath during Roman occupation—sheer inspiration, to do that kind of on-the-ground research."

"I appreciate it," Lenox said. "And I would be pleased to talk about my writings another time. But the young girl is dead, and I really do want to see the matter through—only as shadow support for the Yard, you know."

"I see."

"It shall only be a very few questions."

Eustace Bramwell put his journal aside and nodded, acquiescent now that he knew he was talking to the author of *Hadrian's People*.

"Good," said Lenox. "Good. First things first. Do you have any idea who killed the girl?"

"I can't say that I have."

"You didn't kill her?"

"Sir, if this is the sort of question which I am meant to answer, then this interview is at an end."

"It is a necessary question."

Eustace did not seem mollified. "The impertinence—"

"Very well, very well," said Lenox. He was growing weary of nephews. Jane would sympathize. "Have you heard of *bella indigo?*"

"Of course I have."

"How?"

"I graduated with a first in botany and won a prize in the bargain, sir."

"Of course."

"Are you implying that *bella indigo* killed this girl?"

"It may have," said Lenox. "Have you ever come into contact with the substance?"

"No. Cambridge quite rightly considers it too volatile."

"But Oxford cultivates it?"

"Oxford is less rigorous, in many ways—"

"Yes, yes, thank you. Have you ever been to Oxford?"

"Yes, as a child, and once several years ago to visit my cousin."

"How many years ago?"

"Perhaps three." Eustace lit a cigarette as he said this.

"Are you close with your cousin?"

"Far from it. I visited him as a gesture of familial kindness, and while I was there he nearly had me arrested."

"Did you visit the botany department at Oxford?"

"And acquire enough *bella indigo* to kill the girl? No. At any rate, if you knew anything, you would know that the poison becomes neutral after a year's time, when its use as a fertilizer for certain rare flowers may begin. The chemical structure is, from what we can gather, unstable."

"What were you doing between eleven and one two days ago, on the day Miss Smith died?"

"Not that it's any of your business, but I was painting the entire time."

"Painting?" Lenox asked, leaning closer.

"Yes."

"What were you painting?"

"The view from a window in the drawing room. I was concentrating deeply."

"Did you finish the painting that day?"

"No. I never finished it at all, just added a few hasty strokes the next day to make it look complete. I was tired of it."

"Did you leave the drawing room?"

"Not for a moment. I was absorbed by my work."

"Who can vouch for that, among the others in the drawing room?"

"I've no idea. I wasn't consciously trying to generate an alibi. None of us had an idea that a girl was being murdered, or I daresay we should have been more attentive to people's comings and goings. I myself would have made a point of seeing which other people left the room, if I knew that this sort of insulting suspicion were going to be directed at me."

"How well do you know the other men who are staying with your uncle?"

"Well enough."

"Do you have an opinion of them?"

"Soames is a wastrel. Potts is lower class. Duff, on the other hand, is a man with sound ideas about things. A Cambridge man too, you know. Rigorous standards for the poor. No more free rides. Good about India, too. Very sound."

"Are you close with your uncle?"

"Extremely. More so every day."

"Is he close with Claude?"

"Not at all. Kind, for the family's sake, but sees him for what he is."

"Do you know anything of your uncle's work at the mint?"

"No."

"If I may ask a delicate question, what is your financial situation?"

Eustace reddened. "Good lord. I'm fine, thank you."

"May I ask how?"

"If you must, I receive income from my investments."

"What investments?"

"Uncle Barnard gave Claude and me each ten thousand pounds upon reaching the majority. I invested mine soundly."

"And Claude?"

"I've no idea what he did with his."

"Which of your housemates do you think is most likely to be guilty of the crime?"

"If you ask my opinion, it was some urchin from the streets who wanted to steal from the house. Or perhaps this maid was stealing, and someone taught her a lesson."

"Barring that possibility."

"Soames. Man's a wastrel, I spotted it from fifty yards."

Lenox stood up. "I shan't take any more of your time."

"Yes, yes, well, nice to meet you."

"Please don't tell anyone we met."

"And why on earth not?"

"Your silence will benefit the girl who has died. We must try to remember her claims in this situation."

"I shall tell whomsoever I please. But I shall consider your request."

"You would do the girl a grave disservice. She has had a hard enough fate."

Eustace seemed to falter. "Well, perhaps," he said sullenly.

Lenox left the smoking room without another word. It was the second time of the morning that he had become disheartened at the prospect of the generation to which he was meant to bequeath the earth. Interesting that each of the cousins had called the other a wastrel; neither seemed a particular prize to him, but did that sort of mutual animus have a deeper basis than incompatibility? It might simply have been that they were related to Barnard and were competing for a spot in his last will and testament. An unfortunate thing in a family, that. Lenox thought with some sense of comfort that at least his own nephews, Edmund's sons, wouldn't care about his money. They were bright young lads, polite and kind besides.

∽ Chapter 17 ∽

After an unsatisfying morning, McConnell aside, and an unsatisfying lunch, Lenox made his way not homeward, though in truth he wanted to, but rather to Oxley Crescent, a small neighborhood on the periphery of London. The driver of his carriage, he felt, was beginning to tire of these trips to obscure and occasionally lower-class sections of London and would have preferred to travel solely to Piccadilly Circus and back, but Lenox felt, with some sense of self-righteousness, that the driver's purposes ranked, at the moment, below his own.

As they drove he read the *Daily Telegraph*, the Whig paper, and before too long they had arrived at their destination. It was a street of somewhat better repute than that in which he had found Jeremiah Jones, and also of better repute than that to which he had accompanied Claude Barnard that morning, but he could imagine that it might offend his driver's higher feelings. His driver lived on Hampden Lane.

Lenox, however, thought it a nice quiet street, with small houses spaced close together but not in disrepair, and pleasant little gardens dotted along the sidewalk, and old women sitting on their porches or, in this colder weather, at their front windows.

It was on Oxley Crescent that Skaggs lived, and it was to Skaggs's abode that Lenox had come, in search of a private investigator. Several cases had passed since he had been here, he thought. He knocked twice on the door of a white house with dark shutters, and after a moment a young girl appeared.

"May I help ye, my lord?" she said.

"I'm Charles Lenox. Are you the lady of the house?"

"No, my lord, I'm the girl."

"Is Mr. Skaggs at home?"

"Just a moment, my lord."

The door closed, and a moment later Skaggs himself appeared. He was a man in his late thirties, dressed in a brown suit, with a bald head and a fat face and a long scar across the left side of his neck. He had once been fearsome, and still could be when asked, but in truth he had been tamed by his wife in recent years and had settled down to respectability. He was the private investigator Lenox had been looking for.

"Sorry about the girl, Mr. Lenox."

"Not at all."

"We've only just hired her."

"A significant thing to do."

"The wife was always on about getting someone. We had our third, you see."

"Congratulations, Mr. Skaggs. A boy or a girl?"

"All girls, Mr. Lenox. A pride and a joy, though."

"You're a lucky man."

"Thank you, sir. Will you come in?"

The two men walked into a small room at the front of the house, with only two chairs and a table in it. This was Skaggs's place of business. Lenox sat down, and Skaggs asked how he could be of service.

"Do you know of Roderick Potts?" said Lenox.

"Yes, sir. 'E's often in the papers, sir."

"That's the man. I'd like you to follow him, closely enough to hear and see what you can."

"I can do that, Mr. Lenox."

"Excellent. Here's five days' wages." He handed over nineteen shillings. "Can you begin right away?"

"Yes," said Skaggs.

Just at that moment, a woman walked in the door, dressed in a new bonnet and an old frock and carrying an infant.

"Is this the new baby?"

"It is. Sorry for the intrusion, Mr. Lenox, it'll only be a moment."

Skaggs began to gesture at his wife to leave, but she paid him no mind.

"This is Emily," she said, and offered him to Lenox. "I've often seen your carriage through the front window, Mr. Lenox, but never to meet. I'm Mrs. Skaggs."

"You have my sincerest congratulations, Mrs. Skaggs."

"Thank you, sir. It was an 'ard labor, sir, but all worth it."

"There can be no doubt of that," Lenox said, smiling. "But I'm afraid, if you'll excuse me, that I must take my leave."

"Always a pleasure to welcome you, Mr. Lenox, sir," said Mrs. Skaggs. "Can we have the girl get ye anything?" She blushed when she said *girl*.

"No, thank you, but you have my warmest wishes." He smiled. Then he turned to the husband, who was looking plaintively at his wife, still hoping she might leave the room. "Skaggs, you'll begin soon?"

"Yes, sir."

"He's staying at George Barnard's house in Clarges Street."

"Yes, sir, I know the spot. Straightaway."

"Good. I'll expect to hear from you when anything comes to light."

"Yes, sir."

Lenox bowed to Mrs. Skaggs, nodded toward her husband, and left them in a minor quarrel, which began as soon as he closed the door, about the sanctity of his place of business. On his way to the path he handed the girl, who was on the porch and seemingly daunted by her responsibilities, a sixpence. She curtsied and blushed.

Skaggs was a man who could assume either an air of respectability or an air of disrepute, which made him infinitely useful, and he had ways that Lenox did not of squirreling into situations. For a day or two, at any rate, he could ease his mind about Potts.

The other members of the house? Barnard he could never question. But he would try to waylay Soames tomorrow, perhaps at the Parliament—Lenox was to eat again with his brother, who was so rarely in town; they had agreed after yesterday's lunch—and he felt sure that he could question Soames in a way that didn't appear to be a questioning.

Duff would be a harder matter.

There were a few hours until he was due to have tea with Lady Jane, and no way to fill them effectively. He had done what he could for the day thus far; at least until Graham explained what he had learned from the servants about Prue Smith.

❦ Chapter 18 ❧

Once every so often—not frequently enough to call it a habit but not infrequently enough to call it a rarity—Lenox returned to his bedroom after he had eaten lunch, changed into a pair of pajamas, and slept for an hour or two. It was a nice thing to do when he was tired, or on a cold day such as this one, when the bed was warm. And while he thought it somewhat lazy, and refused to let himself nap other than as a treat, he dearly loved the days when he did.

He changed into fresh clothes when he woke, a black velvet jacket and gray trousers, and read in his library for a while, taking out maps to look at now and then—for he was reading a history of Persia—and waiting for Graham to return so that they could discuss Miss Smith's social habits.

When he got restless with Persia, he opened his letters. There was one from Edmund's wife, full of news about her sons, and another from a correspondent of his in Paris. The only note that he read twice, though, was from Barnard. Written yesterday, it read as follows:

Dear Charles—
I was unsettled after our breakfast this morning, because I felt I
had been abrupt. I hope you will trust the Yard as I do, and that
you will give the business up unless it comes to an unsatisfac-
tory conclusion. Above all, let us be open with each other.

Faithfully,
Barnard

Now this was unfair. Barnard had secrets from three quarters of London. He was known for his secrets. But in all probability he knew he was appealing to the part of Lenox that did hesitate to deceive anybody and was reluctant to conduct a case in such a back-handed way; in short, the part of him that was a gentleman. Though Barnard himself would have felt no such compunction, he knew that the amateur detective would.

So Lenox brooded over this letter, and read it again, but at last he set it aside, determined that the interests of Prue Smith could be favorably compared to the instincts of his own upbringing. The only question that remained with him, after this conclusion, was why Barnard had felt strongly enough to write him. It was another thing to remember, as the case grew more convoluted.

At the end of this conversation with himself, there was a soft step in the hallway and a knock upon the door, and when Lenox called out that the knocker should enter, Graham came into the room.

"How are you, Graham?"

"Very well, sir. The weather is more pleasant today than it has been recently, sir."

"A sight better."

"I have gathered the information which you asked me to, sir."

"Have you? Excellent. Take a seat."

Lenox was already behind his desk, and Graham sat in a chair facing him.

"What have you got?" said Lenox.

"Before I describe what I have learned of the victim, sir, may I add one note to the information I gave you last night?"

"Of course, of course."

"There is one member of the household who is apparently, sir, without question *not* the murderer—or, at least, had not the opportunity to commit the murder."

"Who might that be, besides Miss Smith herself?"

"One of the two nephews, sir, Eustace Bramwell."

"Why, pray, is he so disbarred?"

"Numerous members of the staff who confided in me have confirmed independently that he never moved. He was painting a picture or eating lunch, but he never left the drawing room or the dining room for even the briefest moment."

Lenox sighed. "Whenever I hear that someone is absolutely innocent, Graham, I tend to conclude that I have found my criminal. But I suppose in this case you're right. I spoke with the lad this morning."

"Yes, sir?"

"Offensive, but too essentially snotty and petty to make such a grand gesture as murder."

"Shall I continue, sir?"

"By all means."

"I went to the girl's funeral this morning, sir."

"Did you? I thought of going, but it wouldn't have been quite right—her funeral, after all, not an excuse for me to do work. There are limits."

"Yes, sir. Having known her, however, I felt I could strike a balance."

"Of course, Graham, of course. I didn't mean to suggest otherwise."

"At any rate, sir, between a visit to the servants' quarters at Mr. Barnard's house and the funeral, I amassed a good amount of information.

"The girl's full name was Prudence Smith, sir, and she was born in London. She went into service at the age of sixteen, and at her death she was twenty-four. In the intervening time she worked three years for Lady Helena Adeline and four years for Lady Grey, and for the past three months she has been working at Mr. Barnard's house."

"Of course."

"Her family is all dead, sir, and her strongest current relation was James, her fiancé, a footman. He is from a good family, all in service, and seems genuinely grief-stricken. I may add here that I know his father and do not believe the lad to be in any way a suspect, sir, though of course that is not for me to judge.

"Her strongest acquaintance besides James was a girl named Lucy, whom I believe you have already met, sir, the servant at Lady Grey's house who informed you that Prue Smith could not read. They were very close, having served together a long while at Lady Grey's residence, though Miss Smith was friendly with all the servants in that house and with many of the female servants here.

"This information, sir, is merely preamble to the unfortunate facts which I have discovered. It was uniformly agreed that she was a good girl and did her work well, but I fear she was led astray in the last year. She was engaged to James that entire time, sir, but in the last six months she had begun to have a relationship with a man named Bartholomew Deck, sir, known as Bart to his friends."

"Who is he?"

"A young man of Miss Smith's age who is the proprietor of a tavern that his father owns called The Bull and Bear."

"What do you mean by a relationship?"

"I fear that the two young people were having an affair, sir."

"Is this what *exotic* meant? Was she generally this way?"

"No, sir. I have assembled information in that direction as well, but I thought that the information about Mr. Deck might be more relevant."

"Indeed."

"The other servants thought of her, I believe, sir, not as a lady of ill repute or someone likely to have an affair, but as someone with hopes and ambitions and a sense of possibility that exceeded what most would contend was her excellent position with Mr. Barnard."

"What were her hopes and ambitions?"

"She spoke of moving to the country when she was married, sir, and of having a girl of her own—nearly all the servants remember that—and she spoke of James living as a gentleman farmer. I cannot say whether any of this was attainable, sir, but when I heard these declarations they were very familiar to me. It is rare, but some girls are that way. You may recall Elizabeth, who was in service here some years ago, sir. She was of that ilk."

"Did Prue Smith's friends know about Deck?"

"Only Lucy betrayed any knowledge of the name, sir. I found out by accounting for the people at her funeral this afternoon. The only person unknown to me was Mr. Deck, and when I followed him I saw his place of business and learned his name from a man in the street. Lucy verified for me that they were more than friends, sir."

"Did it strike you as strange that the funeral was so quick on the heels of her death? It did me."

"Yes, sir, me too. I spoke to a maid, who said Mr. Barnard wanted to have a quick funeral—according to James, who made the arrangements—so that the business would be at an end."

"Interesting."

"Yes, sir."

"Do you have an address for this man Deck?"

"Yes, sir." Graham handed Lenox a piece of paper. "The information is copied here, sir."

"Anything else?"

"One further note, sir. You expressed some curiosity about

the changing of candles in servants' rooms. I was assured by a young lady at Mr. Barnard's house that the servants are expected by an exacting housekeeper, a Miss Harrison, to use their candles until the very last."

Lenox nodded, with raised eyebrows. "A tough type."

"Very tough, sir. To conclude, Miss Smith had changed her candles only recently, according to one of the girls I spoke with. She was surprised to hear that Miss Smith had already been due for a new candle, but I managed, I hope, to convince her that I might have been confused."

"Excellent, Graham. Very good."

"Thank you, sir."

"I mean it. I hope it wasn't too unpleasant, you know."

"Not in the least, Mr. Lenox, sir." Graham stood up. "Will you be having your tea in, this afternoon?"

"No, no. At Lady Jane's. Take the afternoon off; have a holiday if you like. Good work all around—thank you."

"Of course, sir," said Graham, and walked out of the library.

With this report, Graham's role in the case was at all probability at an end, and both men knew that Graham would thereafter resume his normal functions, but perhaps it is appropriate, nevertheless, to explain the relation between the butler and his employer, which was by many men's standards—Barnard's, for instance, or Sir Edmund's—unorthodox.

It had begun at Oxford. Graham was raised nearby in a small thatched-cottage village called Abingdon and became the scout on Lenox's stairwell the year Lenox went up. For three years he had remained in that role, always formal—a little too formal, even—and always efficient, until one night. Lenox had been reading late, taking occasional breaks to visit his friends' rooms, when Graham had burst through his door without knocking, disheveled, without a tie on, and clearly overwrought.

"Will you help me?" he had said. And it was in those few

words that Lenox realized how much he liked the quiet, intelligent Graham—indeed, how much he relied on him. He wanted to help.

"Of course." Lenox turned his book face downward and followed Graham out. It was past curfew hours, but Graham led him through a strange route by the college's kitchen and they slipped out undetected.

From there it was a twenty-minute ride in a hired carriage to Abingdon. Neither Graham nor Lenox spoke. Finally they drew to a halt in front of a small white house with a little bit of grass around it, surrounded by miles of farmland which Lenox assumed belonged to the Prince of Wales.

"It's my father," Graham said at last. "I didn't know who else to ask for help."

"Me, of course. How many times have I asked you for help?"

Inside, a single candle threw a dim light over two rooms. The one toward the back was a kitchen with a low straw pallet in it. The front room held a sturdier brown bed, where Graham's father lay, clearly dying.

"I see," said Lenox. "Is there a doctor nearby?"

"Only Colfax, down the road, sir. He wouldn't come."

"Wouldn't come?"

"He's a proper doctor. The village's nurse died last year."

"Where is Colfax's house?"

"First one, half a mile down."

Lenox found a rusty bike outside and rode furiously toward Colfax's house. When he got there, the doctor consented to come after a short conversation, plainly only because of Lenox's accent and appearance. It took about ten minutes of walking.

When they arrived, the elder Graham was dead and Graham was sitting on a chair by the bed, still holding his hand. Colfax offered a brief condolence, took the shilling from Lenox's hand, and left. Lenox sat up with Graham that night, fixing coffee and letting him ramble, and in the morning he arranged for the funeral. Finally, that evening, he went back to Oxford.

Three days later he called in. It emerged after a while that Graham had nowhere to go; the house belonged to a landlord. Lenox saw the defeat in his eyes.

"Well," said the student, "you'll go work for my father. That will be easy enough."

So it happened; and three months later, when Lenox moved to London, Graham went with him. They never spoke of it, but there was an allegiance between them because of that strange week, perhaps even stronger in Lenox than in Graham. He was honored that Graham had trusted him.

Their relationship had always been what was proper and right between two men of their positions: friendliness without familiarity, comfort without excessive fluency. And soon after Lenox came to London, he stumbled upon the Charterhouse case, which involved the loss of some crucial papers in connection with the government, and in the solving of that crime, Graham had played a small but critical role by befriending a young lady in service with the criminal and extracting from her a vital piece of information.

Since then, Lenox had occasionally asked for Graham's help on cases. When he did not, the butler went about his normal work, but when asked he always fulfilled his duty excellently. As in this case, he had an uncanny ability to gain the trust of talkative maids and footmen.

Thus the situation stood. The truth was that they had known each other for more than twenty years and had been through the major events of their lives together, and while there was always a correct distance between them, they each felt at times that it was appropriate to set aside the barrier and act as what they truly were to each other, should all concerns of rank, money, class, and society be demolished—namely, friends.

～ Chapter 19 ～

It was after four o'clock by now; Lenox had been to Lady Jane's and had his tea and his hot muffin, and the two friends had chatted comfortably for a little less than an hour. He told her about Barnard's two nephews and said that they confirmed her worst suspicions about that species, but he did not tell her about the information that Graham had given him about Bartholomew Deck. He had decided to protect her from it unless it became material to the case—which, he feared, was a real possibility.

For her part, Lady Jane told him she had been to the girl's funeral that morning. She had seen Graham, she said, who had only bowed to her. Very few people had been present, and it was James, Prue's fiancé, sitting in the first pew, who wept. Lady Jane did not add that she herself had cried; but then, it was not the sort of thing she needed to add for Lenox to understand.

It was perhaps unusual for her to go to the girl's funeral— Lenox could think of no other woman of her class who would have done so—but Lady Jane simply *was* unusual, in her persistent refusal to remarry, in her close relationship with Lenox, in her ability to do what she felt was right—even if it meant skipping lunch with a duchess to attend a maid's funeral—and maintaining her rarefied position at the same time. It was simply who she was. Her strength was in the integrity of her actions; she never compromised what she believed she ought to do.

They sat together on the rose-colored sofa for quite some time and talked, also, about Jack Soames and Newton Duff, and, more happily, about Sir Edmund and his two sons. Both Lenox and Lady Jane planned to return to the country soon— Lenox to visit Edmund and Lady Jane to visit *her* brother, who sat at the family seat—since her father's death a few years ago— as the Earl of Houghton. They agreed that they would plan their trips to coincide, though Lenox, for his part, wanted a little time to hunt as well.

He left her house at a few minutes before five o'clock. Though it had been a long day, the cold was unobtrusive, compared to the last two days, and he still had energy left. Therefore he stepped into his carriage and directed the driver to the Bull and Bear.

Lenox's mind had that quality which many great minds have—the ability to consider several opposing ideas at once— and, though he felt stifled in the case thus far, he had begun to consider its nuances, the possible relationships that may have existed, in secret, in Barnard's house. And while Bartholomew Deck played no role in the beginnings of these thoughts, Lenox now admitted the young man to his mind as another possibility. It was one idea that was best either to dismiss or to embrace as quickly as possible, which was why he placed the task of visiting the tavern at the forefront of his plans.

The carriage crossed the Thames and made its way toward the docks as the sun fell. At last, in front of an empty pier, it drew to a standstill in front of a large well-lit pub, with a placard of the Queen protected by a bull and a bear on either side hanging above the door, and cheerful noises coming through its windows. Lenox got out and went inside.

It was an old makeshift building, and there was a sign over the bar, to the left, that said THE BULL AND BEAR SURVIVED THE FIRE OF 1666. Several men sat at the bar, rivermen, mostly, who trawled the Thames from these docks, ferrying passengers, searching for treasure, and drinking at the end of the day. Behind the bar were a row of wooden barrels tapped for ale; the last barrel was darker and said MILD in white stencil on its side. There were chairs and tables scattered around the warm room, and at the main table there was a game of nine-men's morris going on. The place served some kind of food; Lenox saw a young woman by the door eating a plate of pickles, ham, bread, cheese, relish, cabbage, and egg.

Behind the bar was a young man, polishing the pewter tankards the beer was served in and, it seemed, crying.

"A pint of bitter, please," said Lenox, and sat down at the bar.

The man behind the bar was handsome and fair, and upon Lenox's request he took one of the tankards he was cleaning, gave it an extra wipe, drew full from the tap of a barrel, and said, "A penny, please," crying all the while. If any of the customers seemed to see anything peculiar about his behavior, they did not show it, much less mention it. Occasionally one of the young waitresses nipped around the bar and kissed him on the cheek, but this seemed to have no effect on him beyond impeding his free movement among the barrels and taps.

To the man on his left, Lenox said, "Do you know why he's crying?"

" 'E's sad," said the man.

"How long has he been crying?"

"All evening."

"Ah."

Lenox stood up and finished his pint. He went down to the darkened end of the bar, where there were no patrons, but several empty stools and a dartboard that had fallen into disrepair. When he was seated, he beckoned to the young man behind the bar, who looked around for other customers and then walked toward him behind the bar.

"Bartholomew Deck?" said Lenox.

"I'm 'im."

"I'm Charles Lenox. I'm investigating the death of Prue Smith."

Deck leaned his head over the bar and continued to cry.

"May I ask you a few questions?"

"Why not," said Deck, with a gesture of futility.

"How did you know the girl?"

"I loved her. Nobody knows what love is."

"This is an unpleasant question, Mr. Deck, but I ask it nevertheless: Did you kill her?"

To this Deck had a not altogether unexpected reaction; he whipped around the bar, and his hands flew toward Lenox's throat. Nobody in the room looked their way. Lenox blocked his left hand but caught a blow on the chin. Then he put his foot behind Deck's knee and pushed him backward, tripping him, and pinned his hands to his chest.

"I know it's unpleasant, Mr. Deck, but I'm afraid it's necessary."

Deck had given way entirely to tears and didn't struggle at all against Lenox's grip on him. Weakly, he called out, "Fa?"

After a moment, a man appeared through the door.

Lenox released Deck, prepared, if need be, to leave as quickly as possible. But Deck only said, "Cover me, would ya?" The older man nodded and Deck began to walk toward the front of the bar, apparently with the expectation that Lenox would follow him—which he did.

Out in the cold air, the young man seemed to sober up. He lit a small cigar and tucked it into the left side of his mouth. "Sorry," he said.

"It's all right. I understand," said Lenox.

"Only, you asking me, did I kill her—"

"I understand. I have to ask it quickly, before someone has his guard up, you see."

"Never, never, never, never."

"You loved her?"

"Always."

Both men paused. Deck stared out at the water, which was sloping gently toward the docks. Lenox followed his gaze.

"How did you meet her?"

"I delivered ale for a party there."

"And she took it from you?"

"No, the old witch did: Harrison. But I seen her."

"Go on."

"She was pretty, I saw straight off, so I went back to the house and knocked on the servants' door, like, and another girl answered, and I asked if I could see the one with the brown hair. That's how we saw each other, first."

"And how long has this been happening?"

"Awhile. Less than a year."

"Did you know she was engaged?"

Deck nodded vigorously. "To that prat. Of course."

"James?"

"Jem. Yeah. Very formal. Had a bit of money tucked away. But she loved *me*."

"Do you have any reason to believe that anybody would have killed her?"

Deck threatened to cry again but quieted himself. "No, I don't."

"How did you arrange to see her?"

"Tuesdays was her half-day, and Jem's was Wednesday, so I saw her on Tuesdays. Her Sundays she spent with him, only since she had to."

"You only saw her on Tuesdays?"

"Well. No, I suppose."

"How else?"

"Did you see her room, like, Mr. Lenox?"

"Yes."

"Did you see her window?"

"Yes."

"She opened it some nights. So I would walk by, and if it was open I would go in."

Lenox looked at him.

"It was open that night. I looked in and—well, there was her body and the police and everything."

"At what time?"

"Late, you know."

"And did you think of speaking to her friends?"

"To Lucy. Who knew about it. She told me when the funeral was."

"Had you had any arguments with Miss Smith recently?"

"Arguments?"

"Disagreements? About her engagement, perhaps? Did she want to break it off with you?"

"No, no, no," said Deck, shaking his head furiously. "The last time I seen her, we had the best of all our times, see. We never talked about Jem or us or anything, but only had a bit of fun, and a bit of love, you know. Oh, God," he went on, and his eyes grew wide.

"Did you have any means of access to the house other than the window?"

Deck quieted. "No. Although I could've got in a dozen ways."

"How do you mean?"

"Anyone could, wanted to cabbage something."

"Cabbage?"

"Pinch. Anybody could have. Through any of the servants' rooms, like, or through the top of the house, or anywhere."

"What was Miss Smith like?"

"The best girl in the world."

"But what else? Was she inclined to make people dislike her?"

"Oh, maybe people as was stupider than her, p'raps, but no, she was lovely, you see."

"Did she ever mention anything about the guests at Mr. Barnard's?"

"No, not to think of. She hated Barnard. Hated Harrison. She went there to be with James, but by last week she wanted to go back to her other place."

"Yes?"

"I didn't, though. Farther for me to go see her."

"She never mentioned anything about the guests?"

"Not—well, she mentioned that one of the nephews was fresh with her, but only in a laughing way."

"Did she say a name?"

"No."

"Have you heard of *bella indigo*, Mr. Deck?"

"No."

Deck dropped the small cigar to the ground and stamped it out with his heel. He crossed his arms.

"Is there anything else you would care to tell me?"

"No," said Deck, and started to cry again. Without another word, he turned around and walked back inside the tavern.

Lenox stepped back into his carriage. It never did to dismiss anybody, of course. But he had seen murderers, and Mr. Deck, at least in this matter, did not belong to their company.

Chapter 20

Before he went home, Lenox decided to stop by and see Jensen at his apothecary. He had been there only yesterday, but he thought he could use another lead. Night had fallen completely over London by now, though a pitter-patter of sleet on the streets shone in the gas lamps along Piccadilly Circus. Nelson's Column rose high in the distance, visible to Lenox as he walked along in the direction of Trafalgar Square. That had been built in . . . was it 1840? Another monument from Lenox's youth. Amazing to think that if he had been born fifty years earlier London would have been so much barer a city, violent and unpredictable, full of gin alleys, without the bobbies or the new Parliament or Nelson's Column. What an era to live in!

Jensen was preparing to close for the night. As he approached, Lenox saw the old man wandering down the aisles of his shop, turning a jar of cream to face forward or making a note on a little chit of paper, probably about replenishing his stock. The front lights were dim. Jensen lived above the store, and Lenox saw bright lights in those windows, as well as Mrs. Jensen, a plump old woman in a blue frock, busying herself with supper and setting out a bottle of wine. For no reason he could think of, Lenox thought of Lady Jane.

He pushed open the door and immediately felt comforted by the familiar smell of wood chips and shaving cream.

"Mr. Lenox!" said old Jensen, turning around. "How are you?"

"Very well, thank you. And you?"

"I must say, my stomach is rumbling. Pork chops, I think." He smiled and patted his stomach.

"Ah. In that case, I can return at another time—"

"No, no! I have what you were looking for."

"Do you then? I'm impressed that you found it so quickly."

Jensen went behind the counter, disappeared for a moment, and returned with a large ledger with the word TRANSACTIONS embossed on its cover in gold letters. He made a great show of taking out his glasses, perching them at the end of his nose, and flipping through the pages carefully.

"How much do I owe you?" Lenox asked.

"One shilling, please."

Lenox nodded and put a shilling on the counter. Then he added another, and said, "As a down payment for my next professional visit."

Jensen pocketed the money and nodded gravely, then took out another, smaller ledger and put a shilling's credit by Lenox's name.

"Let me see here," he said, again scrolling through the larger book. "I always get lost among these lines when I open the book. My wife keeps the accounts, you see. But I'll find it in the end."

Lenox nodded and smiled. "It does smell like pork chops," he said.

Jensen looked up. "And parsnip soup, if I'm not mistaken, with peas and onions on the side." He patted his stomach again. "Ah!" he said, finding the correct entry. "Here we are."

"Yes?" Lenox said.

"The arsenic was from Lymon's, on the good side of Shore-
ditch. You can tell from the crest. Luckily, Lymon is a member
of our little club, the Ten O'clock Chemists. I went and spoke
to him."

"What's the Ten O'clock Chemists?"

"We have a few rooms in the West End, with newspapers and
cards and a good supper of meat on the joint every Wednesday.
About fifty of us. At our meeting yesterday—we meet at ten,
you see—I asked them to look for this bottle—Lymon marks
each one specifically. Arsenic Act of 1861. Otherwise I doubt I
could have traced it; takes the government too long to file all the
records. Lymon sent over the note today."

"Please tell him how grateful I am to him. Sounds like a
charming club, too."

"Full of decent folk," said Jensen, smiling. "Don't mind having my pipe there now and again."

"Who bought the poison then?" Lenox asked.

Jensen peered down through his glasses. "Let me see then,"
he said. "Ah. Does this name ring a bell? A Mr. . . . Mr. Newton Duff?"

Chapter 21

It so happened, when Lenox returned home, that he discovered that for once he had no social obligations. He knew he ought to be grateful for the free time, but almost immediately a sense of restlessness came over him.

Like some men of varied interests and comfortable means, he was rarely bored, but nevertheless he occasionally found himself unsatisfied by the pursuits available to him of an evening. Neither his books nor his maps nor the prospect of a spell at one of his clubs interested him, and therefore he found himself, in the hour before supper, walking vaguely toward the West End along St. James's Street, growing gradually less certain by the moment of any firm knowledge he had about the murder of Lady Jane's former upstairs maid. Newton Duff kept running through his mind. Would the man be foolish enough to kill somebody? And if so, why? Or if not, why had he bought the arsenic and to whom had he given it?

It had now been two full days, as well as the evening of the murder itself, that he had been invested in the case. It felt at once like less time than that and more. He had done a great deal, but instead of the work yielding back to him a series of small discoveries, such as those that comprised most cases, all he could do was pull at the ends of the ropes and hope something would pull back.

This evening, at any rate, there was little more that he could do. He would have his supper and go down to the Devonshire Club later, perhaps, or go to see a few collectors he knew, or even drop by—but no, he felt; no, none of it would do. With the restlessness in his heart increasing every moment, he found his feet turned toward Clarges Street and, without quite realizing it, soon found himself standing across from George Barnard's house, as if by staring at it he could unlock the secrets it held.

For fifteen minutes he saw very little. Indeed, it was hard to discern whether or not there was anyone in the house at all. Barnard's dining room sat to the rear of his living room, whose windows were darkened, and if there was a glimmer, now and then, it might have only been a trick of the eye.

And then three things happened in rapid succession, all of which filled the space of less than half an hour but which it would then take Lenox a great deal of time to piece together.

First, Claude Barnard burst forth from the house, laughing, with a young man Lenox took to be a friend, probably from the Jumpers, a tall fair lad. The two of them paused together on the stoop to fix their cuffs and examine their appearances in the window glass—and in the light pouring through the front door and by an odd flicker of the streetlamp, Lenox thought he saw a small raw burn mark on Claude's forearm. No sooner could he look again than the door was closed, the buttons had been buttoned, the coat donned, and the forearm again concealed, and the young men had turned down the street.

But the moment left Lenox with the peculiar feeling of having seen something revealing without knowing precisely what it was—and without having a chance to learn because it was so quickly withdrawn.

He turned on his heel, and within short order the second thing happened: He felt sure that he was being followed.

It was the sort of thing for which he had developed an instinct. No specific shadow stalked him, but from the corner of his eye he sensed a presence behind him amid the flickering lamps that played along the cobblestones.

This gave him no alarm, but all the same he felt he had better pursue a cautious course. He walked down the street, nodding, once or twice, to men he knew, and planning to seek refuge in the Athenæum, his nearest club. It was unlikely that anybody could follow him inside, unless it was a gentleman who sought a word but felt uneasy about meeting him in public—which was certainly possible.

But as he turned up the steps of the club, the man who had been following him apparently relented, because from behind him Lenox heard his own name called.

"Mr. Lenox!" the voice repeated.

The detective turned around to see James, the footman, fiancé of the dead maid, looking up at him breathlessly.

"James?"

"Yes, Mr. Lenox."

"I understand that you're having a difficult time, James," said Lenox, "but it is unpleasant for anybody to be followed through the streets at night."

"I'm sorry, Mr. Lenox, sir."

"It's all right. What can I do for you?"

The young man looked so anguished, Lenox took a step back down the stoop to stand at eye level with him.

"Something is on your mind?" he said. "Is there anything you wish to confess?"

A moan of some sort escaped the footman's lips. His black hair was uncombed and his eyes were sunken, as if he had not slept since Prue's murder. "No," he said, "no."

"What troubles you, then?"

"Oh, Mr. Lenox," cried the young man, "tell me anything, give me anything to do, anything, anything!"

Lenox softened toward him immediately. "I truly am sorry," he said.

"Anything!"

"In time it will pass."

"But . . . oh, I loved her so very much, Mr. Lenox!"

Lenox thought carefully for a moment. "Very well," he said. "If it gives you comfort, you may observe the inmates of Mr. Barnard's house, watching for any peculiar behavior."

James looked at him. "Observe?"

"Yes. Understand, however, that I will be part of no deception, and that if you come to me, it will not be because I have asked you to. I am only counseling you to do what I myself would do, in your position. You have a unique opportunity to see what you can."

"I shall," said James.

"But not on my behalf. However, if there is anything in the house or in the actions of the people residing there that you wish to report, come to me or go to Inspector Exeter, as you see fit."

"Oh, Exeter, what does he know?"

Lenox tried to smile, but the young man was patently unhappy—and lurking in the back of his own mind was Bartholomew Deck, for whom he had some sympathy as well.

"Good evening," said Lenox, and turned away, not toward the Athenæum, now that he was no longer pursued, but up the street and in the direction of home.

He had walked two blocks, and left James behind, when the third of the three events occurred.

To cut more quickly toward his own house, Lenox had chosen to walk along one of those small, dark, thin streets, closer to alleys than anything, that proliferate everywhere in London, even in the best parts of the city, and that always seem to hold some menace in them until they are safely traversed, after which they seem to be less than nothing.

He was alone in this little alley when suddenly he saw two men coming at him from behind but at an angle, and walking quickly. It would have been better, he later saw, to run away immediately, but in the event he thought only that he had been unnerved by the quick encounters with Claude and James and was being foolish.

The two men were of a similar height, both an inch or two shorter than Lenox and younger as well. From their dress and their demeanor, it was impossible to tell whether they were middle-class or lower-class men wearing their finest, but they did not stick out too badly for the neighborhood—except in a single respect. The shorter of the two men had a very clearly outlined tattoo of a hammer curved around his left eye.

It happened in a quick flash. At one moment they were striding toward him and, the next, one of them—it later seemed to Lenox to be the one with the tattoo, though he would never be sure—had clipped him hard into the wall.

The detective did not lose his wits all at once, and when the second man came toward him he dealt him a hard blow in the concavity of his chest, doubling him over. As Bartholomew Deck had learned, Lenox knew just enough to protect himself. But no sooner had the second assailant fallen than the first was again upon him, shoving him to the ground and kicking him hard in the stomach with the toe of his boot.

It was not the first time that such a thing had happened to Lenox, and yet he felt shock—pure shock. He had been brought up a gentleman, and though he had chosen to wade, occasionally, into an unfamiliar world, a world of hard men, his own essentially genial outlook on life had never left him. The toe in his stomach, therefore, was shocking, and by the time the other man had recovered, Lenox was overwhelmed.

He protected himself as well as he could with his arms, but they rained blows across his shoulders. Only once did one of them hit the side of his face and then quickly corrected himself, as the other grunted "Not the face" and pushed him aside.

Then one of them took out a knife, and Lenox felt a violent fear in his chest. Though the alley was dim, he could see the silver gleam of the knife's edge. Even amid his fright, he tried unsuccessfully to spot something distinctive about the knife.

"Wot now?" said the one with the hammer over his eye.

"That's good enough."

"Let me give him a poke—quick one, in the belly."

The leader seemed to consider this, then, to Lenox's almost uncontrollable relief, said, "No. You'll make a mistake and knife an organ."

"How about the leg?"

There was a noise at the end of the alley, and they looked up.

"Let's get out of here," said the tattooed man, and he spat near Lenox's foot.

The other man told Lenox, "Leave it to the Yard," and then both men ran away, leaving him against the wall: prone, terrified, and breathing heavily, still within less than a minute's walk from his own home.

Chapter 22

Beasts!" said Lady Jane, yet again.

"Yes," said Lenox.

"The absolute beasts!"

"I daresay," said Lenox, wincing as he tried to sit up.

He was on the sofa in his library. Graham stood back, but Lady Jane was perched on the edge of the sofa next to him. Word had somehow worked its way to the next house when Lenox came staggering home, and Lady Jane had rushed into the library and said, "Graham, move out of the way!"

There were very few people from whom Graham would have accepted such a command at that moment, but she was among their ranks. She had been able to do very little in the way of providing Lenox with physical comfort—he had, he thought, a broken rib, but other than that only bruises, albeit painful ones—but she hadn't left anyone in the room in doubt of her opinion of the two men who had done it. She thought that they were beasts.

"Where did they come from?" she asked.

"I don't know."

"Did they try to rob you?"

"No."

"Then why?" She patted his hand sympathetically.

"I think it must be in connection with the case."

"About Prudence Smith?"

"Yes."

"Oh, Charles, I *am* sorry. Be done with it this instant. Please, let's let the man you so dislike do it all, and perhaps he will turn up the person who did it, but please don't do anything further!"

"I fear I shall have to."

"Charles!" She leaned toward him, her hands in her lap and a look of concern on her face. Lenox thought she looked beautiful.

"I'm sorry, my dear, but I have to finish, now more than ever."

"Why, because two cowardly men hurt you? Please, stop your investigation."

"It may have been Exeter himself who put them up to it."

"It couldn't have been, Charles. He's a policeman."

"Yes, but I daresay he caught wind of me trolling around the edges of the case and wanted to warn me off. I made him look a fool with that forgery last week. I tried to beg out of going to the Yard to put it all down officially, but he wouldn't let me."

"Do you really think so?"

"I'm nearly sure of it."

"Then report him!"

"That's not how it's done. But don't worry, my lady, I shan't get into any more trouble if I can help it. I'll equip myself with a rifle or something and wave it around, and nobody will come near me." He made an effort to laugh and winced as he did.

"Oh, don't joke, Charles, it's not in the least bit funny to us, you know."

She looked at Graham, nodding, and he nodded too.

At that moment there was a knock on the outer door, and Graham excused himself to answer it. After a few seconds he announced Dr. and Lady McConnell.

"Oh, Charles, you poor dear man!" said Toto, bursting through the door and kissing him on the forehead. "Are you dying?"

"Not at the moment, at any rate."

"Thomas will make you better," she said, and promptly pulled her aunt away—Lady Jane was her cousin in fact, but Toto had always called her aunt—to the set of chairs on the other end of the room, and forgot about Charles entirely.

"Did Graham send for you?" Lenox asked McConnell.

"No, your neighbor did." He gestured at Lady Jane. "She sent a note."

"Nothing serious."

"I am still a doctor, for all that, Charles. Lift your arm."

For perhaps five minutes, McConnell gently pushed his fingers into Lenox's ribs and stomach and over his waistcoat, checking twice in each case. He then sat in a chair facing the couch, pulled his flask from his hip, and took a sip from it.

"Gin?" he asked.

"No, thank you," said Lenox.

"Your ribs aren't broken, though one of them is badly bruised."

"I thought as much, more or less."

"How much advice will you take?"

"The maximum amount that will not result in any impediment to my work."

"None, in other words."

"You are, for all that, the doctor, Thomas. Have you no advice that fits those parameters?"

McConnell laughed. "I do, I suppose. You must eat soon and then sleep, without delay. Sleep as long as you can. Don't have Graham wake you up."

"I shan't."

"And move about gingerly."

"I shall—or, at least, I shall as far as I can."

"Then you'll be all right, in the end. Who was it?"

"Two men. At the behest of Exeter, I should imagine."

McConnell took another sip. "Do you have any proof?"

"No. One of them said, *Leave it to the Yard*, but that might have been a message from the murderer, or Barnard, or even somebody who wishes me to abandon detective work altogether."

"In that case I should probably do things much as I have been," said the doctor, "but I might carry a revolver."

"I don't like to."

"Give it a miss, then. But I would."

Lenox sighed. "Perhaps you're right, after all." He noticed for the first time that McConnell and Toto were dressed for the evening. He was wearing a dinner jacket and she was wearing a blue evening dress. "Where are you going?" he said.

"To dinner at the Devonshires'."

Lenox sat up. "I was to attend, as well. It had slipped my mind entirely."

"No doubt they'll forgive you. Although not as readily if you hold Lady Grey back with you."

"No, of course not. She and the Duchess have become near friends."

"Quite right. And Toto adores them both, or so at least she tells me."

McConnell laughed tiredly and took another sip from his flask. A stud in his shirt had come loose, but Lenox left it to the doctor's wife to find it. She seemed to sense that her husband was finished, for she patted Lady Jane quickly on the hand and stood up to join the men.

"Charles, old dear," Toto said, "have you been a good patient?"

"A reasonable one, I think."

"And shall you keep Aunt with you?"

"No, of course not."

"Oh, good," said Toto.

But Lady Jane looked at her young friend firmly. "I shall stay here for supper, at any rate," she said. "Toto, apologize to Mary, and tell her I'll play a hand of whist after Charles and I have finished, if she likes."

Toto looked extremely cross.

"It will do no good for you to stand there like an angry cat," said Lady Jane. "Run along."

Toto gave her cousin a grudging hug and once again kissed Charles on the cheek, McConnell nodded his farewell, and then they were gone.

"You needn't have stayed," said Lenox to Lady Jane.

"Of course I shall. I've told Graham to bring supper into the library."

He smiled. They ate very simple food—cold sliced tomatoes, mashed potatoes, and milk—as they had when they were children together. They ate over the side table, laughing and talking the entire time, as outside it began to snow once more.

Chapter 23

As he left Lenox's house, McConnell had apparently slipped a dram of sleeping powder to Graham, who had in turn given it to the patient. The next morning, as a result, Lenox arose at nine o'clock, which, though it might have seemed like the crack of dawn to Claude Barnard, was quite late for the detective. He had slept off much of his soreness, though his ribs were still tender and the cut on his face had swollen. But he had slept well and felt fit for a reasonable day's work. A sort of terror at the memory of the glinting knife stirred somewhere deep in him, but he ignored it.

It had, after all, snowed the whole night through, and there was a fresh white coat over the city. Lenox's bedroom had a broad window with a very comfortable armchair by it, close enough to the fire for warmth, and he ate breakfast in that chair, wearing his robe and slippers. He had only just gotten used to the old snow, which was conforming to the habits of the city's walkways, and while this new coat was lovely to look at, as he sipped his hot coffee and ate his toast, he knew it would only add to the difficulty of getting about.

He sat with his final cup of coffee long after he had put the discards of his breakfast to the side, on the tray on his night table, sipping slowly, snug in his chair, and with the prospect of a long day ahead of him. Occasionally he preferred to give himself half an hour before he started out, and so he did this morning. After last night, he thought it would be all right.

But eventually he stood up, put the cup and saucer next to the tray, and dressed. He asked Graham for his overcoat with the fringed collar, which was his warmest, and lamented again his poor choice of boots, which would no doubt be in tatters after half an hour. Then he put them on.

When he was outfitted, he stepped downstairs. As he arrayed his clothes and his person to his liking in front of the mirror, Graham spoke to him.

"Sir, I was hoping I might have another afternoon off. I have an aunt to visit."

"An aunt?"

"Yes, sir. In London."

"Not in Abingdon?"

"No, sir."

"But you've never visited her before."

"No, sir."

"Inventing aunts now! That's scarcely polite, Graham. What would your real aunts think?"

There was a slight, almost invisible smile on Graham's lips, the sort of thing only somebody who knew him well would spot.

"Is it a girl, Graham?"

"Yes, sir."

Lenox started. "Who?"

"My aunt."

Lenox laughed. "Go ahead, of course. Keep your secrets from me." Turning back to the mirror, he touched the cuts and bruises on his face, which were pretty bad looking, then laughed and stepped outside to his carriage.

He directed the driver to Parliament. There was to be a vote that day, and speeches beforehand, of course, and he hoped to catch Soames on the way in. He knew the man well enough to detain him for a few moments and knew also that Soames so little liked the life of a backbencher that he might even agree to sit for a while.

He went again to the members' entrance, facing the river. On the walkway on either side of the door were two awnings, one green-striped and the other red-striped, the green for the Commons and the red for the Lords. In summer they retreated under their awnings and sat outside with cool drinks.

On this day he went inside, nodding to the doorman, who recognized him, and again faced the choice of going right, to the rooms of the House of Lords and the Queen Empress, or left, to the rooms devoted to the House of Commons. He took a left.

At lunch he had simply gone to the first room, the dining room, but now he went past it. Down here, where there was a whole series of rooms overlooking the Thames, were the places that various members sat in between sessions, to broker deals or talk with their friends or simply have a drink.

There was a large empty library, followed by a periodical room with all the day's papers and journals, and a smoking room, with a billiard table in it and several men waiting about, talking listlessly.

Past that was a refreshment room, which was abandoned now but would be filled that evening with people after a pint of ale or a glass of shandy. Then there was a tearoom, which was more populated, for many people were having a late breakfast, and finally there was a large chamber with many comfortable couches, and waiters here and there, which didn't have a name but was closer to a clubhouse than anything else. It was the room with a door to the hall that led into the House of Commons, and he decided to wait here, where Soames was most likely to pass before he went into the chambers.

He retired to a large leather sofa and read the *Pall Mall Gazette* for half an hour.

While he was carefully reading a report on the conditions of London slums, Soames came along at last, walking side by side with Newton Duff. They had evidently come together from their host's house; Soames seemed to be talking at length about a horse named Adagio.

Duff, who looked as if he was sorry he'd ever heard of horses—or of Soames, for that matter—said a cursory goodbye and stalked toward a group of less frivolous members. Lenox wondered briefly whether a man as smart as Newton Duff could make the error of leaving a bottle that led back to him at the scene of a murder. Yes, he thought—but before Lenox knew it, Soames turned, temporarily at a loss, and saw him.

"Charles!" he said. "Hallo, old chap."

"Jack," said Lenox. "Good to see you."

Now Soames was of a specific type among the English gentry, not altogether a good type or a bad one, but rather one who lived on the periphery of these categories, half in and half out.

He had earned the title of captain some years past, in the army, and he was known to his friends by and large as Captain Jack, or Soaps to his close friends. But he was a gentle man, not at all militant. He had earned his rowing blue at Oxford, in the years before Lenox's time, and his ability with an oar was by all accounts prodigious. He had secured a place in Parliament shortly after coming down, out of a pocket borough belonging to an old oarsman who had admired the young Soames, and from then on he was received throughout London, but in a way he had never quite equaled his early promise, and his life now, though happy enough, was marked, among those who knew him, by the peculiar sorrow of unfulfillment.

He was the sort of man who stayed at his club much of every day, playing billiards or cards as people floated through the room, eating good meals and making much of himself, encouraging talk of days in the old crew or the old regiment, but without any particular present glory to balance it; he was quick, in the way that men of the clubs are quick, but like them he had lost, whether by drink or lassitude, the ability to focus his efforts over a long time or on a large subject. Gradually his interests had begun to turn to the turf; he was now considered an authority on horses and could tell you of this trainer or that jockey. But serious men, some of whom had looked up to him twenty years earlier, no longer took him seriously.

Lenox felt a deep sorrow, in a way, to know that he was in financial trouble, for whatever his decline, Soames was an institution of a sort, and, moreover, his family's money had all been entailed upon an elder cousin, who was unlikely to let it leave his pocket.

But still, all in all, he was a good man and tried to do his duty in Parliament, even amid talk that he would be replaced. His only committee work now happened to involve the mint.

"How are you, Charles?"

"Aside from this," said Lenox, pointing to the cut on his face, "quite all right."

Soames laughed. "Have you been boxing?" he said.

"Rather against my will."

"Have a cigarette?"

Lenox accepted, and gestured toward a pair of armchairs. The men sat down. A waiter came by and asked if they'd like a drink. Soames declined, but Lenox asked if he wouldn't join him in a glass of hot wine, early though it was, and Soames said that perhaps he would after all.

They had been talking of horses, the expert having found a more willing listener in Lenox than in Duff. But in the lull when Soames took his first sip, Lenox said, "And what is this about the murder?"

"You ought to know, from what I gather."

"Why?"

"You were around that evening, weren't you?" Soames said.

"Ah, but Barnard asked me to step back." This was not a lie.

"He did? Tough bird, Barnard. Good man, but tough."

"What do you think of it?"

"The girl?" Soames shifted uneasily in his seat. "I daresay it was one of the servants. One of them started to cry during supper two nights ago, just for an example. Never seen anything like it. Probably felt guilty."

"Perhaps the fiancé?"

Soames looked away. "Perhaps," he said.

"I hear there are two nephews there?"

"Both horrid, old man, really horrid. One of them is a sort of Casanova or something, and the other disapproves of me, I rather think."

Lenox gestured to the waiter for another glass.

"Thanks, Charles," said Soames, watching his cup as it was filled. The wine steamed and smelled of lemon and cinnamon. "Cold out, you know. Got to endure a day of these things on the benches, now. The wine will make it pass. They're asking me to show up more often, you see, even though I don't know much."

"Is there anything at the mint, right now?"

"Oh, no, not really. I only help Barnard, you know. That's why I'm staying with him. Close work." He blushed and didn't say anything else.

"I really am curious," said Lenox, "about what happened to the girl. Spectator's interest, you see." This was closer to a lie.

"I haven't really got any idea."

"What about Duff? He's a hard one."

"Duff? Do you think?"

"Why not?"

"You may be right. In fact, if I were an inspector, he should be where I started."

"Really?"

Soames took a sip and then put the glass down unsteadily. "Oh, yes. Can't think why it didn't occur to me before, actually."

"Perhaps we're overstating it."

"Nothing of the sort." Soames coughed. "Just as a parlor game, of course, it would have to be him."

"Just as a parlor game."

"Well, of course, none of us could have done it, you know, in reality."

"Of course."

"Suicide, I have no doubt."

"That's how it will end," said Lenox. "But as a parlor game—"

"Oh, Duff." Soames finished his wine. "All the characteristics. Dark chap."

"Dark as midnight."

"Yes."

"But then, why not you?" said Lenox, smiling. He hated to, but he did.

Soames stared for a moment, but then laughed. "Indeed, why not? Only, in a game, you know, it's the mental part of the thing, the motive. I'm not too likely."

"Probably not."

"Maybe as a surprise ending."

"You mean, where Duff seems like the man for it but it turns out to be you?"

"Yes," said Soames, and laughed. His face was red. "But in real life—"

"Never, in real life."

"No, no. Preposterous."

"Yes."

There was a silence.

"Well, I'd better get inside," said Soames.

"Good to see you, though."

"Thanks for the wine and all, Lenox."

"Of course."

"Are you meeting your brother?"

"Yes," said Lenox. "In a little while."

"Say hello. Old Edmund. We were at university together."

A sad moment passed. Then the two men shook hands, and Soames went into the chamber.

Chapter 24

After he had interviewed Soames, Lenox was at loose ends. He was to have lunch with his brother in only an hour, give or take a few minutes, so it would be pointless to go home. He decided that he would take a walk.

The new snowfall was already trodden underfoot, and the city had again taken on a dingy aspect, but the air was clear and, if cold, not unbearably so. He decided he would go down by the river.

Every few hundred yards, in this part of London, there was a staircase leading down from the sidewalk that overlooked the Thames. Lenox went down one of these staircases and soon found himself even with the water, on a little promenade lined with short trees that ran for a while just next to the river, much more quietly than the busy street above.

The water was gray and running fast, with drifts of ice eddying down it and snow fringing its sides. A few birds were flying close to the water, and Lenox stopped to sit on a bench and watch them skimming the small waves. The sky was gray and the river was gray. It was the sort of thing he loved, though a sudden ache where he had been hit called him back to the world.

Soon it was lunch time, and he walked back slowly, looking at the buildings of Whitehall.

Lenox's interest in politics dated back nearly as far as his memory. Lady Jane's father had often taken his seat in the Upper House, where Lenox and Jane would watch him speak from the spectators' gallery, and while Lenox was unimpressed with the trappings of power, he was fascinated by the power itself. It amazed him, after his schoolboy lessons of the monarchs and a deeper look into history at Harrow, that the bodies of Parliament controlled the fate of their countrymen. The discourse, which he read in the papers, was seldom elevated, occasionally very low, but once in a while sparkling. He had grown up with the ideal of the great statesmen, Burke, Fox, Peel, and Palmerston, in his mind. And then, he felt, as he grew toward adulthood, that he had fallen into a singularly lucky time, when both Disraeli and Gladstone were coming into their strength as leaders of men. It was a time of great debate.

But it had been a fascination from afar. Sir Edmund, as both brothers had always known, would be the member from Markethouse. The baronet always was. Charles, their father thought, would buy an estate near Lenox House, or, if it were absolutely necessary, a house in London. But leisure would fall to him, whichever it were, as the consolation for having lost a career.

And yet there were times when Lenox walked among the members he knew, or spoke confidentially with his brother or with the half-dozen politicians he had known since childhood, when it occurred to him that there still might be a chance; he still might enter the House. He knew their minds, though suited to politics at the moment, were in the end no sharper than his. He felt that he might be equal to the job.

But for now he was content to walk the halls of power, to ask his brother for morsels of information, to read the paper in the evening, and to say hello to Disraeli at a party or to Russell at a country house where they found themselves together—to move partially in the political set.

No matter, no matter. The case at hand, that was the important thing. He walked back in the direction of the members' entrance at Parliament and then to Bellamy's, with its low windows and old portraits, to meet his brother.

Lenox had been sure he could take Soames unawares and question him almost without his knowing. That such was not the case put Lenox on his guard. And then, Soames's manner had been so peculiar. The way he grasped at Duff's character, his uneasiness at certain questions, and his insistence that none of them would be found to have done it when the facts came out in the clear.

But surely not Soaps the clubman, whom Lenox had known to say hello to for decades, since he and Edmund had been at university together? No, it was the drinking that had rendered him so inarticulate and ill at ease and of such an unhealthy pallor.

Lenox waited for his brother, and at last he arrived in the dining room. They each ordered a slice of hot game pie with sauce, chips, and peas. Sir Edmund, who was in a cheerful mood because he was returning to the country soon, ordered a bottle of port after lunch, and the two men shared it happily, talking not of the case but of Lenox's own nephews, who were good lads, and of minor matters about the estate: its rolls, the steward's complaints, and Darrow Farm, which was the largest tenant farm on their land. Sir Edmund had a living in his hands and wondered whether he should sell it to the highest bidder or, at a lower price, to a cousin of their mother's; both decided that the cousin should have it and come to Markethouse as the rector. The two men occupied themselves with problems such as these, which brothers who are lucky enough to be close may discuss. At the end they talked over Charles's visit, which would come at Christmastime.

"I had hoped to go to the Riviera, you know."

"Oh, Charles, you will plan, won't you? I remember when it was Portugal last year, but you had that case with Meyer the German—oh, and I remember your short-lived dreams of crossing over to America, as well."

"Well, well, one of these days."

"I daresay." Sir Edmund laughed. "But it won't do to get your hopes up again. Be happy to come to the country; we can hunt a bit, you know. I've finally managed to convince Crump"—the butler at Lenox House since time immemorial—"that we need real fires while anyone at all is awake. Though you would have thought I'd suggested we set the old portraits ablaze."

Lenox laughed along with his brother. "I look forward to it so greatly, you know. To see Molly and the boys."

"Yes, well, they only wish you'd come more often. Particularly the boys."

"Yes," said Lenox, and smiled to himself. "Where are you off to?"

"The law and order committee in the House. The Royal Academy's report on banned poisons is coming in."

Lenox had an idea. "Who was responsible for it, in the House?"

Edmund thought. "Young James Hilary. Duff. Alexander Adams. Those three, I think."

"Duff?" For a moment disappointment coursed through Lenox. Was that why Duff had the arsenic? But if so, why buy it in a private shop? Surely the Academy would have given them samples.

After a few moments of further talk, Edmund and Lenox stood up and began to walk back toward the members' entrance, wending their way through the refreshment rooms and tearooms and card rooms.

"You're staying in the House for the evening?" Lenox asked, as they walked.

"I must. Terrible trouble, of course, but they would like it."

"Shall we trade jobs? I'll leave you the task of interviewing Duff."

"Newton Duff?" Sir Edmund grimaced. "Perhaps we'll trade later. Oh! There he is."

Both men had seen Duff, who was a member, settling on a couch in the usually abandoned chess room, surrounded by a set of papers he appeared to be deciphering.

"Would you like me to take you over?" Sir Edmund asked in a low voice.

"Yes, actually. I suppose it may as well be now as ever."

"Unpleasant, though."

"Thank you for reminding me, dear brother."

"Only saying. Here we go."

The two men walked over to Duff, but Lenox had to cough once before the austere member would look up.

"Mr. Duff," said Lenox. "We've met several times before, but I daresay you don't remember."

"I do."

There was a moment of awkward silence.

"Well, I must be off, then!" said Sir Edmund, and shook his brother's hand and walked away.

Duff looked down at his papers again.

"May I sit, for a moment?" Lenox asked.

"I suppose, yes, if you must. I came to this room seeking solitude."

There was another moment of silence. Duff's hard, dark eyes focused relentlessly on him. His hair was dark as well, and combed back, and he had the strong jaw and lean body of someone without much pleasure in his life except work.

"I believe you're staying with George Barnard?"

"I am."

"Some business of a murder, from what people say."

Duff finally looked up, though it was not an altogether pleasant look that he gave Lenox.

"Yes."

"Have they any idea what happened?"

In response to this question, Duff stood up and said, with an iron glance, "I must be on my way, sir. Good day."

Lenox watched him leave with a sigh. Why had he bought that arsenic? He was a difficult man. Other men, whom Duff walked by on his way to the chambers, seemed to wait for him to pass until they spoke again. Curious, his reaction—but hard to say whether Duff merely disdained frivolity or, perhaps, knew Lenox's business, as Soames had, or, indeed, mistrusted his own answers, should the line of questioning have gone any further.

Chapter 25

"Charles, Charles, Charles!" said Lady Jane, rushing to the door to meet him. "Oh, Kirk, call Lucy, won't you?"

She took his hand and led him to the rose-colored sofa, where they sat, but she was in such a flurry of emotions that she stood up almost immediately and paced back and forth in front of the fire, though she would tell Lenox nothing.

It was near teatime, which had become, since the beginning of the case, a daily event for Lenox and Lady Jane. They had always managed to see each other several times a week in the afternoons—and inevitably more in the evenings, for they shared a similar society—but now, he knew, he had a daily mandate to come see her and discuss Prue Smith's murder. He liked it, in a way. Often he took tea at home, as the quietest part of his day, but to be with his friend was no chore. He shouldn't have been surprised, really, that she had become so invested in the matter; but in a way, nevertheless, he was.

The butler, so instructed, clambered heavily down the lower stairs, in his loud way, of which Graham so disapproved, and reappeared a moment later with the young maid Lenox had met once before, who had been Prue Smith's nearest friend.

"Lucy, be kind enough to repeat for us what Kirk overheard you saying."

"I'm sorry to be sure, ma'am."

"Very well. Now let us hear it."

"I only meant it as a bit of fun, ma'am, nothing serious," she said uncomfortably.

Lady Jane stood up—she had been back upon the couch—and gazed imperiously, in the way Lenox always forgot she could, at the young girl.

"Lucy," she said, "I demand that you tell us what you said *now*."

"Yes, ma'am. I only said—leastwise, I only meant to say—as how Prue, she knew one of the nephews, the grand one, called Claude."

Lenox said gently, "She knew him?"

"Well—knew him well, like, sir."

"They had an affair, Lucy?"

Lady Jane sighed and walked toward the fire. Kirk coughed and Lucy stammered out an apology.

"It's all right, Lucy," said Lenox quietly. "It's quite all right. When did this begin?"

"Last month, sir, when Mr. Claude came down to London. He'd nip into Prue's bedroom, sir."

"How often?"

"Often, like, sir."

"What did she say about the matter?"

"Oh, it wasn't serious, sir—she meant to marry Jem, sir, and keep Deck on the side, I guess, sir."

Lady Jane grimaced, and Lenox stood up. "Shall we continue in the hallway?" he said to Kirk, who nodded.

But Jane said, "I'll hear this," with that strength of purpose Lenox knew so well and bade Lucy to continue.

"Well, I guess that's all, m'lady," said the girl.

"Was there anyone else?" asked Lenox. "I shall try just as

hard to find out who killed her, Lucy, no matter what you tell me. She deserved to be killed just as little as the Archbishop of Canterbury does. But I have to know if there was anyone else."

She shook her head with certainty. "No, sir. And even Prue knew it wasn't right, about Mr. Claude, only she couldn't say no, really—and he's a charming young man, sir, you know."

"Indeed," said Lenox. He nodded to Kirk. "Thank you, Lucy," he said, and turned away, and the butler led the maid back downstairs.

He walked to Lady Jane, who had her back to him now, and looked out the window.

"It's really the fault of Barnard's nephew," he said. "The poor girl—"

"You're right, of course, Charles. But it seems awful nevertheless."

"Yes," he said. He took her hand and smiled sympathetically when she turned to look at him.

"Well," she said, still frowning. "Tea?"

"Of course."

They sat again, and Lenox asked how the Devonshires' party had been, to which Lady Jane replied that it had been rather boring, because an ambassador of great reputation and poor social skills had been the central attraction. But she had played a hand of cards and had stayed late with Toto, talking over the new season—the young girls were coming out now—and where it might be fun to stay in the country after Christmas.

"Oh, but Charles," she said at last, cutting him a slice of treacle tart, "you must tell me, have you found anything new?"

"Perhaps," he said. "But it is a difficult case, of course, and it has barely been three days."

"I mistrust that man Duff, you know, and the nephew sounds like the limit, but so does the other one. I bet they all three did it together, just to be awful."

"I'll look into it," said Lenox, laughing.

"Must it have been one of them, though?" she asked.

"Or Potts, or Soames. Or indeed Barnard."

"Nobody else?"

"I grow less sure by the moment. But I am beginning to think that it may have been Soames."

"Not Jack Soames? He's so gentle!"

"It seems possible."

She looked at him wide-eyed.

"Oh, but you're right," he said, "it seems impossible as well, of course. Duff seems more likely." He murmured this last thought.

"No," she said. "You know what you're doing, Charles."

"It's only that it's maddening."

"But you have to solve the case—I know you can—and your getting hurt makes me want it even more."

"I thought you said you'd rather I quit."

"Not anymore. I don't want you to be afraid."

"Thank you, Jane."

"What will you do next?"

"I'm waiting for word of Potts, and I ought to interview Claude Barnard again. And then I will have to wait for the ball, to see if I can have a look at the people."

Barnard's ball was in two days, and Lenox had firm ideas about what he would do there, but he decided not to share them with Lady Jane—which was, indeed, a good decision, because when she remembered that it was nearly time for the ball, she began to speak about another set of subjects entirely, including the possible attire of one Lady Wendall; the prospects of a young girl with great beauty and birth, but without fortune; and the possibility that Lenox, who preferred to stay off to the sides, might be persuaded for once to dance.

Chapter 26

In reality, Lenox was even less hopeful than he told Lady Jane he was. Events seemed to have arrived at an impasse. He had very little access to the suspects, and very little reason to suspect any of them individually—other than Eustace's knowledge of botany. But Eustace was exempt, according to Graham's undoubtedly reliable information.

The only real hope, Lenox felt, was the ball.

He sat down at around eight o'clock to supper, though not in the dining hall, choosing instead to sit at his desk in the library, where he could read. A new book about Peru had come from the bookseller across the way. After the previous evening, when the Devonshires' party had slipped his mind altogether, he had double-checked that there was nowhere to go tonight; and there wasn't. He felt restless again, as he laid aside his fork and knife, but had no impulse to go for a walk, which was natural, one night after his attack, and neither did he much feel like reading or answering letters. Perhaps it was, after all, time to go down to the St. James's Club, where he could read the newspapers in the front room and look at the park through the window, or have a quiet chat.

But the doorbell rang just as he was standing up from his desk so that he might go upstairs and change, and Graham brought forth a most unexpected visitor, one whom Lenox had never thought would dare to ask admission to his house: Inspector Exeter.

"Mr. Lenox," said the tall man, bowing.

His bobby's helmet was tucked beneath his arm, and with his other hand he absentmindedly twirled his mustache. It looked as if he had spent a day on the streets; his cheeks were red and he had snow and mud around his boots, Lenox noticed, although he had tried to wipe them off.

"I see you've come from Barnard's?" Lenox said.

Exeter carefully studied his entire person, searching out the clue that had betrayed him, but it was a game he inevitably lost.

"How do you figure?" he asked.

"The lemon," said Lenox.

"What lemon?"

"Giving off a slight smell. You've had your tea there, I imagine."

"I have."

"George is one of the only men I know who serves lemon whether or not women are present."

"Others might, though."

"And yet I should have guessed you were come from him even without the lemon, you know—which made it slightly easier."

"Tricks," said Exeter, pompously, "are an excellent pursuit for the leisure class."

"They are indeed. Cigar?"

"With pleasure, Mr. Lenox."

The two men sat down facing each other and smoked in silence for a few moments.

"Mr. Lenox," said Exeter, at last, "you are not a workingman."

"No, I suppose not."

"A workingman has pressures on him, you know."

"Yes," said Lenox. "It's true." In one way ridiculous of Ex-eter, he thought, but in another way true enough to give him a moment of inner embarrassment. What poor manners to make Exeter feel stupid about the lemon—about anything.

They fell again into silence. Again, it was Exeter who broke it.

"Would you care for half an hour inside of Mr. Barnard's house when all of its residents are out?"

This was so surprising to Lenox that first he coughed and then he tried to stifle his cough, which led to much more coughing.

"Why are you here, Inspector?" he finally managed to say.

"To make you that offer, Mr. Lenox."

"You will forgive me for saying that it seems improbable."

"Yes, yes," said Exeter, "very improbable. Nonetheless."

"You'll have to explain what you mean just a bit more."

"That's all there is to it."

"A half hour in the house?"

"Perhaps a bit less, if I should change my mind."

"To roam about freely?"

"Yes. I know you're on the case, Barnard's word aside."

"I have never raised this point, Inspector, but I feel that now I must: You seem more likely to hinder my efforts in that direction than to help them. Such has been my experience, at any rate."

"Mr. Lenox, I'm a simple man," said Exeter, leaning back in his chair and shrugging. "I seek no glory, no riches, nor any of the like, you see, and I don't mind a bit of collaboration, if the situation calls for it."

Lenox knew, on the contrary, that Exeter did seek glory and riches and that collaboration was the equivalent, to him, of giv-ing away a pound. Not ruinous, but not intelligent either. But now he saw. There was only one thing that could trump his un-willingness to let the amateur detective into the case.

"You're stuck, then," said Lenox.

Exeter seemed to ponder the idea. "Well, I shouldn't say that, sir. But it is not the clearest case, either."

"You no longer think it was suicide?"

"We ruled out self-destruction this morning or thereabouts."

Lenox laughed bitterly, even though he knew he shouldn't have.

"And what of 'Leave it to the Yard,' Inspector?"

Exeter looked so genuinely perplexed that after a moment a wave of fear reached Lenox; perhaps somebody else had sent the two men to find him. He felt again that pang of fear in his chest, constricting around his heart. The police wouldn't kill anybody—that had been his comfort. But someone else might. For a moment he thought about leaving the room, but he pulled himself together.

"Never mind, never mind."

"It would be tomorrow morning, Mr. Lenox. Three of the guests will be at the House, the two nephews will be at separate engagements, and one of my men will be following Barnard, in case he returns abruptly."

"I see."

"And of course, the Yard will appreciate your insights, Mr. Lenox."

"Of course."

"Well?" Exeter puffed on his cigar.

It had the flavor of a trap or, if not of a trap, then of a foolish adventure, likely to yield more harm than good. And yet it was irresistible. To be able to look into the suspects' bedrooms repelled Lenox in one way, but he knew it was a chance he could not reject. Again, he reminded himself that Prue Smith's interests must triumph over his own.

"I will, Inspector," he said, "on the condition that Barnard shan't know, at least for now."

"You have my word," said Exeter.

Lenox knew what to think of Exeter's word. Nevertheless, the two men shook hands and, after naming a time, ten the next morning, Exeter left.

The real question was why the Yard would be so deeply concerned; the answer, Lenox knew right away, lay with Barnard. But did that remove him from suspicion? It must have been at his prompting that Exeter was working so diligently—his prompting and perhaps his gold, on behalf of the country's gold.

Lenox was too agitated, by the time his guest had left, to settle in for the night. He decided to pay a visit to his brother, so that he might ask him about the mint.

But when he reached nearby Carlton Terrace, where the Lenox family house in London was, Sir Edmund was out. Lenox felt at a loss, until it occurred to him that he might seek out Claude Barnard sooner than he had planned. He walked back to his carriage and asked his driver to go to the Jumpers.

He arrived there a few minutes later. The window that had been broken by a shoe, when Lenox had first come to see Claude, was repaired, and inside there was the sound of loud talking. He could see through the glass a foursome playing whist, and beyond them a billiards table, and after a moment's pause he went inside himself, to find the young man he wanted to speak to.

"Claude Barnard?" he said to the harassed porter.

"Right away, sir. If you'll follow me."

He led Lenox up a flight of stairs and into a smaller dining room than the one on the first floor. It smelled of smoke and was full of dark wood paneling and small tables. The club's insignia was framed on the left wall, but that was the room's only decoration, and Claude Barnard was its only inhabitant. He sat at a table with a plate of simple food in front of him, a few pieces of bread and cheese and a jug of wine, which he was tipping into his glass when Lenox came in. He seemed morose.

"Claude?"

The young man looked up and laughed bitterly. "It is my fate, I see, to be pursued by men whom I scarcely know."

"Surely I'm the only one," said Lenox, sitting down across from him. The porter had left.

"Ah, life would be a good deal easier if you were, my dear fellow." Claude stroked his chin contemplatively. "There's you. There's that horrid man from the police, Exeter. There's my tailor; he's waiting for my next allowance even more eagerly than I am. And then there's that awful footman, who sneaks about like a spy but seems to be deficient in the most basic areas of common sense."

"James?"

"I daresay. I ask you, what sort of man thinks that spying consists of standing in the hallway in front of one's damn bedroom? About as subtle as a slosh on the head with a stick."

There was a pause. Lenox lit a cigarette before he spoke.

"You had an affair with the dead girl, I believe, Claude?"

For a moment, Claude's face was impassive. Then he laughed and threw his hands up in the air. "There it is," he said.

"What do you mean?" asked Lenox.

"Now you know."

"I know what?"

"It's out. Damn, though. Yes, yes, I had an affair with her. What of it?"

"That you concealed the fact seems to make you a likely suspect in the girl's death."

"It does?" He laughed again. "There would be more dead girls than you could count, if I was that sort."

Lenox said nothing.

Claude rolled his eyes. "Yes, yes, inappropriate . . . but of course I didn't kill her, you know."

"You didn't?"

"Dammit, no! I feel horribly broken up about the entire thing. Why do you think I'm dining in this godforsaken room?" He picked up the wine and then put it down again, waving his hand with a gesture of futility. "I tried to act normally, but God—"

"I must ask why you neglected to tell me your secret," said Lenox.

"You're a stranger to me!"

"Yes. But you must have known it would come to light."

"No. I thought it would die with her." Claude lit his own cigarette and shrugged. "I really am sad, you know. I joke, but only because it's so damn hard—I couldn't tell anyone, of course, and I couldn't even go to the funeral. It would be ridiculous."

"Yes," said Lenox.

"At any rate, you know everything now. Tell the world, if you like." Claude chewed morosely on a bite of food.

"Claude, what did you do with the money your uncle gave you? The ten thousand pounds?"

Claude looked at him. "You don't miss a trick," he said. "I invested it. Found a good, only slightly risky proposition in America."

"What is its status?"

"Flourishing."

"You have enough money?"

"Nobody has enough, but I'm decently covered."

Lenox sighed. "I must ask, again, whether or not you killed her."

Again the young man laughed. "You're not much of a detective, are you?"

"Perhaps not."

"I was in the drawing room the entire time."

"Not the entire time. You told me you went out to the washroom. And then you might have enlisted outside help."

"Enlisted whose help? I don't move in your circles, my dear man. The criminal elements are wary of offering their services on the street corner, you know. Not sound business, I expect."

"Claude—"

"Although I suppose I could have asked Eustace to do it. But no—he would have lectured me on civic responsibility and the greed of the lower orders, so scratch that; it would never be worth it. But how about Duff? He's a likely fellow. Or one of the lads downstairs, eating supper below us? All of them are masterminds. I believe Solly Mayfair solved Fermat's theorem last week, on a bit of scrap paper between hands of gin rummy. Or perhaps I asked the Prime Minister?"

"Claude—"

"Or the Archbishop of Canterbury?"

"Claude—"

"The Queen!"

"Claude, it is a serious matter."

He waved his hand tiredly. "Leave me alone, would you?" He began to pour wine into his glass and acted, indeed, as if the older man weren't there.

After a few moments, Lenox stood up, paused for a moment, and then left. It was not the time to ask about the burn on his arm. This conversation was even less fruitful than their first one.

On his way home, he felt more lost than he had since the case began—and, for all that, very nearly sorry for the fellow he had left behind, sitting alone over his modest repast.

Chapter 27

Lenox awoke the next day at half-past seven and devoted the early hours of his morning to quiet thought. He ate again in the armchair in his bedroom, gazing out over St. James's Park and savoring his final cup of coffee, and again he tried to make out the unlinked clues of the case, which sat before him like so many puzzle pieces—but each seeming to belong to a separate puzzle.

He thought it made sense, after a night of turning it over in his mind, that Exeter had come to him. Exeter knew him to be investigating the case already, Exeter would have difficulty on his own, and Exeter would rather ask him for help than fail before Barnard and the world.

After all, there had been a dozen times before when Exeter had at last consented to take Lenox's laurels, in exchange for the pleasure Lenox drew from solving the case. However, it had never been so tense as this, and more, it had never been at a time when Lenox had received so much discouragement, though who knew from what quarter it came.

He asked Graham to fetch the book on Peru from the library and read for half an hour, imagining himself on those distant shores with only a compass and a knife; then, at nine-thirty, he put the volume down and changed from his robe into a suit and from his comfortable slippers into his beleaguered boots.

He met Exeter on the corner of Clarges Street promptly half an hour later. The great inspector was less deferential than he had been the previous evening, but then Lenox gathered that there was an invisible army behind them as they walked, waiting for instructions, and Exeter would be loath, above all men, to show weakness in front of subordinates.

They entered Barnard's house a few moments later. Lenox felt his principles betraying him even as they passed through the doorway, but he steeled his mind with the thought of the unanswered questions that lurked within and made a silent pact with himself that he would no longer worry about whether or not he was wrong to have come. Alas, it was the sort of pact he had trouble keeping. But he was able to muster enough professionalism, amateur though he was, to spend the rest of his time usefully, seeing what he could see rather than quelling his own doubts.

The house was, indeed, empty. The maids had finished their work upstairs, and Miss Harrison was supervising the preparation of the midday meal. And if one of the servants did happen to venture upstairs, not one was willing to stay within sight, much less stop Inspector Exeter in his searches.

"I suppose that the guests have consented to let you search their rooms?" Lenox asked, as they went up the stairs to the third floor.

"No," said Exeter. "Mr. Barnard gave me a key. Less trouble to everyone that way, he said. He just doesn't know you're the one looking, not me."

"Ah."

They arrived first at what was plainly Duff's room, which Exeter confirmed: a well-ordered desk, a spartan wardrobe, and a bureau unburdened by any personal objects other than a medical kit. Curious, that, though there was nothing out of the ordinary in it. No arsenic, for example, though it would have been convenient. Lenox looked into each drawer of the desk and then shuffled quickly through the clothes, briskly checking the pockets of the pants. He scanned the floor, aware of his limited time, and found it bare. Then he left the room, wondering yet again about that puzzling bottle of arsenic.

But he thought better of it once he was in the hallway and, without saying anything to Exeter, he turned on his heel and went back inside. Once in the room, he searched out the four corners and at last found what he was looking for: a wastebasket, which had been obscured by the closet door.

"Too bad!" he said, picking it up. "They've emptied it already."

"You would look through a man's trash?"

"I would."

Exeter shook his head, while Lenox replaced the basket and headed back toward the door. But the Inspector stopped him and pointed to the floor. Lenox turned and saw that a scrap of paper had fluttered to the ground, resting half in sight beneath the closet door.

"Excellent," said Lenox, and picked the paper up. He held it so both men could read it together. Its bounty was small, but interesting:

£? JS?

Lenox handed it to his companion and moved quickly into the hallway and on to the next room. It happened to be Soames's, and while it was considerably less tidy than Duff's, with all sorts of personal oddments lying about, racing forms and suspense novels, in the end none of them were useful, so he moved, still as quickly as he could, to the next door down the hall.

Here he had arrived at Eustace's room, and while it, too, yielded unfortunately little, it gave some idea of its inhabitant's tastes—there were thick, strictly pressed wool clothes hanging in the closet like a battalion in formation, and there were a number of conservative pamphlets, stacked neatly on the desk, next to precisely sharpened pencils and a stack of blue stationery. No paints, which Lenox found strange. The only sign of disorder was a handkerchief, which had been lost beneath the bed and smelled of peppermint and wax.

Claude's bedroom was as little a surprise as his cousin's; it had all the disarray of Soames's room without any of the attempts at tidiness. What clothes there were had been hung neatly by the servants, but evidently he had instructed them not to touch his bureau or his desk, for both surfaces were covered with half-empty wineglasses, small tokens and coins, variously used candles, discarded pieces of cloth, and scraps of paper— most of which turned out to involve gambling debts, either owed by or owing to him but predominantly the former. Either he had collected much of the outstanding money he had won or he was a poor player indeed.

Potts's room came last, and when he entered it Lenox felt his deepest pang of shame. Here was a man he barely knew, who was seen by nobody, whom Lenox in all probability would never meet at a party, for Potts wouldn't be invited, but who might have been anything at all, even nice and kind, at any rate quite undeserving of this invasion.

And then, the room, he thought briefly, was touching in a way. Potts had declined the help of the maids in some matters, Lenox could see, because he had obviously folded his own clothes, and taken great pains, as well, though his work was filled with imperfections. His bed had been made by a professional hand, but the wood by the fire had clearly been stacked by Potts, being different from the woodpiles in every other room— stacked diagonally in the up-country fashion that helped prevent house fires.

But Lenox, in keeping with his pact, pushed all of this out of his mind and tried to push out of his mind even that he was favorably disposed, by the nature of the room, to the self-made man who resided in it.

He looked swiftly over the desk and the bureau, finding only the small things Lenox himself might have had, a cameo of what looked like his daughter and a tinderbox, and then checked through the clothes and to see if the wastebasket had been emptied, which it had. He then scanned the floors but found nothing there.

As a last check, he looked, with trepidation, in a small valise by Potts's armchair. Inside it were a few documents relating to Potts's business and a silver pendant, which might have been, Lenox thought, for his daughter.

And then, feeling in the pouch on the side of the valise, Lenox's heart fell. His hand had grasped a small bottle, stoppered with rubber, of the kind in which he knew poison was kept. He pulled it out. It wasn't identical to the bottle that had been in Prue Smith's room, but there was no need for it to be. That had been arsenic, not the poison that mattered.

"What is it?" asked Exeter.

"I'm not sure."

"Better take it."

The man's stupidity was astonishing. "I think we might leave it here," said Lenox.

Exeter shrugged. "Very well. He wouldn't miss it, though."

"He wouldn't miss it if it weren't important. If it were, he would miss it immediately."

"Something in that."

Exeter, at least in private, did not hold on to his public stubbornness and spoke agreeably when a better idea than his came along—which must have happened to him, Lenox reflected, a substantial amount of the time.

He removed from his pocket a small kit that McConnell had given him, which was comprised of a cotton ball, a small glass jar, and a pair of tweezers. He took the stopper out of Potts's bottle, dipped the cotton in it, using the tweezers, then tucked the sample safely into the glass jar, screwed on the top, and dropped it into his pocket.

"Should we arrest Potts?" asked Exeter.

"No," said Lenox, who was very nearly at the end of his rope. He was hungry as well.

"You'd better give me what you just took, at any rate."

Lenox turned to him. "I shall have the results forwarded to you instantly—but I shall have it analyzed by a man who is superior to your men at the Yard and does quicker work."

Exeter looked affronted. "What's wrong with the men at the Yard?"

"Nothing, nothing," said Lenox. "Do you trust me?"

Exeter merely looked at him, with pursed lips.

"I assure you that doing it this way will yield faster results— within two days, you know. That may mean solving the case faster. Nobody will know that I aided your efforts."

This had the intended palliative effect, and Exeter nodded, though still without speaking.

"Now how much time have I got?" Lenox asked, placing the bottle of liquid back in the valise and carefully setting everything as it had been.

"Five minutes," said Exeter.

"Is that all?"

"No longer, I'm afraid."

"Then show me the staircase to the next floor, please."

"The next floor?"

"Yes, Inspector."

"There's nothing there, Mr. Lenox, but flowers, like."

"The greenhouse is above us?"

"Right," said Exeter. "No use there."

"Nevertheless, I'll take a quick glance."

The Inspector shook his head expansively, as if to say how

little he thought of quick glances, but nevertheless led Lenox to an undersized stairwell at the end of the hall.

"I'll stay down here. We have enough flowers in our garden." Exeter chuckled.

"As you wish," said Lenox, thankful for a moment alone.

The stairway turned at a right angle halfway up, and soon Lenox had lost sight of Exeter. At the top of the steps was, indeed, the door to the greenhouse, but just to its side was another door. A large man stood in front of it, wearing a gray suit but with the air of a bobby.

"May I open that door and look in?" Lenox asked.

"No," said the man.

"On police business?"

"No."

"Are you with Exeter?"

"No."

Lenox thought for a moment, considering which tack he could take.

"Look—are you married?" he said.

"Yes."

"There was a girl murdered here—barely twenty-four—I'm only trying to figure out who did it."

"I'm sorry, sir."

"I already know what's in the room."

"I doubt that, sir."

Lenox pulled a shilling out of his pocket and held it in the air. "My brother is in Parliament."

The man looked slightly impressed but still shook his head, no.

"Please?" said Lenox. "You'll watch the whole time."

The man said nothing.

"Her name was Prue."

"I thought you knew what was in the room. Why do you want to see it?"

"There may be a clue—something vital—that nobody else would see."

The man looked down at him steadily for fifteen seconds and then said, "Oh, all right, but you only have a moment. The guard changes over rather soon."

"Thank you, thank you," said Lenox.

He opened the door partway. He didn't know what he had expected, but it wasn't what he saw—tightly bound packing crates without any visible markings. The room was large but empty, other than the packing crates. The only door was the one Lenox had opened, although, at the very edge, half of a skylight, where the greenhouse ended, peered into the corner—but it was dusted over, and tiny, at any rate.

He looked around quickly. There was nothing to see; the large man had been right.

"Mr. Lenox!" boomed Exeter's voice up the stairs.

He looked around again, disheartened. He had felt with such conviction that this room bore some relation to the case but, if it did, it revealed none of its secrets to him.

Something—he didn't know what—made him glance up, and immediately his dejection ended—for he saw, pushing the dust away from the skylight, a hand. Acting as quickly and as quietly as he could, Lenox drew the door nearly shut, leaving himself a sliver of a viewpoint. The hand continued to brush the detritus from the window away, but at last it was clean and a face was lowered to the glass.

"Lenox!" Exeter shouted at that precise moment—which was just like him, Lenox thought—and the face vanished as quickly as it had come. Lenox closed the door quietly and thanked the guard. He walked down slowly, though his mind was running.

"Anything?" asked Exeter, when Lenox appeared.

"No."

But this was a lie, for in the dusty window he had seen, unmistakably, the pink cheerful face of the old athlete—Jack Soames.

~ Chapter 28 ~

"I see Barnard's been here," said Lenox, taking off his coat in Lady Jane's hallway.

"Charles, you're early," she said. "It's only just after three."

He looked at his watch. "You're right. I'm sorry."

"No, it's quite all right. I was only reading. Are you hungry?"

"Terribly."

She called for Kirk and asked him to bring food and tea to the drawing room.

"Barnard was here," she said, "only I didn't see him."

"Did he leave a message?"

"Only his compliments. And the orchid, of course."

Lenox bent over to smell the flower. Then he stood up and smiled. "Oh, Jane, I'm sorry," he said. "I'm in a black mood, and I didn't know where to go."

"I'm glad you came here, then," she said, and led him to the rose-colored couch. The instant she said it Lenox felt better. "Where did you have lunch?"

"I didn't eat."

"Charles!"

"I went into a chophouse, but I only had a pint."

"Of beer?"

"I was in a black mood, as I said."

"What happened?"

He waved a hand, stood up, and began walking around the room restlessly. "Nothing, nothing," he said. "It's hard to say."

She was silent.

"Why do you think Barnard visited you?"

"No doubt to remind me of the ball tomorrow evening. He usually goes around."

"Shall we go together?"

"Yes, of course—although Toto wants to come as well."

"With Thomas?"

"No, Thomas doesn't want to, and she doesn't care. Nobody will mind her going alone. But you might write to him."

"I might." He picked up a silver vase full of lilies and smelled them. "Jane," he said, "would you believe that Jack Soames could murder anyone?"

"Is that why you're upset?"

"There's nothing certain about it, but it may have been him."

"How awful."

"Yes."

"Charles, what happened? Won't you tell me?"

"I can't until I'm sure. And at any rate part of it is a secret."

"Your brother's secret?"

"Yes."

Kirk came in with the tea and some sandwiches. Lenox felt the sudden hunger of someone who hasn't eaten but doesn't truly realize it until he sees food.

"Sugar?" said Lady Jane.

"Yes," he said. "Just this once."

"How many sandwiches?"

"Twelve, I should say."

She laughed and handed him his tea and then put three of the small sandwiches on a plate, which she laid on the table next to him. It was strange, the new closeness the case had brought them. Lenox almost dared to think about—but no, it wouldn't do.

"What about the others staying with Barnard?" she said.

"Perhaps, perhaps. There are points against each of them. I wish I knew more about Duff."

"Then it isn't conclusive, about Jack?"

"No, it isn't conclusive."

There was a pause. "I have to confess something," Lady Jane said.

"What is it?"

"I don't think Barnard brought the orchid around just because of the ball."

"What do you mean?" said Lenox.

"I think he—well, what you and Toto say about his affection for me—"

"Oh, is that all?"

"Not quite. Do you remember me asking whether I should try to take advantage of knowing him to find something out? I know you said I shouldn't, but I did. I had to try to help, particularly after those men hurt you."

When she said this there was a pang in some inner chamber of Lenox's heart.

"Jane, don't you understand the danger of what you did? I said you oughtn't to try for a reason. What if—what if you had been hurt? I can't think about it." Without realizing it, he had taken one of her hands. "Will you stop now?"

"Oh, yes, you have my word on that. I was absolute rubbish at it, you see. No use at all."

"What happened?"

"We had lunch with him yesterday, Helena Adeline and I, and then I spent really the most awfully boring afternoon at the botanical gardens, where he's a director."

"The botanical gardens?"

"You can't imagine it." She laughed. "It was a trial, listening to

Barnard talk about bark and different sorts of leaves and things. He made me take a couple of them, the beast. He took some, too. Mine are still around somewhere. A cluster of yellowish sorts of leaves. You'll trip across it, I daresay. I felt like strangling him with one of his stupid orchids. The way he went on!"

"And there wasn't anything you found of interest?"

"No, I'm afraid. I stumbled about looking for things in the most amateur way possible, until the housekeeper wanted to murder me and even Barnard began to get suspicious. I suppose he thought it was out of the ordinary for Lady Helena and me to wander off together for half an hour. Really, I was using her as an excuse to snoop. But I was an absolute failure, as I told you."

They were both laughing by this time and Lenox felt he could breathe again. "That's too bad," he said. "Brave of you to try it." .

"Oh, but there *was* one thing!" she said.

"What?"

"What was the name of that poison?"

"*Bella indigo?*"

"He had some."

"What!"

"In his greenhouse, in among the orchids, were a lot of little bottles and things. I took a quick look through them, and that name struck a bell. But it was five years old."

"How do you know?"

"It was dated on the label. But at least it shows there might have been poison like it floating around the house or the green-house."

"Fascinating," Lenox murmured. "He could also have intentionally misdated it."

Lady Jane didn't seem to find it as interesting as Lenox. "I really wasn't much count, Charles, but *you'll* find out what happened." And she smiled at him.

"Thanks." He took a sip of tea and bit into the edge of a sandwich. "My favorite, tomato," he said, and smiled back at her.

Half an hour later, and a good deal more cheerful, he left Lady Jane's and walked the few feet back to his own house. It was nearly four.

He was pondering the greenhouse when Graham met him at the door.

"Sir Edmund is in the library, sir," he said.

"Really?"

"Yes, sir."

"I'll go see him."

His brother had indeed come on one of his rare visits. He was sitting in one of the two armchairs by the fire with a tray of tea things by him, staring out the window.

"Edmund," said Lenox, "what an unexpected pleasure."

"They said you came by the house to visit last night," said the baronet, as he turned and smiled. He had a cup of tea in his hand.

"So I did. Will you pour one for me?"

Sir Edmund did as he was asked and waited to speak again until Lenox had settled comfortably into the other armchair.

"How is the case?"

"Perplexing."

"Who did it?"

Lenox raised his eyebrows. "Hm."

"You don't know?"

"I may, actually, but it's not happy news. By sheer luck, I may have discovered that it was Jack Soames."

"Soames!"

"Yes."

"It's impossible. I could see him having a gambling debt, at most. But cold-blooded murder? It's impossible."

"You may be right. It looks badly though."

"How did you find out?"

"I was in Barnard's house this morning—"

"How did you manage that?"

"Exeter asked me to come. He was struggling with the case."

"That man you hate so much?"

"I don't hate anybody."

"That man, though?"

"Yes."

Sir Edmund looked into the fire ruminatively. "I suppose frogs will begin to fall from the sky pretty soon."

"I daresay."

"We should stay indoors when it happens. Messy business."

"I saw Soames trying to figure a way into the guarded room."

"What!"

"Yes."

"Why didn't you tell me straightaway? We need—we ought to—"

"No, it's safe."

"What do you mean?"

"I saw him through a skylight, and it would have been impossible for him to drag any of the crates through it."

"Then what was he doing?"

"Examining the room. I expect he'll make a try during the ball tomorrow night. If it is him."

"Do you think it is?"

Lenox shrugged. "It's so hard to say. What do you know of his finances?"

"He's washed out, I'm afraid. Oh, is that why—he's after the gold!"

"I think so."

"But he might have been merely taking a walk, Charles. I would think that more readily than that Soames could kill somebody. He might have been looking at those blasted orchids."

Lenox shook his head. "I went to the greenhouse once with Lady Jane. Barnard had a lunch and showed us up there afterward. I saw the row of skylights. First of all, it would be particularly hard and pointless to get there—there's no door, and once you get there there's no view, no stretch of roof to walk across. You have to walk around the entire greenhouse. You have to *want* to get there. And second of all, Soames was looking through the window. It seems too clear to be coincidental."

"Another thing, though," said Edmund, satisfied with his brother's explanation of the last point.

"Yes?"

"The girl couldn't possibly have known, even if she had seen him snooping around."

"Perhaps he thought she knew and became nervous," said Lenox. "I don't think it's in his natural way to be a thief and a murderer. He might have become paranoid."

"Would he know anything about poisons?"

"I don't know. Although he lives near Oxford, of course, and went there with you."

"In my year," said Sir Edmund.

"Yes."

Still, his brother's points were valid. It was good to bounce ideas off of him. Had Soames been *forced* to kill Prue Smith? No, probably he hadn't . . .

"Jack Soames. . . ."

"You must tell me something more of his finances, Edmund."

"I heard it from Robert Camp, but everyone knows, I rather think."

"What did Camp say?"

"That Soames had been struggling along with less than anybody thought and then lost a few bets and had to pay some outstanding debts to tradesmen, and that he went under. More or less. He's living on credit."

"Is it only gossip?"

"I don't know. Could be. At any rate, you heard it, didn't you?"

"From Graham."

"Not one to lie."

"What does he have left?"

"They say very little ready money," said Sir Edmund, plucking another scone from the tray and spreading clotted cream over it. "He could touch his friends for some, I suppose."

"He has a great many friends."

"One has fewer when one needs money, however."

"You're right. It's awful, really," said Lenox.

"Well, it's awful for the girl, Miss Smith."

"Yes, of course."

"At any rate, people live on nothing all across London. It's sad that Soames has fallen over, I grant you, but what do we know about any of it?"

Sometimes Lenox's brother surprised him. "You're right, of course."

"And anyway, he has the Pacific, I suppose."

"The Pacific?"

"Surely you know what that is, Charles? It's much in the news."

"No, I'm afraid not. I don't often read the bits about business."

"He sits on the board of the Pacific Trust, that trading company. They pay him something."

"How many people are on the board?"

"Seven or eight. Actually, it must be seven—they can't have an even number."

"What does he have to do?"

"Vote. He made people cross only the other day, because he was the deciding ballot on something or other, I'm not sure what. I can only say I'm grateful that Father put our money in the five percents."

"I am too," said Lenox, thinking. "Say, Edmund, would you help me at Barnard's ball?"

"Does that mean I have to go?"

"Yes."

"Dash it all."

"Will you or not?"

"Of course I will. I hate a ball, though."

"I know you do. But just think, you shall be back in the country soon, at any rate, and you'll have helped me."

Sir Edmund brightened. "That's a good way to look at it, Charles. Very good." He chuckled and took another scone—but offered the plate to his brother first, who took one, too, even though his hunger was gone.

Chapter 29

Almost as soon as Sir Edmund left, there was a soft tap on the door.

"Yes?" Lenox called out.

Graham came in quietly and stood by the door. "May I have a word, sir?"

"Of course."

"You'll remember that I took the afternoon off yesterday, sir?"

"To visit your aunt, wasn't it?"

"I confess that was a falsehood. I apologize, sir. I didn't want you to stop me from going out."

"I would never have stopped you, Graham. I think you know me better than that, don't you?"

"In usual circumstances, yes. But I was trying to track down the two men who had assaulted you, sir, and I thought you might not like the idea."

"I certainly wouldn't want you to risk your skin for me—but thank you, Graham, it was awfully good of you. What happened?"

Graham took a deep breath. "Well, sir, I had a rather adventurous day."

"Come in and tell me about it then."

The butler had been standing in the doorway, but now he moved to the two armchairs in front of the fire and sat down. Lenox went over to a little table in the front corner of the room and poured two glass cups of dark scotch from a bottle thick with dust. It had an old, stinging smell to it, like hickory. Mc-Connell had brought it back from Scotland after his last trip home. A local drink, aged for twenty-two years and then mulled over fire to concentrate it.

"Here you are," Lenox said, handing Graham one of the cups and sitting down with him. "I'm curious to hear about this adventure."

"My first thought, sir, was that Scotland Yard would be the place to begin, because of the comment the two men made just before they ran off. I spent a little while there and tried to talk to a few men, but I confess I failed."

"Better men than you and I have failed with Scotland Yard. What did you decide to do then?"

"I thought I would go back to the alley to see if I could find a clue. I looked around, hoping for some trinket or piece of torn cloth left behind, but I didn't find anything. Even what blood there must have been was cleaned."

"In the East End it would have lasted weeks, I suppose," Lenox said. "What did you do next?"

"I confess I was discouraged, sir, by my lack of success. I seemed to be running out of ideas. Being at a loss, I decided that while it was not related directly to the assault in the alley, it might be a good idea to return to Mr. Barnard's house, which I imagined was probably the epicenter of all these events."

"Sensible, that."

"Thank you, sir. I had a brief conversation with a young lady I had befriended there; thankfully the housekeeper, Mrs. Harrison, was away. After perhaps a quarter of an hour, there was a commotion, and the coachman leaped into action and began to ready his carriage. From that I deciphered that Mr. Barnard was leaving and decided that, being at a loss, I would follow him."

"And where did he go?"

"To the mint, sir. I suppose to work."

"Alone?"

"No, sir. Mr. Soames was with him."

"Soames! Really! Now why would he have done that? Even though his committee is to deal with it, I wouldn't have suspected he'd have any hands-on role." Lenox took a thoughtful sip of his scotch. "What happened when you arrived at the mint?"

"The gates opened, sir, and both men went inside the court-yard that stands in front of the main building."

"I know it."

"At the same time I noticed a group of four or five men, rather low in appearance, hanging on to the bars around the building. Mr. Barnard and Mr. Soames paused inside the courtyard to talk, and one of these men took the opportunity to yell, ''Allo, Guv'nor!' Soames turned around but Barnard didn't. Soon after that they both went inside, through different doors."

"Different doors? You're sure of that?"

"Yes, sir."

Lenox stared into the fire, thinking. At last he said, "Suspicious of Soames, that."

"I'm afraid I don't understand, sir."

"No matter."

"Shall I continue?"

Lenox snapped out of his thoughts. "Yes, of course," he said.

"I was contemplating a return to Mr. Barnard's house when I heard one of the men—the same who had shouted at the two men—say very clearly the name *Barnard*. Then all at once I saw that another man had a tattoo on his neck. He had been facing me, you see, sir, but when he turned there was a blue hammer on the back of his neck."

"You're joking!"

"I admit that I was surprised too, sir. I decided I ought to follow these men. Well, it was a long walk, through shabbier and shabbier neighborhoods, until at last I recognized that we were in the Rookery."

"You didn't go in, I hope?"

"I did, sir. It was getting dark—you know, sir, how early it gets dark at this time of year in London—but I followed them. Two or three peeled off at one point, but I stuck with the one who had the tattoo on his neck. He was with the man who had shouted at Mr. Barnard and Mr. Soames."

Lenox had been to the Rookery on cases. It was no place to be caught even in broad daylight: narrow streets with tenements on either side; a foul smell mixed with sulfurous coal of people who couldn't wash and lived close together; prostitutes in threadbare dresses laughing ostentatiously and offering their business, while they sipped penny pints of gin; gangs of children roaming here and there, picking pockets and getting cuffed by the men on the streets. The men too, made violent by years of unkind life, were quick to lash out. Suddenly Lenox felt a memory of that night when Graham's father had died. He was awfully lucky, sad though it was, that Graham had called on him.

"What happened next?" Lenox asked.

"After a few minutes they ducked into a bar. I took off my tie and my jacket, scuffed my face with a little soot from the street, and went in after them."

"You did!"

"Yes, sir. Then, I'm afraid, I made an error. I went in and had a pint of bitter, and after I had drained it asked for another. Then, when the barman brought it, I asked him in a low voice, 'Do you know what this tattoo of a hammer means?' The place went instantly silent. The barman simply walked away. After a moment, three men came up and asked who I was and why I was asking questions I shouldn't be. Another man came up and then another. There was only a thin crack in the circle but I decided to dash through it. I was pushed and grasped at on my way out, but I managed to run into the street and around a corner."

"Graham!"

"Unfortunately I had lost my way. So I looked at the last light of the sun and walked west toward it. Pretty soon after that I found a cab."

"I have to say, it was terribly brave of you, the whole thing," Lenox said. He stood up and poured two more drinks. "What conclusion do you draw from it all?"

"First, sir, that the men are dangerous. The Rookery is no happy place."

"Truer word was never spoken."

"And second, I think you ought to consider the possibility of Barnard as the murderer."

"I think perhaps Soames is the interesting case here. Why was he at the mint?" Lenox said. "What did it mean? Barnard's a public figure—in the papers, you know."

"I don't think these sort read the papers," Graham responded, and both men took sips of their drinks and looked into the fire.

~~ Chapter 30 ~~

S hreve, the McConnells' funereal butler, admitted Lenox that evening without explicit reluctance, but with a kind of mute reproach nevertheless. It was remarkable that he and the irrepressible Toto lived in the same universe, much less the same house.

"Mr. Lenox, sir," Shreve announced.

The doctor was sitting in a tiny ornamental wooden chair, in a small alcove along the front hallway but almost hidden from view. He was reading the newspaper, with a glass of gin in his hand and his hair falling untidily over his forehead. The cuffs of his pants were splashed with mud, though he seemed not to notice. He stood up and grasped the detective's hand.

"Why are you sitting out here?" Lenox asked.

"The place is crawling with my wife's friends."

"Really?"

"They're like rabbits, you know. They keep multiplying. Every time you think they're gone, another six of them jump out and ask what you think about some horrible scarf or hat or something. It's absolutely harrowing."

Lenox laughed.

"You won't laugh so much when they start to close in on you."

"Why are they here?"

"For supper. And to try on their dresses."

"For the ball."

"You're going?" McConnell asked.

"Of course. Are you?"

"I shall have to, I think." A look of grim determination came over his face. "But they won't catch me looking at their dresses. Not for all the tea in China."

"I may need your help at the ball, Thomas."

McConnell nodded.

"I need your help now, as well," said Lenox. He pulled the small glass jar out of his pocket. "I found what's on this cotton in Potts's room."

"Is it Potts, then?"

"No, actually. I think it may be Soames."

"Soames!"

"Keep it strictly quiet, Thomas. Only my brother and Jane know."

"I shall. But Soames!"

"I know. At any rate, I may be incorrect, and I need this analyzed." He pointed to the cotton. "Can you do it?"

"Of course," said McConnell.

He took a sip of gin; Lenox almost wished he could say something to stop him.

"How soon?"

"Well—since it's a limited sample, I'll have to be careful. Two days, to be thorough."

"Perfect. That's what I told Exeter."

"Exeter?"

"He let me into Barnard's house. That's how I took the sample." Saying this, he handed it over to McConnell, who held it up to his eyes.

The doctor laughed. "You and Exeter. Miracles will never cease."

"I would have bet ten pounds that they had ceased, right before the moment when Exeter offered me help—but evidently not."

"Let's take this up to the lab, eh, Charles?" said McConnell, shaking the glass jar.

"Certainly."

They spoke as they went up the stairs. It was a narrow back staircase, with cartoons from *Punch* on the walls.

"What do you know about the Pacific Trust?" Lenox asked.

"I don't pay any attention to it."

"Neither do I."

"I keep our fortune beneath the floorboards."

Lenox laughed. "Of course."

"But I know that something happened recently."

"My brother said so, too."

"I couldn't say if it was for good or bad, only that it happened."

"It's probably not an issue, anyway."

They had reached the library; Lenox looked up at the familiar railing that encircled the room, fifteen feet up, and the second level of books behind it.

McConnell walked to the tables with his lab equipment. A strong smell of charcoal lingered in the air, and he said, by way of explanation, "An experiment, you know."

"Successful?"

"Hard to say. The kit I gave you worked, did it?"

"Yes. In fact, I need another."

McConnell nodded. He unscrewed the top of the glass jar, took a pair of tweezers, and pulled the cotton out. Then he transferred it to a waiting beaker, which he shut with a rubber stopper. He stepped back and paused.

"Let's see," he said.

There was a huge cabinet above the desk, perhaps thirty feet long, which Lenox had never seen opened, but McConnell opened it now, swinging out door after door after door. Inside were long rows of bottles, the majority of them marked only by a number, arranged neatly. They must have numbered in the thousands. McConnell looked for a moment and then began to walk to and fro, searching for bottles, pulling one down now and then from the other end of the room until an idea brought him back. It was exhausting to watch. By the end he had a small mountain of bottles sitting on the empty table.

He turned and grinned at Lenox. "May as well be thorough," he said.

"Good lord, where did you get all these?"

"There's a bit less under the floorboards because of them. But when one is passionate."

"I understand entirely."

"I've even got a bit of *bella indigo*, just a bit, although it's two years old. Only good now for plants."

"I know your love for botany."

McConnell grinned again. "Well, well. Each of us has an eccentricity. Look at you, when you don't have a case, wandering around and trying to spot Hadrian." He pointed at the sample Lenox had given him. "Two days—or perhaps less."

"Thank you."

McConnell ordered the bottles to his satisfaction, and the two men walked toward the door and downstairs by the same back staircase, ducking whenever they heard women's voices echo through the house.

❦ Chapter 31 ❧

The next evening, a Sunday, at just past six, Lady Jane and Lenox were standing in the middle of his living room while she helped him affix his buttons properly, smooth down his dinner jacket, and complete all of those offices which a bachelor can occasionally find irksome but which are improved inestimably by a female hand.

Lady Jane herself was already in a plain light-blue dress that was tight around her waist and curved out like a bell below, with a black scarf tied around her neck and white kid gloves to her elbows. She always said that some beauty was offset best by complex and bright material, but that what small parcel of beauty she had was only overshadowed by it; as a consequence she dressed with as few frills as she possibly could and still be à la mode. She looked beautiful.

"We live at an odd time," Lenox said, submitting to have his collar fixed.

"No odder than any other, surely, darling?" said Lady Jane distractedly.

"Much odder."

"Whatever do you mean?"

"For one thing, you and Barnard going to botanical gardens together." Lenox shook his head.

She laughed. "Only one botanical garden. But what do you really mean?"

"Look at us! This ball will be the last word in everything conservative and correct, I don't doubt, and all the unmarried girls will dance with innocent hearts, well chaperoned, and the young men by and large will behave politely and everything will be staid and proper and right, you know—much more staid and proper and right than anything was a century ago—or during the time of the great monarchs—or ever."

"Is that so odd, Charles?" said Lady Jane.

"It is! For us to have such conservative values, values that would have constrained our most revered ancestors in their behavior?"

"I suppose."

"But then," said Lenox, warming to the subject, "at the same time! At the same time, the last fifty years have been revolutionary!"

"What do you mean?"

"Think, my dear, about all the reform. Parliament has granted unprecedented rights to the lower classes, unprecedented—things that would never have been dreamed of: property rights, voting rights—"

"I'm for that, though," said Lady Jane.

"So am I, of course. But how odd a juxtaposition—"

"Finished! Go look in the glass, dear heart."

Lenox went over to the mirror in the corner of his library and saw that she had done a very good job: his buttons were fixed, his tie was neat, and his collar was straight.

"Thank you," he said.

"Don't think of it. Only, you must save me a dance."

"Must I?"

"Oh, Charles, you horrid man. Look. For all of what you've

been saying, you aren't even staid and right and proper enough to assent to a lady's request. We fall behind the age of chivalry in that area, I suppose."

He laughed. "Of course I shall dance with you."

She looked at him crossly. "I withdraw the offer. Edmund will do, instead."

"Very well, but he's used to those country dances, you know. Much more active. No doubt he'll twirl you around, things like that."

"Don't be a beast, Charles."

He laughed again. "I'm sorry," he said. "You're right. May I have the first dance?" He bowed and then proffered his hand.

"You may," she said, and curtsied, which sent both of them into gales of laughter. It seemed like yesterday that they were children, peering through the slats of the staircase at their fathers' dances and then pretending to dance themselves, barefoot on the rugs in a dark hallway.

It was nearly six by the time they were prepared to leave and the dinner before the ball began at seven, so they sat down on Lenox's sofa and passed the remaining minutes chatting amiably until the half-hour struck and then hurried through the cold air—Graham behind them, holding an umbrella over them to block the few flurries in the air—and into the carriage.

Now there were only a few dozen houses in London that were equipped to host a ball and of those four or five were supreme: the McConnells', the Duke of Westminster's, Lady Rothermere's, and George Barnard's. Each house had one or two balls a year, though Toto sometimes threw three, if only, she said, to clear Thomas's sporting equipment out of the room, for he used their ballroom as a sort of indoor playing field for everything short of polo.

But people granted that Barnard's house was unique in one way: He could seat two hundred at table and then afterward comfortably admit several hundred more to his own vast ballroom, which sat in the center of the first floor—above, among many other areas, Prue Smith's bedroom. It was three hundred feet across, with light-colored wood floors. The walls were full of gold columns and huge paintings, and the ceiling was painted with the transit of Venus.

The ball would follow the usual form. Several weeks before, the women guests had received a white card, listing the dances on one side and with blank slots on the other, to fill in a partner's name for each dance. It would be mostly quadrilles and waltzes, but while most balls had a four-person orchestra, people expected Barnard to have about a dozen musicians.

The dinner before the ball was a peculiarity, for some people sought the tickets eagerly while others cared for them not at all; at any rate, there was no consensus on their value though to be sure the lack of any invitation at all, to dinner *or* dancing, would have been devastating.

To the dinner were invited the circle of which Barnard would have liked to consider himself a member: Lenox and Lady Jane's circle, whose de facto leaders were the Duchess Marchmain, Jane herself, and Toto, representing the three generations in descending order.

Barnard was a peculiar case. Great politicians were of course invited everywhere, but it was not clear whether he was of the first rank of politicians. Men of tremendous wealth were occasionally invited, though Barnard was unwilling to class himself with that group. But he was connected, by threads more numerous than strong, to enough of the correct people that he was sure to be invited many places and was sure to have his own invitations accepted. That is, to put it more briefly, some combination of money, birth, and power were united in him that was impossible to classify and was neither enough to disbar him from the first tier of society nor to include him fully in it—for whatever one takes that first tier to be worth.

Of one thing there was no doubt, however, and that was that fashionable London would appear tonight en masse, and when Lenox's carriage pulled into Clarges Street he saw that it was but one of three dozen, making the street quite impassible and in some respect exhilarating, full of the excitement preceding a large well-organized party.

After some deft work by the driver and a gradual movement of the carriages, Lenox and Lady Jane were able to step onto the unfurled red carpet that led to the front door of Barnard's house and, with just a few moments to spare, make the dinner table on time.

The people were of great interest and variety: the men belonged to the upper echelons of art, politics, science, and scholarship and the women were all either beautiful or matriarchal, with very few exceptions. The men wore dinner jackets and shining shoes and the women wore beautiful dresses, usually in gray or blue, with an occasional splash of red.

This was also a time when the symbolism of flowers was in great vogue, and all the young girls carried bouquets with private meanings. Violets meant modesty, and the girls with violets tended to look rather pinched and censorious; ivy meant fidelity, and the girls with ivy looked very happy; forget-me-nots meant truest love, and these girls looked the happiest. They all had pocket dictionaries of these meanings, and when two lovers had different dictionaries, flowers were often thrown tearfully into some poor man's chest, to be followed by explanation and reconciliation.

For the fun of it, Lenox had once asked Toto what his favorite flowers meant, and she had very excitedly scanned her book. "Snowdrops," she had said. "Hope, or consolation."

Dinner was served.

Lenox, like all Harrovians since time immemorial, had been forced to read *Satyricon* in his day, and he remembered well the delicacies at Trimalchio's feast: the dormice dipped in honey, the roasted boar with pastry sucklings at its breast, the hollow side of meat which, when carved, released live birds into the air.

Barnard had not elected to serve such exotic fare, but his banquet was no less complete. There were to be a dozen courses, and in due time they arrived: warm onion soup, bubbling with cheese; delicate strips of hare with cranberry sauce; roasted chicken and a blood gravy; plain English mutton under a blanket of peas and onions; a broiled beefsteak in pastry; a light salad of pears and walnuts; sliced apples dipped in chocolate; a towering white cake decorated with whipped cream; a plate of thinly sliced cheese; a bowl of chestnuts and walnuts; and, last, coffee—all accompanied by what Lenox had to acknowledge was a remarkably good selection of wines, from champagne to German summer wine to dark claret to a light Bordeaux. It was the sort of supper that people would talk about for quite a long time—just as Barnard intended.

Lenox sat with a group of men and women he knew, though McConnell was far to his left and Lady Jane far to his right—two seats to the left of Barnard himself, in fact. Lenox spoke for most of the night with James Hilary, a young politician barely out of his twenties, and Lord Cabot, his old friend, who was too busy eating to be truly coherent but who uttered, from time to time, some authoritative word on whatever subject was at hand.

Hilary was a good sort. He was one of the people who had been working with the Royal Academy to ban certain poisons, and while Lenox couldn't get anything from him on that subject he spoke very fluently about Parliament.

"I expect our side will be in the ascendancy for some time, Mr. Lenox," he said, during the fifth course.

"Do you now?" asked Lenox. "Why?"

"As fewer boroughs become rotten, and the number of people who vote their conscience increases, we must by necessity grow. We are the party of the public. It was more difficult to be so when the public had trouble voting for us, because Lord So-and-so of So-and-so decreed otherwise. No offense, Lord Cabot."

"None taken," Lord Cabot said.

"You may be right," said Lenox.

"I was speaking with Eustace Bramwell before dinner—a most ardent conservative, belongs to my club—and even he acknowledged it."

"You belong to the Jumpers?"

"Yes, indeed, Mr. Lenox. But how would you know the Jumpers?"

Lenox laughed. "Do you mean because I'm so old? I still hear of things, now and then. How well do you know young Bramwell?"

Hilary had laughed too, good-naturedly. "Not well. He and his cousin Claude are rather friends, sometimes thick as thieves, and they belong to the half of the club I don't know much about. Just as in Parliament, however, I expect my half of the club will eventually outlast."

Lord Cabot here made one of his rare comments. "Damn silly club, if you'll excuse me saying, Hilary. Don't see why you can't come to the Travelers more. Your father does."

"We've got good food and good fellows at the Jumpers," said Hilary. "But I do come to the Travelers, now and then. I've got a constituency to work for, though. And to be honest, I feel a bit rubbish that my five hundred miles were only to Germany, when both of you pop round to Jupiter every few years."

He laughed again, and so did Lenox and Cabot, and the conversation, intertwined with the food and the wine, floated along.

All through this chatter, however, Lenox kept his eye on the residents of the Barnard house. Sir Edmund had been invited only to the ball, not to the dinner—it was thought likely that he would decline the invitation altogether based on his neglect of prior invitations—and Lenox couldn't very well pull McConnell away from his seat, so he was forced to observe the men he

suspected on his own, and increasingly his attention was devoted to Soames, down at Barnard's end of the table.

Soames, unfortunately, was quite flushed and appeared to be
drinking too much and eating too little. His dinner jacket was ill-
fitting, or perhaps had merely been hastily donned, for he was
usually a well-dressed man. His discomfort seemed to be palpa-
ble, and he only spoke intermittently, Lenox noticed, without
truly entering any of the conversations around him.

It had taken two hours—and an effort akin to rowing ten
miles—to go through all the courses, but at last people put their
forks aside, took their final sips of water and wine, and began to
light their cigarettes and wander into the maze of drawing rooms
that surrounded the ballroom. Only then could Lenox pull Mc-
Connell aside and say to him, "Keep an eye on Potts and Duff if
you can, Duff especially," before the two men joined Lady Jane
and Toto, who were waiting intently to begin dancing.

Just as the band began to play, however, Barnard himself approached Lady Jane and to their quiet amusement asked her to
have the opening dance with him. She could not but agree and
Lenox was left to the side, where he smoked a cigarette and
watched his friends dancing and, with slightly more focus, also
watched Soames walking unsteadily around the room.

❦ Chapter 32 ❧

S upper had lasted until nine, and the ball had commenced an hour later. It was now eleven, and the chatter on the couches and the clack of shoes on the dance floor were growing steadily louder, as the flow of guests into the party reached its crest. Sir Edmund had come, looking not altogether disheveled, and Lenox had set him the task of watching the two nephews, Eustace and Claude.

Lenox had originally intended to watch Claude himself, but he had begun to feel more strongly by the moment that the murderer was Soames. Thus he devoted his entire attention to his prime suspect. He must have murdered Prue Smith, Lenox thought, because she had tripped over him while he was angling after the gold—and while she couldn't know what it was, he would have been on edge and more likely to overreact. In particular because this would be his first time, really, as a criminal. How had he cadged an invitation to stay with Barnard?

Soames was dancing with a succession of women, but he had grown redder and drunker and visibly less in control of himself, and after a last waltz he had sought rest at one side of the ballroom and taken a glass of champagne to cool himself.

Lady Jane and Lenox stood on the other side of the ballroom. They had just finished a dance together.

"What was that business with Barnard?" Lenox asked, with an eye on Soames.

"Strange, wasn't it?"

"There are probably worse things than dancing with Barnard, but at the moment I can't think of them."

"Don't be mean," Lady Jane said. "I suppose he needed a woman and saw that I met that description, in some modest way."

"You look lovely."

"Thank you, Charles."

"Have you danced with Edmund?"

"Of course! Not half so much twirling as you frightened me with, although he stepped on my foot once. I think he was trying to spy on somebody."

"He's a zealous assistant."

"Tell that to my poor ankle. But listen. If he's going to spy on somebody, I will too."

"I won't have it—listen to me this time—it might be dangerous."

"What about Barnard?"

"No! We'll do fine, McConnell, Edmund, and I. Would you like a glass of water?" A waiter was walking by with a tray.

"Oh, yes," she said. "How can it be so frightfully warm when it's so cold outside?"

She sipped the water he handed her and continued to fan herself. At that moment McConnell came toward them.

"Hot as anything, isn't it?" he said.

"I may step out in a moment," said Lady Jane, "if you care to join me. I'd like a breath of fresh air."

McConnell smiled. "I would, you know, but the boss might object." He nodded at Lenox.

"I'll get Toto to take me then."

"She's with Mary, just over there." He pointed to one of the couches that ringed the dance floor and Lady Jane walked over to it.

"Soames is acting strangely," said Lenox, when the two men were alone.

"You suspect him?"

"Perhaps."

"Brave of him to come at all, if he's gone broke."

"Very brave, if he's not guilty of murder. If he is, I shan't know what to think."

McConnell smiled again. "You do get wrapped up, my good friend."

Lenox looked away from the dance floor for a moment. "I think I should stop doing it if I didn't."

Just at that moment the host came toward them, bearing three glasses of champagne on a tray he had just swiped from a waiter and smiling broadly.

"McConnell! Lenox! A toast!"

"As you say," said the doctor, though Lenox kept silent. Why on earth did Barnard want to toast with them? In all likelihood he was drunk.

At any rate, the three men tipped their glasses and threw down the champagne.

"First-rate," said McConnell.

"Of course, of course," said Barnard. "Are you having a pleasant time?"

"Very pleasant, aren't we, Lenox?"

"Indeed. Thank you, Barnard. One of the must delicious suppers I've ever eaten."

"I've got a new cook. From France, but he does English dishes quite nicely, doesn't he? And then that salad—I'd never had the like before, and I daresay no man in London had either, don't you think?"

He had stepped closer to them, and at that moment, forced to respond to Barnard, Lenox lost track of Soames.

"Anyway," said Barnard, after half a minute, "dance, drink, and be merry!"

He raised his empty glass in salute and walked off.

"Damn," said McConnell. "I lost both of them."

"I lost Soames, too."

"Split up, shall we?"

"Yes. But keep an eye out for Soames above the nephews. He may be planning a theft."

"As you say."

The two men walked away from each other. Lenox's heart had begun to beat faster, and his pace increased as he walked around the edges of the ballroom, praying for his eyes to alight on that familiar visage.

He wended his way through six drawing rooms, each of them impossibly crowded, making sure not to miss a single person as he searched out Soames. Doing his best to nod and smile at everybody without getting caught in conversation, he got to the end of the house, went back through again to double-check, and then nearly ran to the dance floor and walked briskly around it, hoping to catch a glimpse of him.

Some plan must be afoot, he thought at last and, as surreptitiously as he could, he began to creep upstairs toward the room that contained the gold.

He scarcely knew what to expect—perhaps the man guarding the room would be dead? If he was, Lenox didn't think he could ever forgive himself. He hoped McConnell had come upon Soames but thought it more unlikely by the moment.

The second floor had been dimly lit but deserted. Now he was cautiously stepping up the next staircase to the third floor. He had followed the advice of his friends, and now, with a feeling of absurdity, pulled a small gun from his pocket, which he had had as a souvenir from the Plymouth case. If he needed to he could handle it, but he left it half-cocked.

Suddenly he heard a rustling from one of the rooms and

paused on the middle of the stairway to the third floor. The noise seemed to be coming from the second room on his left. He approached it slowly and at last cocked the gun altogether, though he kept it by his hip. He counted to three under his breath, and then opened the door suddenly, with the pistol raised slightly though not enough to be conspicuous.

He had stumbled upon two young people he knew, if not by name then by face, a young girl and a young man. He was holding her hand and whispering to her when Lenox interrupted them.

"Sorry," Lenox said.

"No, no—got lost, you know. . . ."

Lenox withdrew, closing the door behind him, and heard the sound of stifled laughter from the room. Again his nerves heightened; he was on the third floor and walking slowly toward the staircase he had gone up only the day before. But it was dark this time, almost dark enough that he couldn't see anything at all.

He reached the bottom stair and steeled himself against any possibility. Then he took a deep breath, lifted his foot—but at that moment he heard a piercing scream. It came, without any doubt, from the first floor of the house.

He raced downstairs, concealing his pistol as he did. When he was on the second floor, he began to walk down quietly, but he needn't have; the commotion was a hundred yards away, in the hallway leading from the front door to the ballroom. As he got closer, he could see that it came, more specifically, from the head of the stairwell leading down to the servants' quarters.

His first thought was for Lady Jane, but as he glanced around he saw her with Toto, sitting on a sofa, looking concerned but not, like the majority of the party, pushing toward whatever spectacle had aroused their interest.

This left him free to push toward it himself, and with the best manners he could muster he parted the crowd until at last he arrived at the epicenter—where he saw McConnell leaning over into the darkened stairwell and Barnard hanging over him, while several footmen kept the crowd at bay, to its chagrin.

McConnell looked up, for just a second, and turned back—but in that second Lenox must have flickered on the edge of his vision, for the doctor turned around again and shouted, "Charles!"

Lenox pushed his way past a footman and toward McConnell and Barnard.

"What is it?" he said.

They were both examining something, but not until Barnard stepped aside did Lenox see what it was—a body, a male body, slumped on the stairs to the servants' quarters, stripped of its jacket, with a pool of brilliant red blood staining the pure white shirt. Still, the face remained obscured.

"Who is it?" said Lenox.

McConnell stood up, cupped his hand, and whispered in Lenox's ear. "Soames."

Chapter 33

Lenox saw, peering down into the darkness of the servants' stairs, that it was indeed Soames sprawled across them.

At this moment Barnard stepped away from McConnell and Lenox and said in a loud voice, "Please, everybody, return to the party."

Nobody obeyed his instructions, but Barnard walked through the crowd nevertheless, presumably to find further help, perhaps in the shape of Inspector Exeter.

Lenox acted quickly. He asked a footman for a candle, and when he received it he scanned the area. There was no blood anywhere except on those stairs across which Soames was laid. He looked at the foot of the stairs for anything dropped or tracked but found nothing. Then he shone the candle over the walls and saw only a certain amount of blood, which could be assumed to have come from Soames himself. It appeared that no clue was to be found.

"Can we move him?" said Lenox, when he was done looking.

"Yes," said McConnell, "but it will be wet work."

Lenox beckoned to one of the footmen and instructed him to clear the largest table in the kitchen and cover it with a white sheet. The footman walked downstairs quickly to fulfill the request, and Lenox stepped out toward the crowd.

"Ladies and gentlemen," he said, "I fear I have bad news. A friend of ours—Jack Soames—is dead, but we need space, please, to give his body the treatment it needs."

Whether this broke the spell or people were galvanized by the news, the crowd broke out into a high buzz, and people began to walk loosely here and there, seeking out special friends, no doubt talking to each other about Soames's financial downfall and perhaps speculating about suicide, though it was the farthest thing from McConnell's or Lenox's minds.

The doctor, with the help of the footman who had prepared the kitchen table, gingerly lifted the body and asked Lenox to close the door behind them. The three men stepped down the narrow staircase and went to the right. Standing in the kitchen, alone, was Miss Harrison.

"Not in my kitchen," she said.

"Ma'am," said Lenox, "with all due respect, we must place him here."

"Not in my kitchen," she repeated. "Henry, stop helping them."

The footman looked at McConnell in confusion.

"Henry," the doctor said, "stay with us, and if you lose your job you can come work for me at ten pounds more a year. Miss Harrison, I am sorry to say this, but we have little time to accommodate your willfulness. Consult your employer, if you truly wish."

That said, he and Henry placed the body on the table, while Miss Harrison vanished down the left hallway, her skirts flying behind her.

"What is it, Thomas?" said Lenox.

McConnell gingerly unbuttoned the dead man's shirt, removed the suspenders, and revealed Soames's chest, which, though stained with blood, still jutted out proudly, as if in elegy of his former athletic greatness.

"Henry," said the doctor, "bring me a basin of hot water and take another white sheet and tear it into short strips."

"Yes, sir," said the lad, and ran off to do so.

"A knife, I think, not a bullet," said McConnell.

A little breeze of fear passed through Lenox's mind as he remembered the knife the two men in the alley had shown him. But he ignored it and said, "Yes. We would have heard a bullet."

Henry returned with the basin and the cloths, and McConnell cleaned the area around the wound with expert care until they could see three long, jagged red cuts, all in the region of the heart, now cleansed of the gore that had matted his chest.

"How long a knife?"

For lack of a better tool, McConnell had taken his pen to lift back the edges of the wounds. "Fairly long, six inches or more, I should say. Somebody was below him, I think, and thrust upward, through his ribs."

"Below him on the stairs; it makes sense," said Lenox.

"Exactly."

"All three wounds are the same?"

"No, these two are alike," said the doctor, pointing to the lower two cuts. "The third wound came after death, or near the end, and was only a glancing blow."

"How big a man?"

"It wouldn't matter. He had leverage. Even a strong woman could have done it, if she had taken him by surprise."

"How long ago?"

"Ten minutes at the most, I should say."

"Who screamed?"

"A maid found him, and Barnard asked for my help. She was the one who screamed."

"Did you see him after we left each other?"

"No, alas. I couldn't find Potts or Duff either, for that matter."

"I hope Edmund saw something."

"Yes."

"Could anyone else from the party have seen anything? Anyone who wasn't purposefully looking?"

McConnell shook his head. "No. Nobody was even near the hallway. Somebody lured him there, I suppose."

"It must have been someone he knew. No witnesses, then?"

"I don't think so."

He turned to the footman, who was standing a little way off. "Henry, explain to me how the servants were stationed tonight. It seems absurdly dangerous for someone to commit a murder here if there were servants coming up and down the stairs all the time."

"Actually, sir, with respect, that would have been the best place. The servants' quarters was going unused, sir."

"What do you mean?"

"We were set up in a room just behind the dining room so the food could be served hotter and quicker. And then, it's a narrow staircase, so there would have been delays, like, Sir."

"How did you cook in there?"

"An extra oven. And we served drinks from there, where they were cooling under ice."

"Who came up with that idea?"

"Mr. Barnard, sir."

"Who would have been out in the main hall, closest to that door, among the servants?"

"One man outside, in case of late arrivals, sir. Several at the entrance of the ballroom, though that'd be facing the dance floor. Nobody was departing yet, sir, and near everybody had come."

"Damn. Smart of whoever did it—a deserted place in a crowded house, and an easy escape through the downstairs."

"Lenox?"

"Yes, Thomas?"

"What motive occurs to you?"

"I'm not sure. Might it have been to cover up Prue Smith's murder?"

"I suppose," said McConnell, though he sounded unconvinced.

"Thomas, keep guard over the body, and see if you can find anything else. Henry, ask the servants what they saw, say the police would like to know, and then tell them you think it was self-murder."

"Suicide?"

"Yes. Do you both understand?"

The two men nodded, and Lenox nodded back.

"Now let's look through the pockets," Lenox said. He and McConnell systematically went through all of Soames's clothes, finding only the usual things—handkerchief, a pocket watch, and a little money. No key, because he was staying here with Barnard, and no personal objects.

Lenox sighed. "Still, I think we're close," he said. "I have to see my brother."

～ Chapter 34 ～

Sir Edmund had the same thought. He was standing at the head of the stairs, trying to convince a phalanx of footmen that he was in fact one of the men assigned to help in the case, without avail.

"Charles!" he said, when he saw Lenox open the door. "Tell them!"

"Will you have a cigarette with me outside, Edmund?"

"Dash it all, Charles, no. Tell me what happened!"

"Outside, Edmund."

"Oh, all right."

The two men walked past the crowd and through the front door to the stoop, where it was lightly snowing. People were leaving, so they stood off to the side.

"What happened to the two nephews?" asked Lenox.

"I lost one of them, Charles. I apologize."

"Quite all right. McConnell lost both of his. Did you lose Claude?"

"Claude? No. The other one, Eustace."

"You mean to say you had your eyes on Claude the entire time?"

"Well, ever since you asked me, at least."

"What happened?"

"The two were talking but just for a second, and then Claude seemed to strike Eustace—I must say, they don't seem to like each other—and then they diverged, and I could only keep up with Claude, who you said was more important."

"Yes," said Lenox. "You did well."

"Thank you. Who did it?"

"I don't know. The only people we can account for are Soames and Claude, the two men I thought were most likely to have killed Prue."

"Claude might have done the first murder anyway, mightn't he?"

"No, I don't think so. It was the same murderer. The chances that there would be two murderers in a single house—with a giant pile of gold in it—are too remote."

"Who does that leave?"

"Eustace, Duff, Potts. Barnard, I suppose. A servant. Someone I've never even considered."

Lenox dropped his cigarette, smothered it with his shoe, and gave a sad sigh.

"I've bungled it badly you know, Edmund."

"No, you haven't, Charles. You'll get it."

"I know next to nothing about Potts. And I haven't worked on Duff nearly enough."

"This is the part you're cleverest at, though, Charles."

"Thank you for saying so."

"Really, it is."

"Yes, perhaps."

"Is there anything I can do? As far as Soames? Poor fellow. . . ."

"Yes, it's awful," said Lenox. "But no. Not unless you care to keep an eye on Duff or Potts—or, better still, sneak up to the fourth floor just to make sure the gold is still there."

"I will."

"Thank you."

They both went inside, Lenox in a downcast frame of mind, searching for the clue he had missed, the step he glided over, the mistake he made that had perhaps cost Jack Soames his life.

Just as he was about to go back downstairs, Lady Jane tapped him on the shoulder.

"Are you all right?" she asked.

"Yes, are you?"

"Awfully sad, of course. But listen, I know what a rush you must be in. I followed George around—Barnard, I mean."

Lenox sighed. "I suppose I can't stop you. Remember the Charterhouse case, when you kept helping?"

"Of course," she said.

"What happened tonight?"

"I saw you go upstairs, you know, and started to worry a little bit, so I tried to watch him from near the stairs. Well, almost right after you walked upstairs he brushed right by without seeing me. I couldn't tell if he was following you or going on his own. So I followed him, you know, and then when I was on the first floor and he was headed toward the second I called after him."

"What did you say?"

"I just called his name. He looked reluctant, but he came back. Then I said I had been getting away from the madding crowd for a minute, but would he dance with me? I had to throw over William Carstairs, but that didn't matter. At any rate I dragged him back down. We didn't dance, but he said he'd be right back. Then, within about thirty seconds, the maid screamed."

"Were you watching him?"

"No, I headed back to the stairs to catch you up, I'm sorry to say."

Lenox paused. "Let's talk it over later." He turned away, but then stopped and said, "You know, I can't think of any other woman I know who would have done that. You're awfully brave."

"Oh, nonsense," she said. But in her face a look of happiness rose briefly and then disappeared.

Lenox ducked through the footmen, who grudgingly allowed him passage, and back downstairs to the servants' quarters. He saw the light burning in the kitchen and caught a glimpse of Mc-Connell, who was still examining the body. But instead of walk-ing toward him, Lenox turned left and went back to Prue's room.

What had he missed? What, in this room, revealed the mur-derer? He opened the door, candle in hand, and saw again the narrow bed, the plain desk, and the drawing on the wall.

He also saw that the window was open—still open since he had examined the room? Probably not. It seemed unlike Miss Harrison to allow a draft in.

And then all at once Lenox realized what must have hap-pened. The murderer must have lured Soames near the service stairwell, killed him there, and then, instead of going back up through the party, gone down—down through the servants' quarters. He would have been bloody—*wet work*, McConnell had said—and his escape would have been this way.

But through this room, or through the kitchen? It might have been any of them, unless the murderer happened to know about the window in Prue Smith's room and knew it was still unoccupied. This fact increased the odds that the murderer was someone living in the house, someone who had been in Prue's room before. Claude? Whoever it was, he would have had to gam-ble that the servants were upstairs or else stayed in the kitchen as he got away.

It was the open window—he was by no means certain, but he had a hunch that it had been the means of exit, too. Eagerly, he lit the candle on the desk—the new candle—and set it next to his so that the room was bright. He looked carefully over the floor for a footprint, a drop of blood, anything. But he found nothing, and again his heart sank.

Just to be thorough, he looked in the drawers of the bureau and examined with particular care the entire area around the window. Still nothing.

Out in the hall, he heard Exeter's booming voice, asking Mc-Connell who he thought he was. There was nothing else Lenox could do that evening. Exeter would be in command of the situation. Terrified, of course, that a Member of Parliament had been murdered, but in command.

Lenox sat on the edge of the bed, cursing to himself. He had mangled the entire case. Motive, he thought—he should have begun with motive. Why would anyone kill Prue Smith, if not for love or money? To keep her quiet. Suddenly the wine and the food caught up with him, and he felt heavy and tired.

The bed creaked as he got up, and its noise gave him one last thought. Sinking to his knees, he took the candle and held it underneath the bed. Last time it had been bare; this time, he saw with a start, it was not. He reached into the far corner to see what had been hurled back there—a dark indistinct object—and pulled it out to find his fingers bloody and a long wet knife in his hand.

～ Chapter 35 ～

At that moment Exeter walked in the door. Lenox looked up at him and held out the knife, as if he were presenting him with something as innocuous as a glass of wine.

"I've found the weapon."

If Lenox was expecting applause for his discovery, he was sorely mistaken in his estimation of Exeter.

The man seemed to get even larger. He didn't speak straightaway but stepped into the room and paced back and forth on a tight line.

"This looks very black against you, Lenox," he said, dropping his standard politeness.

Lenox sighed, realizing what was going through Exeter's mind.

"Exeter," he said, "I don't want to be short with you, but you'll vex me terribly if you don't stop being an ass."

"Very black indeed," said the Inspector.

Lenox sighed again. "I'll explain it, then. For the past ten minutes, I've been in the kitchen, inspecting the body with my friend McConnell. Do you really think that if I had committed a murder and successfully hidden the weapon in plain sight of several other people, I would be so daft as to come back into the *first* room the police were liable to search, where another murder had been committed, and hide the knife there? If I ever turn to crime, Exeter, I shall do better than that, I assure you."

There was a cloud of doubt on the large man's brow, but he came back. "That might have occurred to you only after you put the knife in here. Perhaps you're getting it back now. Or perhaps you wanted to be found, finding it. Many murderers call in the body."

"You think me that stupid, Exeter? My heavens, I was called to the stairwell from the party, and from the instant I got there was among people." He waved a hand. "This is nonsense, and we're wasting time. Here is the weapon used to murder Jack Soames." He laid it gently on the desk.

"I suppose you're right," said Exeter finally. "Can't be too careful, though, Mr. Lenox."

"Quite all right. Now, shall we get to work?"

"What do you have in mind?"

"You ought to send two constables to the fourth floor. I can't tell you why, but you may trust me. My own brother is there now."

"Why?"

"As I said, I can't tell you."

"Afraid we can't do it, then." Exeter looked as if he got some happiness from denying the request, after having been shown up.

Inwardly, Lenox sighed. "Please, Exeter. Remember. The credit will be yours. We have to work together." Together, indeed.

For a moment Exeter pondered this new tack. "All right," he said. "The fourth floor?"

"Yes. I think the murderer escaped through this window. I'll check outside for signs of him, though I doubt there will be any."

"And what shall I do?"

"The force has the manpower I don't, all the bobbies up-stairs with Barnard. If I were you—though I'm sure you've thought of it already—I'd assemble the guests who are still here and ask them what they saw. Get ten or twelve men, if you can. This is now a double murder case, if I'm not mistaken."

"Two men to the fourth floor, and ten questioning the people upstairs? Probably in the line of what I should have done, the questioning upstairs."

"Yes. You're acting very sensibly, Exeter. And perhaps, if you like, you should have the constables who question the guests look at their wrists and their shoes for blood or dirt. Particularly their shoes. It's a wet night, but the guests all entered directly from their carriages. They should have clean shoes, unless they went through this window."

Exeter, feeling a part of the plan now, said, "Very well. But you must share anything you know with us."

"As always," said Lenox. "Now go. Quickly, man, quickly. I'll take this knife to McConnell. He'll be able to examine it."

Exeter left, and on his way out began barking at his subordinates.

Lenox walked down the hall to the wide kitchen and presented McConnell with the knife.

"See if this is the murder weapon," he said, and smiled at the doctor's astonished look. "I'll return as shortly as I can."

He went up the servants' stairs and passed as quietly as he could to the front door, avoiding all conversation. Then he went outside, pulled his collar up, and counted down the lower windows, which opened onto the street, until he found Prue's. He stopped about ten feet from it. Here was the area to examine.

There was a great deal of brilliant light coming through the upper windows because of the ball, and he could see the sidewalk very clearly. The last few coachmen were the only people outside, and they were huddled in the small shelter between the broughams and carriages, smoking and talking. Lenox was alone.

He began by looking at the windowsill. He had glanced over

it on the inside of Prue Smith's room and seen nothing but the old scuffs, a probable result, he thought, of Bartholomew Deck's late visits. On the outside were the same scuffs, but he saw something he thought might be new: a very slight black scuff, of the kind a black shoe might have made when it scraped against the sill. Perhaps there had been poor traction on the slippery sidewalk, and the person bolting from the room had stepped hard with his back foot, coming outside. Every man present tonight, of course, would be wearing well-polished evening shoes. It was very little. But it lent credence to the idea that somebody had recently come through the window.

The cobblestones were wet, but unfortunately they didn't betray anything. There was no rock dislodged, no further black scuffs, and certainly no footprints. Lenox could see that his own faint footprint disappeared the moment he lifted his shoe.

There was nothing else in the area. He walked fifty yards in either direction on the sidewalk and saw no marks or objects; then he went back and walked through again, looking very carefully, and occasionally stooping to the ground, and on this second go-through he did find a yellowish leaf of a rather odd shape. He would have ignored it if it hadn't been very near the window. There were no trees in the area, but it could easily have been trammeled to and fro until it had made a journey of several blocks. And yet it didn't appear hard-used or stepped on, and though it was clearly nothing, Lenox put it in his jacket pocket.

Now this was a disappointing blow. He had hoped against hope for something conclusive. Still, there was the black scuff, which looked fresh and seemed to bear out his idea of an escape through Prue Smith's room.

But here again he was disappointed, when he thought it through. The person who had killed Soames had known Prue's room; it was too big a coincidence to think that a stranger would have randomly picked her door out of a dozen others, including many nearer the stairs. Yes, it seemed conclusive. But there you ran against a wall. The only person absolutely certain to know Prue's room was Claude, because he had been behind closed doors with the girl. Even Barnard might not remember precisely which one was hers. But it happened that Claude was the one person entirely free of suspicion in this instance. Edmund had been firm: Claude Barnard had never left his sight.

Lenox refused to give in, however. He went inside and checked with McConnell again; yes, it was the same knife that had killed Soames; yes, anybody of any stature could have used it; no, it had no particular provenance. Anybody might have bought it at any store that carried such things, probably one of the Army and Navy Cooperative Stores around the city. In storybooks, Lenox thought, it would have had some definite origin: a curved Indian knife with a ruby in the hilt, or something of the sort. He laughed as he walked back up the stairs. He noticed that the blood on the upper stairs was already cleared away.

A hand fell on his shoulder as he came out into the upstairs hallway again. Lenox looked around and saw it was the footman, James.

"Tell me anything," said the young man.

"I'm sorry," said Lenox. "I'm still working, though."

"Anything, anything," he moaned.

"As soon as I discover anything," Lenox said, patting him on the back. He walked into the center of the hallway, where he stopped and looked around.

Was there anything else to do that evening? No, he thought. The body would be removed soon. He would speak with Exeter in the morning. So after going downstairs to tell McConnell that he would be in touch the next day, he went upstairs and walked to the front door, wearily, to leave. There he heard a familiar voice.

"Charles!"

He turned around and smiled, both inwardly and outwardly. "Oh, Jane," he said. "You needn't have stayed." She was sitting in a chair by the front door.

"Nonsense," she said. "Have you your coat? We'll go back together."

He smiled again. "Yes, yes." And he held out his arm, which she took, and they walked out through the snow together, to find their carriage home.

∽ Chapter 36 ∽

Lenox woke up the next day with a terrific hunger, despite the previous night's banquet. He was instantly sad about Soames, when it came back to mind, but he had slept well nonetheless. For the first time he felt recovered from his back-alley skirmish. The cuts and bruises were still there, but they were faded and didn't hurt.

He ate a breakfast of eggs, toast, dark coffee, and a large orange. He read the final chapters of *The Small House at Allington* in bed as he ate, going through both the food and the book with great relish, and when he laid the book down he felt satisfied. After feeling more and more depleted in recent days, he felt that he had taken his small break, now, and had a great deal of energy again.

He rang the bell, and Graham entered his bedroom.

"Sir?"

"Hullo, Graham. Beautiful day, isn't it?"

The sun was pouring richly through the windows.

"Indeed, sir."

"I'll need all the papers, if you don't mind. The regular three and then all the ones I don't read as well. Even the *Post* and the *Daily Standard*, if you please."

"Very good, sir. I shall bring them back in just a moment."

"Thank you. Oh—and would you send round a note asking my brother to come visit me?"

"Yes, sir."

"Only if he's not in the House this morning."

"Yes, sir."

"And I'll want my carriage just before lunch. I'm to eat with Dr. McConnell."

"Very good, sir."

"Thank you, Graham."

The butler left, and Lenox stretched his arms behind his head for a good long think. He puzzled through the recent events and came to some tentative solutions. Only after Graham had returned and left the newspapers on his bedside table did he break out of his reverie. He had an idea. If only he could be sure, he thought. . . . Well, there was plenty of time to test it out. He did feel that there would be no further deaths.

In turn, he examined each of the articles on Soames. Primarily they were sketchy and quick, because the murder had been late at night, but he knew he should read them anyway. They were by and large redundant, with few if any details altered between them. They all emphasized the victim's athletic glory, his military service, his consistent work on the Liberal side, and his popularity among friends and acquaintances, and all of them expressed shock and anger at the recent trend of violence in England but ended by assuring readers that Inspector Exeter was on the trail of the murderer and he would soon bring the criminal to justice.

The note in *The Times* summarized these accounts as well as any:

Late last night, the distinguished MP for Renton and former Oxford Blue, Jack Soames, was murdered in cold blood at the annual ball hosted by George Barnard. Guests at the event, which is generally considered one of the high points of the London season, were shocked to hear a piercing scream in the hallway of Mr. Barnard's house, and moments later Mr. Soames was discovered at the head of a stairwell leading to the servants' quarters. The police would not reveal the manner of the death but acknowledged that it was not natural. Inspector Exeter, who has taken the case in hand, said only, "We're well on the track of the criminal, and anybody with any knowledge should step forward immediately."

A junior constable admitted to The Times that there were copious amounts of blood at the scene. Society gentleman Thomas McConnell, husband of Lady Victoria McConnell, née Phillips, who happens to have medical training, performed the immediate postmortem, but declined to comment.

Readers of The Times will observe that this is the second act of violence in a very short period of time at Mr. Barnard's house, following the poisoning of the housemaid Prudence Smith; the two events seem to be linked. Mr. Barnard commented, "It's a terrible thing. Soames was a good fellow. And it was a wonderful evening, before the whole mess." He went on to say that he had no idea who was committing the crimes, but he felt safe in his house under the protection of Inspector Exeter.

Meanwhile, of course, fashionable London is in shock. "He was such a good sort," said Lord Stearns, and others echoed this sentiment throughout the evening. Soames first came to public prominence on the oars for Oxford, leading them to three consecutive wins in the boat race during his time at university. Some readers may recall how he seemed single-handedly to pull them back into the race in his final year, after the team had been overtaken by the

Cambridge eight. He also earned a blue in rugby, which he only played recreationally but at which he nevertheless excelled, and boxed as an amateur at Oxford.

After coming down from university, Soames entered the army, where he became a captain. Within his regiment, said Colonel James Waring, he was well-liked and well-respected. He behaved heroically in a minor skirmish in the East and was discharged because of a wound earned in battle. Almost immediately after leaving the military he was elected to Parliament as the Member from Renton. In that governing body he has had a long and distinguished career, advising Party leaders on manners of finance, reform, and trade, and though he never held office he would no doubt eventually have ascended to some position in a Liberal government.

Soames was a bachelor who lived in the West End. Friends said he was an affable man, well liked by all. Lord Stearns echoed this general opinion, saying, "Soames could no more have an enemy than I could. It must have been a mistake—a horrible mistake—as I see it."

Soames, in addition to his Parliamentary duties, sat on several boards, most notably that of the Pacific Trust. His name has been in the newspaper lately because of his work for that company. Readers will remember that he represented the deciding vote on the matter of reinvestment; he voted against releasing a large amount of capital to shareholders. While this angered individual investors in the company, who would have realized an instant windfall, many in the financial world agreed that the board's decision would pay out in the long run and that any loss of immediate wealth would be compensated in the future. Insiders fear that Soames's death will mean an overturn of the vote, which is set to be reaffirmed two weeks from now, after discussion, because it is generally thought that the conservative Sir James Maitland will fill the vacant spot on the board. Maitland has made it known that he would have voted differently from Soames.

Soames was also an excellent horseman and traveled among the best country houses for the shooting and the riding. "He will be missed," said Lord Stearns. "He made any shooting party better."

Until the police release a report, his friends will have to wait for consolation. As is customary, Parliament will conduct a tribute to him on both sides of the aisle, and the Speaker will offer a eulogy.

"He had high potential," said Newton Duff, MP, a friend. "The country is losing a valuable servant."

Lenox read this with mild interest. He paid closest attention to the quotes. Stearns was a good fellow, but it surprised him to hear Duff's praise, never given lightly.

The rest of the papers added very little except for a penny paper called the *Post*, which was of low repute but high circulation. It offered the same eulogistic tone, the same descriptions of Oxford, the Army, Parliament, and the Pacific Trust, but at the end it contained a variation:

It is painful to bring up now, but we must be True to our faithful readers and write that there was some gossip out of turn concerning the late Member's finances. To put it plain, People have been whispering that Soames was at the end of his means and that the Creditors, though they could not touch him while Parliament was sitting, as the law demands, were prepared to land on him as soon as the session was over. People spoke, as they will, of the Turf, and of expensive habits on *slender means*—in short, it was widely reported that he had no further money left.

It is the honor of the *Post* to report otherwise. A confidential Source at a certain bank revealed that Mr.

Soames had been continuing at his usual rate of getting and spending. In point of fact, this rumor was incorrect; in truth, Mr. Soames was very comfortable, as befits a former Hero on the oar and a distinguished Member of Parliament. We are glad to put the rumor of the only blemish on this fine man's character to rest, especially as it would be hard to hear Mr. Soames ill-spoken of after his death. *The Post*, as usual, has now Set the Record Straight.

This last phrase was the paper's motto, which they repeated in nearly every article, whether it was relevant or not.

Now here was an interesting fact. People far and wide had said that Soames was definitely broke—far and wide enough even to reach Lenox's ears, and Lenox was by no means a gossip. Everybody had mentioned it, here and there, as a known fact: his brother, Lady Jane. And yet, if *The Post* was to be believed—and rag or not, it generally was, Lenox found—it was all false. It was really a rather remarkable thing.

He had laid down the last of the papers and was again thinking, his hands behind his head, when Graham knocked once more and entered.

"Sir Edmund Lenox, sir," he said.

"Downstairs already?"

"Yes, sir."

"Drat. I need to dress," he said, getting out of bed. "Tell him I'll be a moment. Offer him some tea, please, or some breakfast if he hasn't had any. Oh, and give him those papers," he said, gesturing to the nightstand.

"Yes, sir."

Graham left, and Lenox put on the clothes that had been laid out for him on the armchair; black cloak, gray pants, and a homburg. He took the time to tie his tie neatly but otherwise rather rushed, so it was only a short time later that he went downstairs to join his brother.

~ Chapter 37 ~

Have you glanced over the papers yet?" said Lenox, coming through the double doors of the library.

Sir Edmund was sitting in one of the two armchairs before the fire.

"It's really terribly cold out," he said crossly.

"Oh, Edmund, I'm sorry," said Charles, trying not to smile.

"Well, all right, all right."

"Those are the demands upon the investigator, you know. Harsh weather, for one."

Now this seemed to appease Sir Edmund. "Really?" he said. "By Jove, yes, I suppose that's right. Well, at your service, then." He mimicked a salute.

"Have you looked at the papers?"

"Oh, yes, the papers. Well, *The Times*."

"Not the *Post*?"

Sir Edmund shuddered. "Gracious, no."

"Take a look at it," said Lenox, sitting down in the other chair and gesturing at the papers Graham had left on the small table between them.

His brother studiously looked over the article and went so

far—which Lenox had admittedly not thought he would do—as to open the paper and read the entire story.

"Most interesting," he said, after a moment. He was smoking his pipe while Lenox smoked a cigarette. "Yes, very interesting. Although the popular gossip has been wrong before, Lord knows."

"Millions of times. But I find this intriguing. What triggered this particular gossip? Was there any event? Any indication?"

"None at all, I think," said Sir Edmund. "In fact, I remember it only started when he won a bit at the Derby. People said it was a good thing he had."

"How odd, really! Isn't it?"

"I don't see why—"

"Well, leave it, then," said Lenox. "Would you like anything to eat? Or a cup of tea?"

"Coffee would be lovely. I'm due back at the House this afternoon, and I shall have to stay awake, I suppose."

Lenox called for Graham and ordered a pot of coffee.

"Now, Edmund, I called you over this morning."

"I know you did. I had to walk across half of the South Pole to get here. Hyde Park too."

Lenox laughed. "It's for a good reason, I think. I'd like to hear an exact account of your evening before they discovered Soames."

"Poor chap," said Sir Edmund, ruminatively. "Well, ashes to ashes, I daresay. Now, let's see, my evening. Yes. Well, I arrived only in time for the dance, as you know. And you told me to follow those two cousins. I was perhaps overzealous at first—don't laugh, it's not kind—and followed too close upon them, because Claude kept looking at me and making faces."

"Faces?"

"Yes, like an animal. So I backed off a bit. I got a glass of wine and sipped it pretty slowly and watched them. Claude danced with any number of girls, whereas Eustace seemed to be lecturing elderly men about something or other, I can't imagine what."

"I can," said Lenox.

"You'll know, then. Well, that was how it went. They only talked one time—in the doorway between the ballroom and the salon. For ten seconds or so. Then Claude hit Eustace, rather hard. Most uncousinly."

"Why, I remember you hitting Cousin Ronald on the nose!"

Sir Edmund reddened. "Totally different situation. And it's ungentlemanly of you to bring it up."

"Well, it was ungentlemanly and uncousinly to hit Ronald in the nose!"

"Dash it all, if Ronald would insist on commenting on perfectly nice parlor maids all the time, it's not my lookout what happens to him."

"Oh, yes, that's when you loved that parlor maid . . . what was her name . . . Mary?"

"I did not love her at all. A fine manly affection, yes. A fondness for the extra dessert she slipped me now and then, certainly."

Lenox laughed. "I apologize. Will you tell me what happened?"

Sir Edmund tried to master his emotions and deliver the rest of his report. "After that, I tracked only Claude, because Eustace went into the salon, and you had told me Eustace was less important."

"I did. Now. You've done very well, Edmund, but there remains work to do."

"There does?"

"Yes. I need you to spend whatever time you can in front of Barnard's house."

"What?"

"Specifically, in front of Prue Smith's window. Fourth on the right."

"The window?"

"Yes. Look through the window, see if anyone enters, see if anyone's lurking—however you can."

"But I shall be noticed!"

"No, you shan't." Lenox walked to a chest in the corner of the room. "Wear these," he said, and he held up a houndstooth suit with mud all over it.

"You can't be serious."

"Oh, yes. Clean on the inside, my dear brother, and warm as a button. Wear a low hat. Scuff your face—I use tobacco ash. Come back here before you have to go to the House, and then—when you can—go round again."

Sir Edmund took a great deal of cajoling, but gradually Lenox convinced him that he could imitate a loafer and was earning his stripes as a detective.

At last, after half an hour and several more cups of coffee, his brother went upstairs to change into the clothes. Graham fetched him some ashes from the grate, and when Sir Edmund came back down again he looked fairly convincing.

"I look all right?" he said.

"For the part, perfect," said Lenox. "Graham, bring a flask of brandy for Sir Edmund, please."

"Yes, sir."

Lenox wrote a quick note on a piece of paper. "If any of the constables trouble you, ask them to give this to Exeter. It says you're there on my behalf."

"If you're sure, Charles," said Edmund.

"Positive. Now, take this flask," he said, as Graham returned. "Brandy will keep you warm and also give you the proper smell. But don't get tipsy."

After a few more minutes of reluctance, Edmund left. Lenox chuckled to himself for a moment. But he was glad that Edmund was going. The murderer was bound to come back for the weapon if he had any wits about him, and Lenox had specifically omitted this fact when he talked to Exeter. A constable by the door of Prue Smith's room would have scared anybody off almost instantly. It was a long shot, but maybe Edmund would find something. It was a job he would usually have asked Skaggs to do, but he was waiting for Skaggs to complete his work on an equally pressing business: an investigation into the altogether mysterious Roderick Potts.

❦ Chapter 38 ❧

In one of their many conversations since the beginnings of the case, both brief and long, Lady Jane had said something that had rankled in Lenox's mind. Specifically, she had said he had a responsibility to inform James, the young footman, about Prue Smith's true actions. Her argument was that it would save him suffering; it would allow the young man to make a clean break with the past, even if his immediate reaction was of deeper grief. The truth would bring him peace. Or at any rate, he wouldn't live a half-life, unwilling to love any girl as he loved the ideal of Prue.

In response, Lenox had said that James would indeed be devastated, but the devastation wouldn't dissolve as quickly as she thought. There would be no answers about Prue's behavior that would satisfy him. While he might forget her sooner if he was told about the maid's affairs, he might also pore over them endlessly, withering away in jealousy, self-doubt, and the strange mixture of hatred and love that devolves upon someone in grief who learns an unpleasant fact about the object of his worship.

And this quick argument—not even an argument but a

considered exchange of ideas—had remained with Lenox longer than he might have thought.

Then he found, as so often happens, that the subject on his mind was confronted by the situation itself. Soon after Edmund left, James knocked on the door and was admitted to the library while Lenox was deciding what to do next.

This was really too much, Lenox felt. Grief, he forgave. But the young man was dogging his footsteps and in a very real way impeding the progress of the case. Perhaps the time had come to follow Lady Jane's advice.

Lenox had been sitting at his desk, and he stood up when James came in. The young man was extremely pale, and because his hair was black the contrast was shocking. His face seemed even gaunter than it had, and his hawkish features, in particular his long melancholy nose, had grown pronounced with lack of sleep and food.

"James," said Lenox, gesturing toward the chair in front of his desk.

"Mr. Lenox, I truly am sorry, sir, only—only—I can't get it away from me."

"James?"

"Like her ghost—not a real ghost, mind you—but like a ghost, all the same."

Lenox looked at him with sympathy. "I understand."

The young man laid his head in his hands and moaned. "It's agony," he said.

"I'm so very sorry, James. I truly am. She must have been a remarkable girl, if you love her so."

"A gem, sir," said James, barely lifting his head to speak.

Here was the moment. Time to tell him. Lenox was on the verge of thinking that Lady Jane had been right. The young man looked as if he would pine away into nothingness. Why, he must have lost ten pounds already.

"James—"

The young man looked up, and Lenox was very nearly prepared to do it, to reveal Prue's betrayals of him with both Deck
and Claude. But at the moment his will failed.

It was not that Lenox reconsidered Lady Jane's position, or
even that he considered anything at all. It was an entirely instinc-
tive decision. Even if the suffering would be greater through the
years this way, he hadn't the heart to be so cruel, to dash this
young man's certainty, his grief, his true pledged love, because it
was the right thing to do.

Here was a characteristic that Lenox came up against in himself sometimes, which even vexed him in rare instances. It could
be cowardice or compassion; he cared little what it was called.
It was in him, and that was all.

He went around the desk and put his hand on James's
shoulder.

"I know it seems as if you've lost the only girl you'll ever
love," he said, "and I know it seems impossible that your life
will ever be happy and contented again, and I know each hour
seems blacker than the last. I know all these things. But don't
become black inside. You may think you're left with nothing,
but you still have your memories of her, and you have time.
Sorrow is all very well but, as the church says, darkness never
lasts, and light always comes. Even when it doesn't seem so,
my boy."

James lifted his head. "I suppose," he said. "I suppose."

"I promise." In truth Lenox didn't know. But he made the
promise anyway. "You must try to live, James."

"Aye."

"It will be all right."

"There's no more I can do, sir? Nothing?"

"I'm afraid not. But we'll get him, sooner or later. I promise
that, too."

James stood up, bowed slightly, and walked out of the room

without saying anything. Lenox sighed and leaned over with his hands on the desk, looking out at the snow on the sidewalks and the people walking along, and eventually he saw James come out, looking very dark against the white of the landscape in his heavy black coat.

~ Chapter 39 ~

Only a moment later the doorbell sounded again, and Graham's light footsteps echoed along the hallway, while Lenox pricked his ears and wondered who it was.

Graham opened the doors of the library. "Newton Duff, sir."

You could have knocked Lenox over with a feather. It appeared that today the case had decided to come to him. But then, he reflected, as he waved for Graham to admit the visitor, that was often how it came out at the end; and though the ideas in his mind were elusive, he knew the end was near. Briefly he wondered about that arsenic. Was this a man capable of murder?

He stood up to receive the Member from Warwick Downs, and the two shook hands. Lenox gestured toward the armchairs by the fire and then followed Duff as he went over to sit down.

"Would you like anything to eat or drink?"

"I take nothing between meals, sir."

"Water?"

"Yes, please."

"Graham?" said Lenox, and nodded. "May I help you, Mr. Duff?"

"You may help me, I may help you; at any rate, I am here now, and we shall see."

"As you please, of course."

There was a moment of silence, and Lenox took it to study the man in front of him. Anybody's first impression would have been the same: a hard jaw, black hair, thick eyebrows, a rigid posture, and a well-fitting old gray suit, with a gleaming pocket watch that he checked as he sat down. But the eyes—well, the eyes were shrewd and quick.

Lenox broke the silence. "You plan to stand in another borough, Mr. Duff?"

Duff started. "Have you been in my business, then, Lenox? But I've told nobody! Damned cheek!"

"No, no, not in your business beyond the present case, I assure you."

"Well, I am. What of it?"

"Nothing at all. But your father is dead, is he not, for some years? The country all knows that."

"Well, what the deuce does that figure?"

"Since I have known you, your pocket watch has been a present from the electors of your borough. And now I see a pocket watch with your father's initials, which are as famous as your own. You have evidently had the watch for some time, because he is dead, but have chosen not to wear it until now—when, I would suppose, you have no further reason to ask the favor of the Warwick electors."

Duff nodded grudgingly. "Yes, I am returning to my hometown this next election. It was always one of my desires to do so, though Warwick Downs has treated me very well. At any rate, Mr. Lenox, enough of this."

"Quite so. How may I help you?"

"On the contrary, sir, I think I may help you, if you will listen. In return, the solving of this case will be a benefit to me."

"I'll listen gladly," said Lenox.

"Very well. I must ask you, then, if you are aware of the unique contents of Mr. Barnard's house. I doubt that you are, but I may be willing to inform you."

As he had once before, Lenox removed a gold coin from his pocket and held it in the flat of his palm.

"Exactly," said Duff. "I suppose you're not as hopeless as I originally thought."

Lenox laughed. "High praise."

"Well, then, I may as well tell you that in addition to the guards, who merely stood watch by the room, Jack Soames and I were guarding the money from the mint by observing the activity of the house."

"Guarding it? Really?" Lenox was surprised.

"Yes. No doubt you asked yourself why we were staying there when we both had our own places of residence—and when both of us preferred our own homes to visiting."

"Yes, I did."

"A few of us in government agreed that the money needed more than armed police officers; it needed people on the spot. We kept it dark from most people, even in the party. The ball was a convenient excuse. Barnard protested at first, arguing that his own presence in the house, as an officer of the mint, surely constituted protection. The very fact that we had chosen his house, after the attacks on the mint, seemed proof to him. There was nowhere else, you see, from Buckingham Palace to Parliament itself, that seemed more anonymous yet safely public. But he came around eventually to the need for another presence in the house. I immediately volunteered, of course, as I am involved in the finances of the country—second to the Exchequer in that regard, I may say."

Lenox was much taken aback but continued his questioning. "And Soames?"

"Not a leading political light but loyal and undeniably patriotic.

Also a military man and handy with a pistol. I may fairly say that it appears to me he was murdered in the line of duty."

"Yes, it seems possible," said Lenox, in a low voice. At any rate, this would explain Soames's face in the skylight, looking over the crates of gold. "And it accounts for your praise in *The Times* obituary this morning, which struck me as odd."

"Just so. At any rate, I may say that we have been successful, despite the unfortunate murder, and the money, which will be released to the public in a day or two, seems safe thus far."

"Thank you for telling me."

"You're welcome. But I have come for another reason, as well. That man Exeter suspects me."

"Does he now?"

"Yes."

"How do you know?"

"Surely you think me equal in wits to Inspector Exeter, Mr. Lenox?"

Lenox laughed mirthlessly. "Yes, yes, far lesser men than you are his superiors, I'm afraid."

"At any rate, I thought it best to come to you."

"If I'm to be honest," said Lenox, "I'm not certain I don't suspect you."

The fury in Duff's face was complete and instant, but he seemed to control himself. "What do you mean?"

"Why was a bottle of arsenic that belonged to you found in the murdered girl's room?"

Duff seemed to relax his anger. "Is that all?" he said.

"That's all," Lenox answered.

"That was connected with my work for the committee from the Royal Academy on banned substances. It's rather a large problem. Children accidentally eating cheese left out for the rats, that sort of thing. Particularly over in the Rookery, where super-vision is less stringent. We need to revise the 1861 Arsenic Act."

"That doesn't explain the poison, Mr. Duff."

"Surely you understand what I'm telling you?"

Lenox sighed inwardly. "Yes, I do. But why go and buy a bottle yourself?"

Duff waved a hand. "To see how easy it is to acquire. I'm actually rather pleased you were able to trace it. That means the chemist must have written my name in a ledger somewhere. . . ."

"What did you do with the poison afterward?"

"I had about ten bottles from various apothecaries in my room and asked the housekeeper to dispose of them. The murderer must have gotten it from her. . . . I say, you do believe me? After all, I've come to you now to talk directly about this subject."

Lenox looked thoughtfully at the fire with his fingertips together. "That is what puzzles me, Mr. Duff. If I may be frank, you have never seemed to like me."

"I disregard your profession as sheer nonsense, particularly for a man of your birth, sir, if I am to speak plainly."

"That is precisely what I mean. Why come to me now?"

"Surely you know, sir."

"I confess myself baffled, Mr. Duff."

"Your brother."

"My brother?"

"Yes, Sir Edmund. A man whose opinion I respect as highly as any in the land."

Lenox was flabbergasted. "My brother, you say?"

"Yes, indeed. Surely you realize how vital, in recent years, Sir Edmund has become to the Party? People underestimate him, I suppose, because he is so gentle—but no, a sharper mind does not reside in Parliament. I may fairly say that the Prime Minister and the Cabinet could not lead the Party without his advice."

"But he holds no office!"

"He refuses them all."

"And comes so infrequently!"

"Comes only when called. He is reluctant to take credit. But surely this is not as important as the business at hand, Mr. Lenox?"

Lenox shook his head. "No, no, of course not."

"What ought I to do about Exeter?"

Lenox, though still distracted, managed to say, "Nothing, nothing—leave him to me."

"I shall then," said Duff, and stood. Lenox stood too and walked him into the hallway. For the first time, the two men shook hands with something akin to warmth. "Perhaps I've underestimated you," said Duff.

"Perhaps," said Lenox, smiling. "Good day, Mr. Duff."

"To you as well," said Duff, and left the house.

A slight draft came in as he left and hit Lenox, rather bracing him. The newfound mysteries of the case would emerge momentarily—but first, a moment to consider his brother!

As long as Lenox could remember, Edmund had been intelligent, but that quality in him was always dominated by his unfailing kindness and cheerfulness. Lenox was himself the same way, to some extent. But gentle Edmund, with gravy on his tie? His life had always been devoted above all to the hills of Sussex and to his hearth.

Still, men must serve their country, their father had always taught them, and as strongly as Lenox remembered the lesson, Edmund must as well.

He returned to the armchair and lit his pipe. Duff . . . that aspect of the case deserved a good think. But Lenox couldn't stop considering his brother.

To think that Edmund said so little! And to have sent him out, that very morning, in a beggar's costume—one of the leading political figures of the day, according to Duff! Lenox would most certainly press his brother the next time they were together.

❧ Chapter 40 ❧

It was nearly lunchtime; Lenox decided to eat in. He asked Graham for something simple, and when he went into the dining room, half an hour later, he found beef in sauce with peas and potatoes, as well as a half bottle of wine. He refused the wine and drank water instead, because he wanted to keep his mind clear.

After he had eaten—it was an excellent meal—he had a thought and went back to his desk in the library. There was a cigar box there where he had assembled the small items that constituted the clues to the case, and he opened it and pulled a scrap of paper out. It was the one he had found in Duff's room, which read £? JS?. It occurred to him that it must have been shorthand for Jack Soames and referred to the money.

Was it all a blind? Duff's unexpectedly confiding in him was out of the ordinary—and anything out of the ordinary mattered in a case like this. It was worth thinking about, particularly after his elaborate and too-convenient account of the arsenic. Had there been a flash of fear across his face, mixed with the obvious anger, when Lenox brought the little bottle up? Duff was too smart by half. . . .

Another knock came on the front door, but this one he expected.

"Mr. Skaggs," said Graham, admitting him without asking leave from Lenox.

Skaggs was dressed very tidily, in a black coat and thick gray trousers, which looked awfully warm to Lenox, who was still seeking a solution to his perpetual misery in cold weather.

"Mr. Lenox," the man said, and tipped his cap.

"How are you, my dear man? And how is your youngest daughter?"

Skaggs grinned. "Fairly flourishin', sir, fairly flourishin'."

"I should think so, with such an excellent mother."

Now he blushed a bit. "Well, yes, never a finer woman—"

"Now, how has the work gone, Mr. Skaggs?"

"Well, as far as it goes, I suppose, sir."

"I don't quite get you, I must say."

"Well, Mr. Lenox, if I've assumed correctly that you're investigating Miss Prudence Smith and Mr. Jack Soames—I gathered as much, because Mr. Roderick Potts, the man you asked me to investigate, was residing in the mansion where they died—then I may or may not be useful to you. However, I think I can definitively strike him from the list of suspects, though I'll leave you to judge that."

"Good heavens! This is certainly more than I had hoped for, Mr. Skaggs."

Again the investigator tipped his cap. "Thank you, sir."

"How can you say so?"

"Well, sir, you gave me the assignment of tracking Mr. Potts and learning what I could. Here are the facts, in a nutshell, then: very rich, indifferent to social status, in fact altogether wary of it, exceedingly kind even to his most distant acquaintances and relations, a widower, one daughter, the apple of his eye, donates great sums to charity, but tends his business still."

"All in all, a perfect suspect."

Skaggs grinned. "Aye. At any rate, I figured I ought to learn more. Why was he in the house, specifically?"

"Yes, exactly."

"So I sought employ in Mr. Barnard's house myself."

"Skaggs! You didn't!"

"Indeed, the ball being an excellent excuse, I was hired as an extra footman, and I worked up to and during the ball. One of a fleet of temporary servants. Chap in the hiring agency owed me a favor."

"Excellent!"

"And that is why I can say with definite assurance that he did not kill Mr. Soames. I followed Mr. Potts throughout the party without my eyes leaving him once."

"Skaggs, shake my hand. You have a very bright future, you know." The two men shook hands.

"Thank you, sir," said Skaggs.

"Now why *was* Potts staying at Barnard's house?"

"The way I saw it, he might still have had a hand in things, so—I'm not ashamed to say—I eavesdropped. And it cost me my job, too, sir!" Both men laughed at this. "The housekeeper caught me; I wasn't sorry to see the back of her by the end of it. But I learned the truth. It appears that Mr. Potts plans to give away half his fortune. He's taking such action because his daughter is engaged, and he will give it away in her name. She's to wed a farmer in the north—a nice fellow, who reminds Mr. Potts of himself. Of what you might call the working-class background. Disregarding the money."

"What! Not a duke?"

"Certainly not. When speaking to Mr. Barnard, Mr. Potts most vehemently decried the earls and such who had come courting. Said he was above all that. The farmer is educated, like his daughter, and a gentleman, but by no means an earl, from what I overheard. He said his money had grown heavy on his hands, and he saw such poverty around him that he felt it right to give it away. He seemed to indicate that he might give away a fair percentage of the remainder in the rest of his life. He was speaking to Mr. Barnard as one of the first men of finance in the land."

"Human beings are remarkable, Mr. Skaggs."

"That they are. At any rate, Potts was not at all pleased with Barnard's advice—namely, to keep it. This was during the ball. And Mr. Potts left in quite a huff, saying he would seek counsel elsewhere."

"Fascinating."

"As I said, sir, it is possible that all this is a blind, but he had no reason to know that he was being overheard, and all in all he seems the most honorable man I've ever known. Oh, a glint of hardness in him. It's hard to make money without that. But good at bottom, you see, Mr. Lenox."

"I do indeed, Mr. Skaggs. I do indeed."

Lenox was thinking to himself of how he had rifled this kind man's room and felt sick at the memory. But it passed; he scratched Mr. Potts from his list as well, thought he might send a present to the engaged couple, and felt mildly better.

The two men spoke for another moment, and then Lenox thanked him, paid him the balance of his bill, and bade him goodbye. Then—just as Skaggs walked through the door—Lenox noticed his boots—the finest boots he thought he had ever seen.

"Mr. Skaggs, if I may—where do you find boots such as those?"

Skaggs turned around, briefly puzzled, but then smiled and said, "Ah, yes. Cork-soled, sir, and lined with thick flannel, and extra rubber for dryness. Very snug, even in the snow." He tipped his cap. "Linehan's, on Crown Street, sir, and not a bad bargain either."

To Lenox this sounded very near to heaven. He said goodbye with a smile, and the moment the door was closed he donned his old inadequate boots and his greatcoat and jumped into his carriage, telling the driver, "Linehan's, Crown Street," before he forgot.

Chapter 41

His business done, Lenox set out for McConnell's house.
"What can you tell me?" he said when he arrived, skipping straight past hello.

"Not much."

"I see."

"Come upstairs?"

"Yes, of course."

They walked to McConnell's private room and then went down to the end of it, where the doctor kept his four or five large tables, his equipment, and his cabinets full of bottles.

"Mr. Potts," McConnell said, "is not your man—at least not on the strength of the sample you gave me from the bottle in his valise."

"No?"

"What he had was a bottle of very nasty poison."

"What?"

"Poison for insects. Perfectly harmless for human beings." McConnell laughed. "Sorry for the joke."

"Why would he have it?"

"Ah, I asked around. Bit of an amateur entomologist, I

understand. Studies bugs, you know. I think he made a study of northern water beetles that the Royal Academy published."

"Ah."

"The knife gave nothing away either. Relatively clean. No fingerprints, although they would be inconclusive, anyway. Drenched in blood, of course. No powders. Nothing out of the ordinary."

Lenox sighed. "It's all right," he said. "I am close to a solution; I can tell I only want a missing piece. But that piece!"

"I'm sorry, Charles."

"Quite all right, quite all right. Well, I must be off." He thrust his hands into his jacket pockets and began to walk back toward the door with McConnell at his side.

But then he felt something at the bottom of his pocket. "Hang on a moment." He extracted the object; it was a crumpled leaf, the one he had discovered by Barnard's house. "I don't suppose you know what this is, Thomas?"

"It looks like a leaf."

Lenox chuckled. "Could you find out what it is, though?"

"Yes, of course. It will take me an hour or so. I must look into a few books." He pointed upward, at the library that surrounded the balcony of the room.

"Will you come over when you do?"

"Yes, indeed," said the doctor.

Lenox handed the leaf over gingerly. "I'll be off, then," he said. "You shall find me at home. I plan to smoke my pipe and solve the case."

"Ambitious."

"As ever, Thomas. Well—goodbye."

"You'll find your way out?"

"Oh, yes, of course."

Lenox left McConnell hurrying back to his tables, where he would place the leaf between two glass sheets. He soon found his carriage again, said goodbye to the somnolent Shreve, left his salutations to the lady of the house, and went home.

Once there he removed the boots, found his slippers and a comfortable old jacket, and, as he had promised, lit a pipe and sat before the fire, thinking. Here was the problem: Effectively, he could remove every suspect from suspicion: Potts, Duff, Claude, Eustace, Soames, poor devil, and Barnard himself, who would seem to have no motive whatsoever and who also lacked opportunity, for he had been on the spot immediately after Soames's death. He couldn't have gone through the window and come around that quickly.

He smoked his pipe, waited for visitors, and mulled it over. But he didn't have, any longer, the feeling of being blocked. He felt instead as if he were circling closer.

About an hour after he had arrived home, McConnell came in, looking flushed from the cold but pleased.

"I've got it," he said.

"Yes? Already?"

"I was lucky to find Tilney in—but let me begin at the beginning."

"Would you like a cup of tea or anything?"

"Certainly—I skipped tea."

"Graham?" said Lenox, and the butler withdrew.

"Japanese maple, my dear Charles. Called *Acer palmatum*. An exceedingly rare tree here in the West. Many of the leaves look like normal maple leaves, you know, but as you can see"—he took the two plates of glass with the leaf between them out of his pocket and handed them over—"these are lace-leaf, more deeply cut and of a different shape."

At this moment the tea came in and each man took a cup, as well as a piece of toast.

"How did you find this out?"

"I went around to an acquaintance of mine on Bond Street. I doubt you know him: John Tilney. Cares for no company but that of his oldest friends, who are all, like him, past seventy, but I daresay he has made as close a study of trees as any man in the kingdom. He has a virtual forest of exotic trees at Talliver Point, his house in the country. Fascinating old man. And now, this is the interesting part: He says they're hardy trees but susceptible to English frost. As a result, only the botanical gardens here in London stock them—and those would have gone bare some months ago. So somebody has preserved this leaf for at least a month."

"Fascinating," said Lenox, as the wheels revolved in his mind.

"It is indeed. Something I never would have imagined knowing, you see."

"Nor I."

"And you know, Barnard has an interest in rare trees."

"Yes," said Lenox thoughtfully. "And I know for a fact that he was in the botanical gardens recently. Eustace might have been too." He sighed. "Or anybody, for that matter."

McConnell smiled. "There is great pleasure in true work, Charles. At times I almost think of returning to it full-time." He was flushed now with excitement, not cold.

Lenox paused. "It makes me happy to hear you say that," he said quietly.

"But at any rate, I must be off. Thanks ever so much for the tea—and for all the interesting pursuits of the case, sad as it is." McConnell stood, shook hands, and went quickly on his way.

Lenox ran his fingertips over the glass and began to ponder, but at that moment the front door opened again—it seemed to be off its hinges, practically, it had opened and closed so often that day—and Lenox went into the front hall to see who had come now.

Chapter 42

It was Edmund.

"Charles! I've just seen McConnell."

"Yes, he was here."

"Charles, I've never had such a thrilling day in all my life!"

Lenox laughed. "Yes, I can see," he said.

Edmund was still clad in the rumpled clothes and brownish hat that Lenox had given him, and his face was still scuffed with ash here and there, which concealed his identity very well, as he said cheerfully, and he had rolled in some trash so he would smell dreadful.

But where you could see his face, his cheeks were bright pink and he was plainly beaming.

"I've missed my vocation, Charles! I would have made an excellent detective."

"You make an excellent panhandler, as well. What did you discover?"

Edmund waved his hand. "Nothing, nothing. I mean to go back after the session this evening. But the sheer excitement of it! Eluding Exeter! And Barnard went straight past and didn't even look at me!"

"You mean to go back? I really don't wish to put you to so much trouble, Edmund."

"Trouble! I would rather Parliament burned to the ground than give up the evening I have planned. Yes, a quick bite— perhaps a sandwich—and then out to patrol the area. Oh, Charles, you should see how I explain myself to the police who try to remove me! I wouldn't trade it for all the money in the funds!"

And then it happened: All the loose strings came into Lenox's hand, and he felt with all the force of his mind, which had never fallen so short as in the past few days, that he had it. The minute puzzle pieces he had collected so carefully at last fit together. "You've given it to me, my dear brother!" he shouted. "Yes, it just may work! I would kiss you, if you didn't smell so awful!"

Sir Edmund's face fell.

"Why, what's the matter?"

"Oh, nothing, nothing!" Sir Edmund said. "I'm very pleased, Charles. What did I say?"

"Oh, a trifle—never mind it."

"So I shan't have to go back out? What excellent news, Charles. It was beastly cold."

Lenox understood immediately. "Oh, no, Edmund," he said. "You must by all means go out this evening. I apologize for your discomfort, but I must impose upon you. It is vital that you continue your work."

"Vital? Are you sure?"

"Oh, absolutely. The cold can't be helped. I myself have boots that seem to be made of paper—but no, we must go forward."

"Very well," said Sir Edmund.

"And now I shall go," said Lenox, gathering together his effects.

"Good, good, excellent. May I take a bath, though, do you think? Your house is closer to Whitehall."

"By all means, Edmund. And remember, I'm counting on your help."

Very solemnly, the baronet said, "Oh, yes, indeed. I certainly shan't fail you."

A moment later Lenox's carriage rattled down Hampden Lane and out into the West End of London, along the snowy streets, through a dense afternoon fog that reached up to the starless sky above.

Shortly thereafter he knocked on the door of his friend Lord Cabot, with whom he had shared a pleasant evening at the Travelers the evening after Prue Smith's death. He walked into his friend's study behind the butler.

"Cabot," he said, without bothering to say hello. "You know the keeper of the records, don't you?"

"Why, Lenox—well, yes, I do. The son of Colonel Waring, my oldest friend."

"Will he do you a favor?"

"Yes, of course: anything legal."

"Without delay?"

"Yes, of course. But why the rush, Lenox? Are you quite well?" Lord Cabot was very fixed in his habits and thought of Lenox, who moved in the fashionable world and had his detective work besides, as a positive dervish.

"Yes, very well—arisen out of the murky fog, I daresay. Come with me?"

After a moment's cajoling, Lord Cabot assented, and then took his time preparing to go outdoors; in truth, he had planned to stay inside all day and further catalog his collection of Chinese pottery, his main passion. The catalog was badly outdated, poorly compiled, and neglected many fascinating recent additions; so he told an impatient Lenox, who in quieter moments had listened with great interest on the subject.

Soon he finished his lecture and then took a long time finding his cloak and searching for his hat, all to Lenox's silent frustration. But at last they went out to Lenox's carriage and began to drive toward the Thames, near the Cleopatra Needle, where the Hall of Records was.

This large building was made of the old white Roman stone, with marble columns, and had a series of steel doors in front. They went into one of these and asked for Colonel Waring's son, who was named Morgan. He was an agreeable young man of thirty or so, already risen to a prominent position and, so Lord Cabot had assured Lenox on the ride, destined for great things. Young Mr. Waring said that Lenox could certainly look through the records. Soon Lord Cabot had bid his goodbyes, and Lenox had at his fingertips the financial records of the entire market for the last century, which had been kept in earnest after the "South Sea Bubble."

The Bubble was the only reason any of this existed, and for that he was thankful. Lenox remembered his grandfather telling him of *his* father's boyhood memories of the Bubble, back in the early 1700s. What happened was simple. King Philip V of Spain had agreed for the first time to allow a very small number of ships from England to travel to the ports of his empire, and the South Sea Company was formed (with the consent of Parliament) to send these ships across.

But people quickly forgot that the agreement permitted very few ships and, picturing the mining of huge untapped gold deposits in Chile and Peru, not to mention other as yet unknown opportunities, they began to invest their money heavily. Almost instantly the company was worth millions of pounds, despite the fact that it didn't even own a ship and had no goals it knew to be attainable. The delusion of the people investing in the South Sea Company had been unbelievable: merely a hope and a wish, spurred on by other people's certainty and greed.

Then, in September of 1720, the bottom of the stock fell out. A few people sold at the top, but nearly everyone else sold at the bottom because there was so little demand and, of course, no regulation of the price. Poor families were ruined and sank to destitution. Rich families saw their worth drop severely. The malaise lasted years, and the terror of investing lasted generations. Nearly every financial rule of the modern day came from that single company's missteps, as well as the conservative market of Queen Victoria's reign.

Lenox thought of all this in passing and thanked his lucky stars that there were papers to go through. A young clerk named Throckmortin was assigned to help him. The lad seemed very censorious at first of the interruption to his usual schedule, but only until young Morgan Waring told him to look sharp, because he was taking a special interest in Lenox's progress.

The room in which the records were stored was dark, with only a few small high windows, and though it was clean there was a smell of mustiness in the air. It was a large room, as well, brimming from floor to high ceiling with paper, and after his initial excitement Lenox was daunted by the task ahead of him.

He spent from three until six, combing through documents relating the financial history of the Pacific Trust. From what he could gather, it was a company devoted to trading overseas commodities in Europe at favorable prices. Like the East India or any of these companies, it was relatively sound. Since the Bubble Act, all such companies had needed a royal charter, which was only stingily given. But what the Trust did wasn't of interest to Lenox. He was looking only for a name.

He worked diligently but unsuccessfully. It was difficult work because the order of the papers shifted from alphabetical to chronological seemingly at random, and even the now-attentive clerk was flagging by 6 P.M. So Lenox sent his coachman around to Fortnum & Mason for a basket of supper, which he and Throckmortin shared in the dim quiet of the hall of records, seated at a small table. There was a tureen of soup, and then a side of roast beef, which they ate with a fine claret as complement.

Throckmortin was supporting his parents, he told Lenox, and

hoped for advancement. His ultimate aim was to become head clerk at a large financial firm. Lenox listened carefully while they ate their dessert, a large buttery peach tart, and then the two men began their search again with renewed vigor.

Ten minutes later, Lenox found the first relevant document. It was dated from several years ago, but it had either been misplaced or filed according to someone's cryptic system. He shouted happily when he scanned it and asked the young clerk to help him on a few points so he could be sure. The clerk confirmed his suspicion.

"Just as I thought, just as I thought," Lenox said.

And then, his fortune suddenly reversed, a second document presented itself only twenty minutes later that again revealed what Lenox had suspected.

"Shake my hand, young man," he said, "shake my hand. We have done good work—very good work—and you have served the City of London this evening more so than even you usually do, I think."

"Proud to, Mr. Lenox," said the clerk. "I shall always be happy to work with you."

Lenox then left, with cheerful salutations, and Throckmortin cleared the last work from his desk and went home to his mother and father, who were worried and had overcooked the dinner.

Perhaps it is worth relating that the next day, though busy, Lenox remembered his young friend and sent his mother two fine legs of lamb and a case of his own favorite port for Mr. Throckmortin, Sr. And though it would take many years, the clerk's final words were prescient, for he would help Lenox in the case of the Queen's amulet, which had further implications than at first it seemed to, and rang through the court at its successful conclusion.

Chapter 43

L enox rode back home through the streets of London, just after eight. Yes, it all fit, he thought. The leaf, the candle, the alibis of the suspects, the peculiar use of *bella indigo*, the stories about Soames's finances, the windowsill, the knife, the wax on the floor, the newspaper articles, and the relative safety of the mint's gold. There was one thing he hadn't figured yet, and that was the identity of the men who had attacked him. But no doubt it would come to him in due course.

He sat by the fire, smoking his pipe, and played with the pieces so they fit exactly in his mind. He sharpened the edges of the impression that he had and tightened the case. It might pass in court—it might—but he would have to hope for a confession, because he had little doubt that good lawyers would be involved. Yes, well, it was nearly time to call in Exeter, but he owed somebody else his first allegiance.

"Graham?" he called, and the butler entered the library. "Graham, will you ask Lady Jane to step over? I would visit her, but there are a few things I want to show her, and I must wait for my brother to return."

"Yes, sir," Graham said.

A few minutes later, Lady Jane walked into the library, tug-
ging at the fingers of her gloves and smiling.

"Charles, how are you? I'm due at the Duchess's, you know."
She was wearing a gray evening dress.

"Can you give it a miss?"

"I can certainly be late. Why?"

"Will you sit down?"

"Of course," she said, and came to the couch. "I came over
for tea this afternoon, you know, but you weren't here."

"Would you believe I was performing the offices of a junior
clerk?"

"Your excuses to avoid seeing me are becoming a trifle
overblown, I think."

He laughed. "I suppose. But I would do it again; I've solved
the thing."

Lady Jane reacted in an unexpected way to this news: she
turned pale and didn't speak. At last she said, "Oh, Charles, I
am grateful."

"Of course. I asked you over because I have to wait here for
Edmund, but I wanted to tell you right away."

"Thank you, yes, of course. Oh, what a relief." She sighed.
"Well, who was it?"

"May I walk you through the case? I'm only coming to it
myself."

"Yes, of course."

Lenox put his fingertips together and puffed on his pipe,
which he kept between his back teeth. He narrowed his eyes,
looked into the fire, and waited a few moments to speak.

"Very well," he said, at length. "Let us begin with the most
remarkable fact of the case."

"By all means," said Lady Jane.

"Usually, when there are two murders, either the killer is a
maniac or the second murder is committed as cover for the
first."

"That doesn't seem particularly remarkable."

"It wouldn't be, if that were the case here. But instead I've come across something unique in my experience. The *first* murder was designed to cover for the *second*, the murder of Jack Soames five days afterward."

"I don't really understand, Charles—only a little."

"I didn't either, you see. I didn't tell you, but in the days immediately after Prue Smith's death I was at a loss: everywhere I looked was a dead end, every string I tugged on was limp. I exhausted the honor roll of normal motives, and each of them was empty."

"I could tell," Lady Jane said. "That was why I decided to spend some time with George Barnard."

"Is that why? I'm sorry I drove you to it."

"Not at all."

"It was only after Jack's death that I began to make headway— and then things came quickly, as they do in most murder cases. In other words, I could only begin to solve Prue Smith's murder after Jack was dead, sadly enough. I wish it weren't so, but it is."

"Yes, I see," said Lady Jane. "But then who *did* it, Charles?"

"I'm coming to that—forgive me if I go slowly; I am piecing it together still. Very well. Let me proceed.

"It appeared immediately that the list of suspects was short. *Bella indigo* is extremely costly and, though I kept this to myself, there is a still more persuasive reason that limited the list of suspects: It took McConnell a full day to identify it, and he's an expert. Only someone with real expertise, or at least an aficionado's knowledge, would have used it."

"Or somebody who knew such an aficionado."

"Ah, correct; you're quicker than I was there. Well, I asked Barnard's housekeeper—and also asked Graham, as a separate corroboration—to identify people with access to Prue Smith during the relevant time. The list was short: Duff, Soames,

Eustace Bramwell, Barnard, Roderick Potts, Claude Barnard, and of course the house's servants."

"It seems as if you passed over the servants?" Lady Jane said inquiringly.

"I did. I discounted them because of the cost and obscurity of *bella indigo*. Just before Soames's death, I began to think of going back to them, particularly to the young man who was engaged to Prue Smith, but then a fresh trail emerged. Therefore it was down to these several people.

"Roderick Potts could not have committed either murder. He was watched at the time of Jack Soames's death, which made him extremely unlikely to have killed Prue, but I couldn't discount it—until this morning. I had forgotten that Potts is a very fat man, in somewhat poor health. It took quick light feet and an agile body to walk down the stairs quietly, kill someone quite physically, and then, too, to sneak through a window. Not conclusive—but combined with all the facts, fairly near it."

Through this explanation Lady Jane listened patiently.

Lenox leaned back and chewed on his pipe before continuing. "After Potts we have Duff. I suspected him from the start, I'll admit. That the bottle of arsenic was his seemed at once damning and yet impossibly easy. And just this morning he paid me a visit, which, depending on one's perspective, either exonerated him entirely or made him my first suspect. I think if I had not had something like an epiphany, I should have followed his trail—but it was unnecessary. And something else occurred to me as well. I told you of the valuable possession secreted in Barnard's house; Duff was there to protect it. So he told me, and it would be such an easily discovered lie that it had to be true. Well, if he had murdered two people to steal it, and then stolen it, even Exeter would think of him first. No, I think it would be improbable even if I hadn't solved the case.

"We are left with four people: Jack Soames, Claude Barnard, Eustace Bramwell, and our acquaintance, Lady Jane, George

Barnard. Exclude Jack Soames, and we are left with three names. You may call me the stupidest man on earth, if you please, because I should have narrowed it to these four straightaway, and even when I did I picked out Soames. Surpassingly feeble of me. My only excuse is that the motive was so strangely inverted.

"Now, who did it? I'll tell you—"

But the revelation would have to wait at least a few minutes longer. Sir Edmund, again in his unattractive attire of the morning, had burst into the room, out of breath and very evidently bearing news.

"Charles . . . Charles," he said, panting. "I saw him . . . he looked up . . . I hid myself out of his sight . . . where I could see. . . ."

He stood up, having been bent over, and collected himself. Lenox, too, had stood, and now clapped his brother on the back. "Excellent! Excellent!" he said.

"I was—"

"May I guess?"

Edmund looked surprised. "Yes, of course."

"A man came into the room, moving very quickly, and knelt to the floor."

"Why, yes!" Edmund was wide-eyed.

"He looked under the bed and then ran his hand across the floor, several times."

"Yes, right again!"

"Then he stood up, much disconcerted—he may have even stood there for a moment—and then ran out as if struck by lightning."

"Why, Charles, are you making a fool of me?"

"Oh, Edmund! Not for all the world."

"Do you know who the man was, then?"

"Why, I imagine I do. Was it Claude Barnard?"

Edmund looked at him with amazement. "Yes—yes, it was."

Chapter 44

The three old friends were seated on the two leather sofas in the middle of Lenox's library, with Graham in attendance. It was bitter cold outdoors, with a high wind, but there was a large bright fire inside and the room was pleasantly warm.

Edmund and Lady Jane sat opposite Lenox, who had tapped his foot restlessly throughout the evening and stood up every few minutes to tidy something on a bookshelf or tend the fire. Both were used to seeing him this way at the end of a case, slightly nervous, slightly dogmatic, checking and rechecking the facts he knew.

Still, Edmund was disappointed, and after a moment of silence, he said sorrowfully, "I suppose my work has gone for nothing, then. Oh, it's all right, Charles," he said, when Lenox put his hand out. "It was interesting nevertheless. Top-notch."

"Gone for nothing? Edmund, don't be mad. It was unkind of me to steal your story, but I was too excited by it. As for your work going for nothing, I've spent the last hour figuring out how to make any of it stand up in court. Gone for nothing? I don't think all the papers in a year could have brought me better news. To have your corroboration—absolute corroboration, in a way."

"Really?" said Edmund, slightly cheered.

"Yes! Absolutely indispensable, dear brother."

"It *was* rather thrilling."

"Nothing, literally nothing, short of a confession, could have helped me more. I was hoping you would see something exactly of the kind when I sent you out."

Edmund was now recovered and turned to Lady Jane. "Oh, Jane," he said—for of course he too had grown up with her— "you would have been surprised to see me out there! Completely in disguise!"

Lady Jane, who had been taking in Edmund's attire, made a bit of a face and said, "I say this as one of your oldest friends, Edmund. You don't look your best."

"I daresay—but all worth it."

She smiled, then turned to Lenox and said, "It was Claude, then?"

Edmund nodded, but Lenox put up a finger. "No," he said. "No, not exactly."

Now Edmund, who, poor soul, had endured many ups and downs in the past minutes, said, with some confusion, "Why, what do you mean?"

"Claude, you may remember, has the airtight alibi of your witness at the ball, Edmund."

"I could have been wrong," said Edmund.

"You weren't. Claude didn't kill Jack Soames."

"Drat," said Edmund.

"Claude poisoned Prudence Smith in cold blood, but his first cousin, Eustace Bramwell, murdered Jack Soames, also in cold blood, on the evening of the ball."

During the silence that ensued, Lady Jane and Edmund sat very still, while Lenox, who, truth be told, had a touch of the dramatic in him, went to his desk, took a pinch of shag from his cigarette box, and relit his pipe before returning to sit.

"Separately?" said Edmund, at last.

"No, in utter concert, to the extent that each of them had an airtight alibi for one of the murders, which did throw me off the trail for a while—and if it had been left to Exeter, I think the Yard would have missed it altogether. Exceedingly clever lads, and a clever plan. I've seen things of the sort before—the Von Olhoffen brothers. Usually one is the mastermind and persuades the other."

Lady Jane was still silent, and Lenox realized that he had briefly forgotten why he first became involved in the case.

"I'm sorry, Jane," he said.

After a pause, she said, "No, I thank you."

"It is better to have it solved."

"Yes, of course," she said.

For a time all three were silent. At last, Lady Jane spoke again. "How did you figure it out?"

Now, with both Edmund and Jane still sitting and Graham standing by the door, Lenox rose to pace the room as he answered the question.

"It was very obscure—very. But as I was explaining, Edmund, by this morning I had narrowed it to the two cousins and their uncle.

"And then, as usual, a series of small and large things began to draw together in my mind. I found a leaf, a rare leaf, with no business being there, quite near the sill of Prue Smith's window, where Eustace escaped after murdering Soames, and later I remembered that at our first meeting I had seen bunches of sprigs and leaves in his pocket. You see that with many botanists: out collecting, I supposed, and thought little of it then. But it returned to me."

"That might have been Barnard, though," said Lady Jane. "You remember he took me to the botanical gardens."

"Yes, you're right. It complicated things. But the other clues sorted out that confusion."

"What other clues?" Edmund asked.

"There was the candle. I noticed immediately when I first

went over that Prue Smith had an unused candle in her room. Graham, remind me what the maid told you?"

"She said, sir, that candles are meted out very stringently by the housekeeper."

"Exactly. That was more than useful, it was significant. It was only because you found that out, Graham, that sometime later, when I happened to see Claude with his cuff unbuttoned and saw a small burn on his forearm, I started to wonder."

"Prue and Claude must have fought," Graham said carefully. "The spots of wax on the floor. Sir," he added, as an afterthought.

"Exactly. McConnell and I found spots of wax on the floor of Prue Smith's room. I think now she died because she had overheard Claude and Eustace discussing Soames and confronted Claude, with whom she was close. During their fight perhaps they struggled, and tipped things over—including, as Graham agrees, the candle, which left wax on the floor and burned Claude. Perhaps she was holding the candle to give them light. At any rate, the two young men must have seen this to be a clue—the mangled candle—and replaced it. They, of course, could have all the candles they wanted, living upstairs."

"But if they were having a fight," said Edmund, "wouldn't poison be a rather roundabout way of killing her?"

"You're right," said Lenox. "I think Claude must have persuaded her to hold her tongue for a little while. I would guess she said yes reluctantly, and gave them enough time to poison her.

"Incidentally, I found something else suspicious: a handkerchief in Eustace's room, under his bed, that smelled of peppermint and wax and may have had a residue of wax on it. My guess is that Eustace cleaned his cousin's arm with his own handkerchief and then kept it—knowing his alibi for the murder of Prue Smith was secure—in case he should need to blackmail Claude or, indeed, turn him in with the handkerchief as evidence.

"And there was something else as well—young Hilary, the

MP. I sat next to him at the ball, and in passing he said that Claude and Eustace, who belonged to his club, seemed *thick as thieves*. I didn't think of it until just recently. He also mentioned—but several minutes later, so I didn't connect it— that they had come into money.

"I should have noticed this right away, and I should have noticed other things as well. Their alibis were too good. To hear that Eustace painted for an arduous amount of time, very noticeably not leaving the room in his supposed intensity—and then to hear from him that he had slapped on the rest of the paint the next day? Why be so fastidious and then so sloppy? For an airtight alibi, which the next day was no longer necessary to maintain. I should really have noticed this straightaway. Whenever an alibi is too good, it bears investigation."

"Same goes for Claude," Edmund said. "Maybe it was a bit too easy to follow him around, now that I think of it."

"You may be right," Lenox said. "Though you did an admirable job, they themselves, you said, noticed your attentiveness. He made faces at you, I recall."

"That's right," Edmund said.

"That seems incorrect though," said Lady Jane. "Why tell Edmund they had seen him?"

"Overconfidence," said Edmund.

"That's right," Lenox went on. "When they met briefly and Claude hit Eustace, they must have very quickly hatched a plan for Claude to be easily followed and Eustace to disappear. After all, Eustace had his alibi; Claude was the one under suspicion. But don't feel badly, Edmund. They fooled me far more easily than they fooled you."

Lenox tapped his pipe thoughtfully against his hand. "But why?" he said. "Why all of this? Why murder Soames, and even murder someone to get to Soames? What power did he have?

"I had concluded that the valuable thing in Barnard's house would be very difficult to move, which is the first thing a burglar thinks about—consider the everlasting popularity of diamonds—and that murdering Prue Smith and Jack Soames wouldn't even begin the job. I'm speaking to you, Edmund."

"Absolutely right," Edmund said. "Especially in a crowded house. You would need twenty men to walk inconspicuously through the house. The party would have been a bad time for it."

"Exactly. Why, then? First, we knew that Claude and Eustace came from poor branches of the family. But in fact, as they had both willingly admitted, they had received ten thousand pounds from their uncle upon reaching the majority. They were financially secure. And I suspect Barnard has done equally well by his brother and sister. He has a great deal of pride, so I imagine he supported them less from generosity than from the dislike of being shamed by the poverty of his family."

"I remember his saying to me that his nephews were set for life," Lady Jane said.

"Did he? That seems like the sort of thing he'd say. However that was, the two nephews had *some* money. Eustace said he had put it in the railway fund at four percent and Claude said he had discovered an opportunity in the Americas. Well. They could expect more, no doubt, upon Barnard's death—but I think neither wanted to be a workingman until then. Note that they still live with him, when most young men want their own digs. It is a fact to stow away, and I shall return to it in a moment.

"What next? I recommended the newspapers with the notices of Soames's death to Exeter, and he blithely ignored the advice; predictably, they became the crux of the case, in my mind.

"Why, when he was completely solvent, did people say that Jack Soames was ruined? Who started that rumor? It was a diversion, I would guess. The two lads started it. My guess is they told their uncle, who, as all three of us know, can be a gossip after a glass of wine. They knew as well that there was"—he looked at Edmund—"that valuable thing under their roof. Perhaps Prue had discovered their plan to steal it some weeks before the ball and was only quiet about it because of Claude's begging, and at last they decided that it was too risky."

"Why didn't you suspect Claude straightaway, if I may ask, sir?" This was Graham.

"They handled it cleverly. Until Soames was killed, they needed a way to remove suspicion from Claude, who would have no alibi for murdering Prue Smith. Perhaps it was a sense of humor, or perhaps they figured Soames to be stupid and friendly, but I suspect that they led Exeter (and me) in the direction of suspecting Soames. They spread it about that he was a ruined man, knowing the mind of a detective is constantly in search of motive. And the real motive was in fact *not* the valuable thing in Barnard's house, which took me even farther afield and left the nephews plenty of breathing room until they could kill Soames, by which time both of them would have an alibi.

"But this is speculation. Let us return to fact. I doubt many people read in the *Post* that in fact Soames was not ruined—but I did. That set my mind clicking. And more importantly, I think all of you *did* read *The Times*. Think back on it—or on any of the reputable reports. They all emphasized the same points: athletics, service in Parliament, social circle, *and his recent service on the board of the Pacific Trust*. It is this last that I realized today was most important. Edmund, you yourself tipped me off."

"How did I manage that?"

"You said you wouldn't give all the money in the funds for something or other, and I saw I had been missing the plainest clue all along. The valuable item in Barnard's house, as I said, was not the object of the crime. It was the Pacific Trust.

"There is a lesson to me in this. Apparently, the vote of the Pacific has been one of *the* stories of the past six months in the financial world. Graham, you tried to get me to look into it—all credit to you. I should have listened to you."

"I recommended it for the wrong reasons, sir."

"But you were on to something. I rarely read the financial

news. Perhaps I even think myself above it, if I'm to be honest—
the City and all of that. A huge mistake, which I only caught by
the grace of God. I shall read the financial papers thoroughly
from now on. Graham, make me do it if I start to slack, would
you?"

"Yes, sir," said Graham, his eyebrows a little raised, a small
smile on his lips.

"The Pacific Trust—well, I shan't bore you with details. It is
a company that has been extremely successful, and its shareholders have received steady dividends while the price of shares
tripled. But there are very *few* shareholders. The minimum investment is eighteen thousand pounds. Now, very few people in
England have eighteen thousand pounds, and even fewer have a
margin comfortably enough above that sum that they are willing to invest it in an extremely speculative venture.

"Here Soames comes in. Suffice it to say that he sat on the
board and represented, about a month ago, the swing vote in
a decision that had to do with the basic fate of the company.
There was a pile of revenue sitting in the bank: would they release it to shareholders or would they reinvest it? If they were to
release it, an investment of eighteen thousand pounds would
have become a clear 180,000 pounds, not counting dividends
already received. However, the company would essentially have
dissolved, and the shares would be worth almost nothing. Still,
many shareholders favored this.

"If they reinvested it, the second option, the Pacific Trust
would become nearly the most valuable company in England.
An investment of eighteen thousand pounds would have yielded
a payoff of the original eighteen thousand, as a large one-time
dividend, while shareholders maintained their shares, which
would have instantly become more valuable and presumably
grown and grown. But no further income would be available to
the shareholders for, say, twenty or thirty years.

"Virtually every outside observer favored the second option, saying that in the long term the generated wealth would exceed even the alluring 180,000 pounds. Virtually all shareholders favored the former. Soames's vote was, as I say, decisive; the company decided for the payout of eighteen thousand pounds and the solidification of the Pacific's status—the choice that led to long-term stability.

"It was a good deal either way, really. By Soames's vote, an investor received his original investment back and still owned the shares, which would become infinitely more valuable in the long term. Eventually, most shareholders accepted this fact. Two who didn't were Claude and Eustace."

"What?" said Edmund and Lady Jane, nearly at the same time.

"They had taken the twenty thousand pounds from their uncle and invested it in the Pacific. I spent all afternoon searching through the Pacific files and at last found what I thought I would, a certificate of joint ownership. They invested the money together four years ago—jointly, which the company permits. They did not, as they had said, invest in the four percents and an American company, respectively. And where there's a lie, there's motive."

"How did they know so much about money?" Lady Jane asked. "Did their uncle help them?"

"I suspect it was Eustace who prompted the action. Claude would not be averse to speculation, or so he strikes me, and Eustace seems deeply interested, I think, in living the life of a gentleman. Smart, too. He hates the feeling of inequality that was instilled in him by his rich uncle. So does Claude. One hundred thousand pounds each from the Pacific Trust would have ensured that neither of them would be forced to work again, and given each of them a clear five thousand pounds a year for life, which is very handsome for anybody, you'll admit.

"But if they had received ten thousand pounds each, with no guarantee of more for a few decades, they would have been in a bind. Most men in England could live their whole lives on that sum. But not two young gentleman with a taste for luxury in London, when certain young noblemen live from quarterly payment to quarterly payment on seven thousand a year."

"The Marchmain boys on even more," Lady Jane murmured.

"Precisely. Such a sum would by no means guarantee either of them a life of certain ease. A good amount of money—but not one that would have allowed them to shoot, to own a string of horses, to travel, to live in London and the country, and to marry above their station. Titled ladies, say. Which was, I suspect, what both of them wanted."

"They must have discovered how Soames would vote when he went to protect the mint, poor chap," Edmund said.

"I think you're right. They would have followed the vote closely—and they would also have known, as I learned from *The Times* after Soames's death, that James Maitland had been virtually promised the next vacancy on the board, being one of the company's chief investors, and that he favored the more investor-friendly option.

"What happened then, we know. They planned to murder Soames, under the favorable condition of a ball, which adds confusion to any incident, and with the false lead of the valuable object in Barnard's house, which would divert any detective. Prue Smith, who served upstairs, must have been in the hall near midmorning, when the servants were eating and the other people in the house were out, before everyone gathered for lunch. I imagine she had nipped upstairs to visit Claude. Claude and Eustace thought they were alone; somehow discovered they weren't; placated Prue Smith, cajoled, browbeat, I don't know, but in one way or another convinced her not to tell. Now that I consider it, I think they must have told her they were only imagining something out loud that they would never do. She would have wanted to believe in Claude. She shouldn't have, of course, but I think she did.

"I believe that's all. I think there's little danger that the two young men will leave town. They think, particularly with Exeter bumbling around, that they're off scot-free. After all, they both have alibis. But indeed we know that their alibis don't hold up—and Edmund's experience tonight proves it conclusively; just why I sent you, dear brother."

Both Lady Jane and Sir Edmund had a few small questions, which Lenox answered or made his best guess to answer. Finally, when they were satisfied, the detective stood up.

"Will you please send notes to Inspector Exeter and Dr. McConnell, asking them to stop by this evening?" he asked Graham.

"I shall send for them immediately, sir."

❧ Chapter 45 ❧

Soon thereafter, Edmund went upstairs and took a hot bath, while Lenox showed Lady Jane a new map he had ordered: Persia. He would travel south, from Isfahan to Shiraz, he told her. She laughed and pointed out that it was a long trip and something would always detain him, but he stubbornly refused to acknowledge the fact. He said he would hire a guide, and he and Graham would take the mountain train, which was new and quick. He asked if she would like to come, and she said no, thank you, but that she was eager for the day when they went to Italy together, which they had long vowed to do. It was where she had gone on her honeymoon.

"Oh, Charles—Venice! Did you ever go?"

"No," he said. "Only Rome."

"It's wonderful. And Florence, Siena—how vividly I remember it!"

He smiled as he listened to her tell him about the places she had gone when she was young and married, but really he was thinking about something else entirely: how he thought her more beautiful now than he had even at her wedding, when she had been only twenty and radiant.

Soon Edmund came down, looking significantly cleaner and happier. He looked at the map of Persia, too, and commented that perhaps his brother would actually go this time.

There was a knock on the door just after Lenox carefully folded the map and put it back in the old umbrella stand. He met Graham at the door and offered to open it himself, expecting McConnell or Exeter.

Instead, covered in a thin layer of snow, eyes bloodshot, Claude Barnard stood on his doorstep.

"Mr. Lenox? May I have a word?"

"Why, yes," Lenox said, taken entirely aback. "Graham, please show Mr. Barnard into the back parlor. I'll join you momentarily," he said to Claude.

He quickly went back to the library. "Claude Barnard is here," he said, giving them no time to respond. "Jane, you stay here, or go home if you'd rather. Edmund, you come stand by the door to the back parlor, if you please. In case he attempts any violence, I shall give the old call." This was a bird call they used to have when they were children. It could mean "Look!" or "Here I am!" or "Help!"

"Yes, of course," said Edmund. "Of course."

"I would ask you to sit in, but he may be volatile."

"All the more reason, Charles."

"No. I absolutely forbid it, if you'll allow me."

Edmund shrugged. Within minutes, Lenox had entered the back parlor and Edmund was stationed by the door.

Lenox paused for a moment when he went in. It was a small room, rarely used, filled with mistakes: a poorly designed chair, an uncomfortable desk, a mediocre painting. Its only saving grace was a small window, looking out onto the small garden by the house. That was where Claude stood, smoking a cigarette, his hands in his jacket pockets.

He looked sorrowful—and leaner by a noticeable measure even in the last two or three days. He didn't hear Lenox enter, and for a moment Lenox watched, saddened. He felt very little pity, to be sure, but all the young man's charm had become melancholy.

"Mr. Barnard?" Lenox said at last.

Claude turned. "Oh, hello, Mr. Lenox. Cold day, isn't it?"

"Yes." There was a silence. "Would you like to sit?"

Claude nodded, and the two men sat in ugly horsehair armchairs facing each other.

"I'm afraid I can't compliment your taste, Mr. Lenox."

"I rarely come into this room."

"Ah—yes."

"How may I help you, Mr. Barnard?"

Claude laughed bitterly. "Help me. Well, well."

"Shall I put it another way? What would you like to say to me?"

"I feel as if I live in a dream, Mr. Lenox. Everything has gone so—so wrong."

"Yes, it has," said Lenox.

Claude looked up sharply. "I'm not certain that you know."

"On the contrary, I know it all."

Now the young man's look changed to astonishment. "All of it? Surely not."

"Yes, I assure you."

"Will you tell me?"

"You and your cousin Eustace murdered Prudence Smith and Jack Soames in order to realize the benefit of your shares in the Pacific Trust."

Claude shook his head. "Yes, I see you do." He sighed. "My last solace was to come to you of my own will, and now I don't even have that."

"On the contrary," said Mr. Lenox. "You did. You might easily be across the channel. But that is by no means an exoneration."

"Exoneration? I tell you—" He broke off and lit another cigarette. After a moment, he spoke again. "Yes: I come to you of my own free will. I've no doubt I'll hang. Anything but living a moment longer in this nightmare."

"Eustace was the instigator."

"Eustace . . . Eustace. You wouldn't think it, Mr. Lenox, but behind those tedious opinions and miserable manners he can be the most persuasive fellow in the world."

"You had better begin at the beginning," said Lenox.

He took a puff of his cigarette. "If you know it all, I don't see why I should humiliate myself in recounting it."

Lenox heard the edge of stubbornness in Claude's voice, and instead of lecturing him, said softly, almost shrewdly, "It starts with your uncle, doesn't it."

Startled, Claude looked up. "Yes," he said slowly, "I suppose that's true. Uncle George." Suddenly, as if spurred on by the possibility of a sympathetic audience, he spoke in a torrent. "You wouldn't believe it. He's—he's positively cruel to the rest of the family, for one thing. Gave us money to save himself from embarrassment, you know, but then he lorded it over all of us, played us against each other. Made our parents enemies. That was the reason Eustace and I first became close. We hated him."

"Go on," said Lenox.

"I suppose, objectively, he was good to us—gave us pocket money, paid for university, let us live as we pleased with him. But I can't explain his constant references, alone or in company, to our indebtedness. It was horrible."

"And then he gave you money, didn't he?"

As if realizing he had let on too much, Claude slowed to a sullen pace. "Yes, he gave us a bit of money."

"And what did you do with it?"

"You know that already, I suppose."

"You can explain your feelings, though. All I know are the facts."

Again drawn out, Claude said, "He gave us ten thousand pounds each. When he did that, Eustace came to me."

"He went to you?"

"We were united in our dislike of our uncle, but I still didn't like my cousin. Still, he was irresistible. Said he had found a way for us be rich, both of us, and we both knew he was rather brilliant about things of that sort. I think he managed his own family's budget from the age of six or seven, saved them from that awful cycle of wealth and poverty I went through. Our uncle only sent remittances erratically, you see." A shadow of childish anger passed over Claude's face.

Lenox, again subtly urging the lad on, said, "He painted you a picture, then?"

"He convinced me. He said we would never have to work in our lives! And of course he was right. Even if we had accepted the board's decision and managed well, we could have survived on what we had, not to mention the stock's growth. But he had filled my head, you see, with these visions of absolute opulence"—Claude stubbed out his cigarette on the open windowsill and ran his hand through his hair—"until ten thousand pounds didn't cut it anymore."

"There were debts, I gather." Lenox offered Claude another cigarette as he said this.

"Why fight it," Claude said bitterly. "You know already. I had been drinking too much, you see, and I owed for cards, and had bills outstanding that would have forced me to live very stringently. From the ten thousand I would have had, perhaps three or four thousand left. A large sum of money, to be sure, but by no means enough to live on as I wanted to live. Or no—as I wanted to show Uncle Barnard I could live." Again that shadow of anger across his face. "Even living very cheaply, I would have run through it in five years."

This was the moment, Lenox knew. Had to be handled carefully. "And Eustace had a solution. . . ."

Claude paused but then nodded. "At last he convinced me. He said if we got Soames off the board, we would be rich: all of my worries, my family's worries, all of Uncle Barnard's snide comments—gone. One hundred thousand quid apiece at one go."

"It wasn't murder at first, was it?"

"No, not at first. To begin with, we merely spread it about that Soames was a drunk and had no money left. We thought perhaps he would be put off the board on the strength of public opinion. I fear we made his life miserable, poor sot." He looked at Lenox almost defiantly when he said this, but the detective's face remained impassive. Claude went on in a burst. "It didn't work—and gradually, you see, Eustace convinced me that our very lives depended on it. As I told you, it was like a dream. I ask you, to murder somebody? I had money enough, all the friends in the world, a rich uncle if an autocratic one—how could I have been brought round? The insanity of it! It only dawned on me after Prue died . . . and then my life depended on it. I couldn't go backwards, Eustace kept saying."

"Go on."

"No. I've said too much. I don't even know what protection you can give me." He stood by the window, still smoking.

Lenox murmured, "It must have been difficult, murdering a girl you had known—perhaps even liked."

"Liked?" said Claude sourly, turning quickly back to Lenox. "I liked her, it's true. . . . Do you remember seeing me dine alone, in the upstairs of the Jumpers? I think that moment was when I really saw what had happened. When I woke up. I saw what an insidious, awful person my cousin was—truly was— for the first time. I felt such sorrow, then. It's no excuse, none; but it's the truth."

"What do you mean, you woke up?"

"You see, when I killed Prue, I didn't really understand it. Eustace gave me some poison or other; he had cadged it from our uncle, plus a bottle of dummy poison that was in the housekeeper's room." Lenox nodded to himself. "He's the one who knows botany—said he used it on plants. I would never have known. I barely scraped a third at Oxford. She had over-heard us talking about Soames, I guess. And she trusted me enough, poor Prue, to confront me." He stubbed out his sec-ond cigarette and accepted another from Lenox. "It didn't seem real, the poison. I didn't really connect it with Prue's death, as strange as that sounds. It was just a little bottle that looked like medicine."

"You had fought, hadn't you?"

"Fought?"

"And then you had to keep her quiet long enough to poison her after the fight." Seeing that Claude meant to protest, Lenox said, a little more sharply, "Come now, the struggle where you were burned."

"You do know it all, I see. We did fight. In whispers, so as not to be overheard—but she was awfully angry. I did get burned. But in the end I convinced her to stay quiet until I could per-suade Eustace to give it up. I said it was just talk."

"So you tricked her?"

There was a long silence; Lenox knew this was the moment when Claude would either try to flee or break down. Slowly, without moving quickly, he pulled a dusty bottle of rye and two glasses from the hideous wardrobe some aunt or other had left to him. Claude wasn't the first suspect he had brought into the back room. He poured the rye slowly into two glasses and of-fered the young man one of them. Claude looked at it, paused for a fraction of a second, then took it and had a sip. With a crack in his voice, he went on.

"It tortured me to do it. I drank heavily that morning. But that wasn't the real reason I went through with it. That only helped. I was jealous, you see. The thing was that I really liked—nearly loved—that maid." He laughed, with such incredulity on his face that it almost seemed he was speaking of someone else, some other set of events. Lenox thought of Deck and James, their dif-ferent reactions. It was obvious that Prue had some quality that all three of these men had more than loved—they had been obsessed.

No longer needing Lenox's frequent prompting, Claude went on. "And Eustace—oh, he was clever—he told me that morning about the man from the tavern sneaking into her room. Deck. I don't know how he figured it out, but I was filled with anger. It ate me up. I went downstairs . . . I put the poison in her glass of water . . . lurked in the hallway. Watched her drink it with something like happiness, you know. Then I replaced the candle, put the note there, and left some other bottle I was to leave. And that was it."

"And once you had done that, you had to help with Soames."

Claude looked at Lenox with something almost like surprise, as if he had been talking to himself. "It's true," he said. "I didn't have an alibi for the time when Prue died, so I needed the alibi for the second murder. I was contrite but I didn't want jail, you know, or the gallows."

Lenox sat back in the chair. It was snowing hard now. Claude was still at the window, and now, with neither of them speaking, there was a deep silence in the night.

"The gallows . . . no, I suspect not. It occurred to me for a moment that you might be trying to trick me—that really it was you who led Eustace on. But that's not right, I see. It was essential that *you* commit the bloodless murder, the easier one, the one that didn't seem real. Your cousin must have known you couldn't push a knife through a man's ribs and drove you as far as you could go." He paused. "No, I don't think the gallows. Twenty or thirty years in prison, most likely."

As if smacked back into reality, Claude said, "Thirty years?" He looked shocked.

Lenox nodded. "It's time to wake up truly now, Claude. It wasn't all a joke."

After just a second, Claude made his move. Lenox had been half expecting it, but was still caught off guard. Claude pushed him out of the way and bolted toward the door. There was no time to make the call; Lenox only gasped out "Edmund!" as loudly as he could. Then he roused himself from the floor (there was still a hint of ache in his body from the beating he had taken) and ran for the door. On the other side of it, Claude was struggling in Edmund's arms, which were wrapped firmly around him.

❧ Chapter 46 ❧

McConnell had arrived and heard the entire story from Lady Jane. Graham had a note from Exeter saying he was on an excellent trail and had no time to come over. The four friends spoke quietly in the library about Claude, who was now more calmly sitting in the back drawing room, locked in by the door and the windows.

"You had better let him sleep in one of the bedrooms," said Lady Jane, "and then take him in tomorrow. There's a blizzard."

Lenox hesitated at first and asked if he would do the same if Bartholomew Deck had murdered Prue Smith and Jack Soames. But gradually the other three convinced him to do the generous thing. It was the last night Claude would spend comfortably for some years.

So Lenox relented and allowed the young man his hot water bottle and soft bed, locking the guest room door from the outside, and the next morning, though he refused to eat with the lad, had breakfast sent to him upstairs. He could only imagine his guest, sitting in an armchair in the luxurious bedroom, eating the last truly good meal of his early life.

Exeter's hot trail had gone cold and he finally came over,

where he heard the story, promptly said he thought it was something "very much of the sort," bemoaned the lax morals (perhaps correctly) of the young "aristos, who never had to earn a
pound," and took Claude into custody. Claude had pressed his
suit himself and neatly tied his tie. He looked very somber, but
also somehow relieved.

The next matter was to find Eustace. He was not at Barnard's
house, where McConnell and Lenox first looked. Nor was he
at any of the several clubs he belonged to. They went back to
Barnard's, then, and asked to be let into Eustace's room. It still
seemed occupied, but the possessions in the room had thinned
out since Lenox last looked there, and finally the ever-charming
Miss Harrison reluctantly told them that Mr. Bramwell had left
with a trunk, saying he was on a trip home for a few days to
check on his mother.

Lenox and McConnell stood for a moment in the entryway
of the house, talking, after hearing this news and walking downstairs. They thanked the housekeeper and stepped outside onto
the freshly coated sidewalk.

"I suppose we shall have to follow him up there," said Lenox.

"Yes," said McConnell. "He can't know anybody's after him."

Lenox paused at this and then cried out, as fast as he could,
"Come with me, come with me—there's no time to lose!"

Without asking for an explanation, McConnell leaped into
his carriage, which had four horses at Toto's insistence, and
beckoned Lenox to follow him.

"Where?" he said, when they were both in.

"The head of the river!" shouted Lenox, "and fast as can be!"

"A ship?" said McConnell, as they rattled quickly along the
cobblestones.

"Yes, yes, a ship!" said Lenox. "Oh, how stupid I've been!
How stupid, all through the case! To underestimate such an intelligent man! Oh, I shall never forgive myself, Thomas!"

"But how do you know that he's on a ship?"

"A full trunk? To visit the North for a few days? No, no, no. And the trains out of England leave too irregularly and too slowly, but there is a ship every day, and we could scarcely hope to catch a ship as we could a train! Everything indicates it, Thomas. He must have followed Claude to my house and realized the game was up."

They arrived at the dock very quickly and ran through the small building where people bought tickets, waited, and said their goodbyes. Yes, there was a ship, the man at the ticket counter informed them, bound for Egypt, and then on to Asia, and yes, there were still berths available.

They ran to the dock, and Lenox scanned the deck of the ship while McConnell looked at the passengers still on dry land.

"Nothing," said the doctor as the crowd thinned out, and Lenox, too, saw nothing.

"Last call!" the captain shouted out, and at the same moment McConnell yelled and pointed. "There he is!"

It was Eustace Bramwell, standing on the foredeck of the ship, unmistakable, dark-haired and wearing a gray suit. He hadn't even thought to hide in his room until they had gone, so sure had he been that Lenox wouldn't decipher his plans. There was a yelp behind them, but their eyes remained fixed on Eustace.

Lenox ran over to the captain. "We need to get on," said Lenox. "There's a criminal on board!"

"Are you the police?" the captain asked.

"No, but we're surrogates," said Lenox.

"Sorry. Ship's off limits." He prepared to walk up the gangway himself, but a last passenger streaked toward it, while McConnell reasoned without avail to the captain.

The last passenger anxiously handed his ticket over. He had absolutely no luggage.

"Third class," the captain said, tore the ticket, and pointed up the gangway. He managed to resist the implorings of Lenox and McConnell, even forcibly repelling them once, and after five minutes of waiting for more passengers, he himself went up to the deck of the ship and cut her loose.

Lenox stood there, then, feeling hopeless, while McConnell walked off to make futile contact with the police, but then he saw something. It was the last passenger, who had rushed onto the ship without luggage. The man's eyes were firmly focused on Eustace, and he only looked back at Lenox once. When he did, he pointed at Eustace and made an inquisitive face. Lenox nodded; yes, that was the murderer. He knew he was sealing Bramwell's fate but he nodded anyway.

The man was dressed in a pitch-black suit. After Lenox's nod, he walked slowly toward Eustace, stopping a few feet away and gazing intensely, hatefully, at him. It was James, the footman, Prue's fiancé. And Lenox saw with clarity the inevitable course of events. He waved McConnell back to him as the ship slowly began to move and told him not to make any further effort. He pointed out James and Eustace, feet apart, and told the doctor what he knew would happen.

He sent word to Egypt to look for Eustace but expected no results. And six days later, when the ship docked in Cairo, he was no more surprised—when the captain remitted the following message to the English authorities, which was then repeated in the papers—than he was surprised that the sun rose in the morning.

Very little is known of the death of two men who were sailing with the HMS *Britannia* on a course for the Far East. On the first night of the voyage, they washed overboard very late at night, according to the captain. One was a first-class passenger, the other in third class. Authorities believe the man from first class to be Eustace

Bramwell, one of the two murderers in the Jack Soames case, which was so ably cleared up by Inspector Exeter before more life was lost. The incident is believed to be an accident. . . .

∽ Chapter 47 ∽

A few days later, Lenox turned his thoughts to his Christmas visit with his brother, due to begin soon. He still wanted to take Edmund to task after Newton Duff's revelatory comments, perhaps that evening over supper and a bottle of their father's wine. And of course Lady Jane would be there, just a few miles off with her brother, in the house where she had grown up.

For now, though, Lenox was in a place that offered even greater measures of bliss than Lenox House, the home of his childhood. He was in Linehan's, Bootmakers, Crown Street, in a respectable middle-class neighborhood by Leicester Square. Not the type of place he would have found on his own, he thought. Thank God for Skaggs.

"Yes, three pairs, cork-soled, two black, one brown, all lined with flannel," he said, repeating his order. He had come in two days earlier, and now his boots were ready.

"Packed up?" asked Mr. Linehan, a jolly, rotund, white-haired man.

"No, I shall wear the brown pair, please."

"Would you like us to wrap your old boots?"

Lenox shuddered. "I hope never to see them again."

Mr. Linehan laughed. "Well, I guarantee these, Mr. Lenox. You're at the right place. I admit I don't think much of the boots you're wearing."

"Nor do I, Mr. Linehan. I can't abide them for another moment."

Mr. Linehan laughed again, took the offending boots, which Lenox had slipped off, and offered the brown pair, designed specifically for his feet from the measurements that Lenox had found much pleasure in seeing Mr. Linehan take.

Lenox put on a fresh pair of socks, which he had brought especially, and then the boots, and wasn't disappointed. Instantly warm, but soft—yes, this was all he truly needed. He gave his profuse thanks to the cobbler, received a bag with the other two pairs, blessed Skaggs for his practicality, and walked onto the street, where, despite the new snow, his feet remained warm and dry. It was a heavenly feeling.

He had two more errands before the evening trip to Lenox House. The less pleasant first. He directed his coachman to Bow Street and Scotland Yard. Today was the day of Exeter's promotion. In combination with the diminishing crime rates in the West End, his bailiwick, there were the Marlborough forgery and the Jack Soames case to his credit.

Though it was cold, Lenox saw that Exeter and William Melville, the head of Scotland Yard, were standing on the sidewalk by the gates before headquarters, addressing a crowd of maybe fifteen journalists and a few citizens. There were a few moments of remarks from each of them, a large grin on Exeter's face the whole time. Lenox didn't mind especially, though he felt slightly duped.

After the remarks were over, the journalists milled about, taking pictures of the principals and of Exeter's young family. Lenox shook Exeter's hand without receiving much attention. But after the majority of the pictures were taken, Exeter brought a young boy of perhaps eight to see Lenox. They moved off a bit to the side.

"This is my son, Mr. Lenox. John."

"How do you do, John?"

"What do you say?" Exeter said, addressing the boy.

"Thank you, sir," the boy said.

Lenox's and Exeter's eyes met. Lenox offered his hand, Exeter shook it, and the detective and his son walked away. Climbing back into his carriage, Lenox thought, Ridiculous, in a way. But as they drove, he couldn't help feeling a little moved.

Their second stop was at the Clark Lane storefront of Mr. Kerr, travel agent.

"Mr. Kerr!" Lenox said, walking in. It was a dusty room but well lit and cluttered with papers, itineraries, and maps.

"Ah. Mr. Lenox."

"Yes indeed, Mr. Kerr."

"Come to plan a trip?"

"Just so, Mr. Kerr."

The elderly man laughed sourly. "Don't see the use. You never go anywhere; I never make any money!"

"Why, Mr. Kerr, I did in fact go to Moscow, only a few years ago."

"Nine."

"Well, work will come up, Mr. Kerr."

"Not for me, with such clients!"

"Ah! Now there you're incorrect, if you'll excuse me saying so. One word, Mr. Kerr: Persia. What have you got?"

"What've I got? Empty promises! What about France?"

"Well, well, I had to cancel. But Graham came by with fifty pounds, did he not?"

"Aye, aye," said Mr. Kerr, begrudgingly but slightly mollified.

"Excellent. Now, what have you got in the way of Persia? I was thinking of a four-city tour, if you can manage it, with a native guide. I may go off the beaten path a bit. . . ."

The conversation began to grow concrete, and very slowly Mr. Kerr pulled out the proper maps and said that yes, perhaps he knew a man who was familiar with the Persian countryside. Gradually, as he always did, Lenox drew the grumpy old man out, until by the end they were equally excited. Often people told him he should go to a different agent, but Lenox liked their ritual and stubborn Mr. Kerr's gradual acceptance of Lenox's good cheer. And then he had one quality that Lenox judged him for beyond all others: Mr. Kerr, too, loved to plan trips. He had found his métier by being the sort of dreamer Lenox was when it came to travel.

Lenox left an hour later with several papers in hand and promises to return after the New Year to plan things more specifically. Who knew if he would get to Persia—but as he planned, he always believed that this time he really would.

On the way home, he asked to be dropped at the end of Hampden Lane and walked happily up the street with a little arrangement of flowers in his hand. They were forget-me-nots, and he left them with Kirk, along with a note that said, *Thank you for everything, and see you soon!*

He then walked back to his house, next door, still gratefully warm of foot, and walked up his own stoop contentedly. He received a telegram when he came in.

Claude Barnard had just pled guilty to charges of murder at the Assizes, saving himself a trial, and received twenty-five years in prison, commuted from hanging on the strength of Lenox's private advocacy of compassion to the judge.

It may as well do to explain his fate now, as his cousin's has already been determined. Claude did in fact receive 200,000 pounds, his shares and Eustace's, when the board of the Pacific Trust voted again—despite the public's futile insistence that Jack Soames's memory be honored by his last vote. The cousins had arranged that ownership of their joint stock would transfer to the remaining cousin upon the death of one, or, upon the death of both, would be split equally between their families.

The money tantalized Claude for the first year in prison, when he could only spread a pound here and there for better meals and a private room. But gradually, after the passage of some years, he grew content with his lot and even wrote a treatise, "On the English Prison," which was well received, for there was only a dim memory of his crime and ample evidence of his contrition.

Then, in his tenth year in prison, Claude began to distribute his money among charities he chose quite carefully. When he was released after nineteen years for good behavior, he had given away all but forty thousand pounds. There was conjecture that he was trying to pay his way out of his memories, and this may well have been true, but the orphans and troubled women who received the money looked for very little motive, and even if he was guilty of assuaging his guilt with his gild, it didn't change the fact that he did an immense amount of good.

He was forty when he again became a free man. He took small but comfortable rooms in an obscure part of the city and traveled to warm climates in the winter. At forty-five he wrote another treatise, called "On the Alteration of Man's Will"; it is not too much to say that it became a minor classic in its time and was still occasionally being dusted off, even after his premature death, of drink, at fifty-three.

Lenox saw him only one more time, on the streets of London. It was on a warm sunny day in June, near the entrance to Hyde Park. Claude seemed unable to speak, and when Lenox said, "I'm glad to see you've turned your fortune to the benefit of the city," Claude merely nodded and then ran off very quickly, stooped over, carrying a number of books under his arm.

Chapter 48

Lenox arrived home in his new boots and went into his library. There he carefully tidied his desk and pulled out a few last books he had forgotten to ask Graham to pack. Then he gave the room a last good look and shut the doors.

Graham waited in the front hallway. After Lenox had looked here and there to make sure things were in order, and even gone up to his bedroom, the two men left for Paddington, where they caught the evening train to Markethouse.

Graham had sent their luggage forward the day before but had brought the morning papers, which he read, while Lenox gave another effort to *De Rerum Natura*, which he had detested at school, where he had been forced to learn it by rote, but now thought he ought to try again.

Faithfully, he read a great deal of the volume, laying it aside only when evening began to overshadow the landscape and the train drew into Sussex, the part of the country he recognized the best. For half an hour he looked out of the window, his thoughts strumming quietly along.

When they were close to Markethouse, Graham said to him, "Have you looked at the *Daily Telegraph* today?"

"I flipped through it earlier."

"The business section, sir?"

"Well, no."

Graham raised his eyebrows ever so slightly.

"Tomorrow," Lenox said, waving a hand.

"There's an article just here, sir, which might be worth looking at."

"I'm not really in the mood."

But Graham insisted in his quiet way. "I can't quite put my finger on it, sir. Perhaps you might."

Lenox took it reluctantly and scanned the headlines, then turned inside, where he read the agony column and the notes on London crime. Finally, keeping his promise, he turned to the financial page. He read the long stories and even glanced at the smaller ones, so that the most remote names of people and companies in the news would be stored away in the attic of his mind.

But the article that truly grabbed his interest was what Graham had pointed out, a very short column of print at the bottom of the last page. This he read again and again, with his brow furrowing, clutching the paper close to his eyes, for the light had all but failed.

He scarcely took his attention from it even when Graham and he left the train and stepped into the waiting carriage. And in the carriage he doggedly studied the little corner of the paper until at last, halfway through their journey to Lenox House, which was a good twenty minutes from the station, he threw the whole thing down and buried his face in his hands.

"Sir?" said Graham.

"By jove, what a fool I am, Graham," Lenox said. "You were absolutely right. Give me a kick in the trousers if I don't listen to you again."

"What is your opinion, sir?"

Lenox read it aloud, as much for himself as Graham.

The *Daily Telegraph* has learned that the nation's money was in good hands for two weeks: Mr. George Barnard's. Most readers will say that this has been true for some time, to which the *Telegraph* replies that we mean the statement literally. After the series of assaults on the mint, which police now think was done by members of the Hammer Gang, quick-acting members of the government, including Lord Russell and Mr. Gladstone, consulted and decided that the money due to be released for circulation would be best concealed in a strongroom in Mr. Barnard's house. There it resided safely until Tuesday, when it was released under supervision into popular use. Indeed, £19,100 was lost, though Mr. Barnard attributed this to assaults on the mint, saying the government was lucky not to lose more and the preservation of the remainder of the money was due to their quick action. The missing amount was coinage stored in one crate. The *Spectator* adds that while £19,100 would be a large amount for most individuals, in matters of government it is insignificant, bearing in mind that the total sum of the gold successfully stowed away was approximately £2,000,000.

"Odd, I agree. What do you see in it, sir?" Graham asked.

It had been less than a week since Claude Barnard's guilty plea at the Assizes, and during that time something had bothered Lenox. He was certain in his conviction of the lad's guilt, and certain of Eustace Bramwell's death, but in the back of his mind he realized that there were dark spots in his understanding, and he had worked his mind over them ceaselessly, if quietly, like a stream wearing away a stone.

"There was a second plot line in the Smith/Soames case, Graham," he said, "running with a faint pulse beneath the actions of the cousins. Oh, to have missed it!" He pounded his fist on the seat. "And now the footprints will be gone."

"May I ask what you mean, sir?"

Lenox, though, was already lost in his thought. "How far back . . . ?" he muttered, and then, a moment later, he shook his head, and said, "Very possibly. . . ."

He spoke again a few minutes later, at the beginning of the long driveway to the house, which ran for some miles through a dense grove of trees. "You know, Graham, I've fallen into the trap of thinking that I'm clever." Graham said nothing but gave that same small raise of his eyebrows. "I ought to have paid closer to attention to Barnard."

"Yes, sir?"

"Yes, of course. The immediate obfuscation—the insistence that it was suicide—and then the exchange of bright young Jenkins for bull-headed Exeter, and finally our odd breakfast together and his insistence that I stand at the edges of the case. Stupid me, I ignored it—took it for his usual ill grace."

"What was it, sir?" Graham asked.

Lenox sighed. "It was he who stole the money, Graham. I have little enough proof, but I know it in my bones. He stole the nineteen thousand and who knows how much else?

"You remember, of course, the men who attacked me. I think you were right to begin with. When that man muttered Barnard's name, it wasn't because Barnard's a public figure."

"I agree, sir. As I said before, they did not seem like men who read the society pages."

"Exactly. You had it all along—he sent them. I also believe he organized the original attacks on the mints. The hammer tattooed above the man's eye—of course I see it now; he was in the Hammer, the gang that runs out of the Rookery. No wonder that's where the chaps led you. I should have seen it before— daft of me. Led by a fellow named Hammersmith, who controls most of the organized theft in East London. Some of its more powerful members have that tattoo as a mark of loyalty. It's considered an honor in those circles.

"Why attack me? It was absolutely necessary that I stay away from the case. Barnard could handle Exeter; he couldn't handle me. But why attack the mint? It was too well guarded. He could guarantee bad guards occasionally, because he runs the mint, but it was too risky. So Barnard himself suggested keeping the gold in his strongroom. Newton Duff mentioned to me when we met that Barnard had initially wanted no guards in his house; he felt he could guard it alone. Is there anything more transparent? I say again, I have no proof, but I feel utterly certain.

"And then the sum! Nineteen thousand pounds. A clerical sum, a sum that would be missed but not thoroughly investigated. A sum a gentleman could live off of for years and years, but not a sum so ostentatious as to arouse much curiosity. I wonder, Graham—how many times has he stolen such a sum? How many times has he squirreled away a few hundred pounds, then a few thousand pounds, as his status rose? All the time, mark you, serving so well as to be above suspicion."

Graham began to speak, but Lenox held up a hand. "No, Graham. I know it. Everything tells me. The great mystery of George Barnard's money—I've got it. Nobody has ever known, not even the men who always, always, know such things."

The carriage slowed to a stop as they arrived at the door. "I can't prove it yet," said Lenox, "but I will."

He didn't open the door to the carriage for a moment.

"It is quite possible, sir," said Graham.

"It is beyond possible, Graham. It is a certainty. And you should take more pride in it—you were the one who forced me to read this and who followed those thugs to the Rookery."

"What will you do next?" Graham asked.

"I must track down the men who attacked me; I am certain now that it was Barnard who sent them. Claude would have mentioned it, you know, if he and his cousin were responsible for the attack. And Eustace, I would guess, would have thought his plan too clever, estimated his own intelligence too highly, to resort to such things. His plan was already working. Barnard is the only answer.

"But he has gone a step too far. He should have left the money alone, after I began to look into his household." With a look of determination, Lenox said, "Yes, he will regret that. He should have laid low."

Only then did he step out of the carriage and greet his brother, his sister-in-law, and his nephews.

⁓ Chapter 49 ⁓

It was now nearly a month later. Lenox had grown accustomed to living in Lenox House again and felt happy, pottering about during the days and sleeping well during the cold nights, back in the heart of his family, back in his childhood home, reading quietly and eating well and resting his mind. He had made a bargain with himself that he would only begin to think about Barnard when he went back to London, which wouldn't be for some time.

One Sunday at midafternoon, he had just come back from a long walk through the grounds. He had taken to doing this every day. He would walk past the thickets of old trees at the end of the park, which he greeted like friends, and then across the stream that divided the park from the wild acres of the property, where he and Edmund had played as children. After perhaps three miles, he would reach several large rented farms at the south end of the estate, which buzzed with activity even through winter. Horses grazing, vets examining the pregnant cows and dogs herding the rest of them, rows of chicken coops where the farmer's wife went every afternoon to find a new batch of eggs. It was a life he loved. He would watch for a while and then turn around and head for home.

Back now, he paused briefly in the parlor to warm his face and hands at the great hearth. His feet, of course, were quite warm enough, thanks to Mr. Linehan.

It was a large solid house, divided into two wings and shaped like an L. In the older wing were the great hall, where the family portraits were, and the chapel where the family had been that very morning. But the bedrooms there, because they were small and medieval, went unused. They all slept in the new wing.

Lenox was staying in his old room, which Sir Edmund reserved for his use alone. It was attached to a good-sized study, where he kept a few duplicates of his favorite books, histories of the Roman Empire and journals on English archaeology, plus pictures and papers from university, which he sifted through now and again. It also had a desk and a small fireplace, and he had his morning tea there, writing letters in his robe and slippers before joining the family for breakfast.

Warmer now, he leaned his walking stick against a wall before going off to search for his brother. He would probably be in his library, where he usually stayed when his family was gone, and Molly had taken the boys over to town to see a play. The two brothers were alone in the house.

Strange to think of it as Edmund's library; it had always been their father's, where the young Edmund and Charles had gone, in season, to be chided, praised, or punished, from their earliest years to their time at Harrow and then Oxford. But now it was cluttered with the things of the ninth baronet, blue books from Parliament, letters, and a portrait of Molly. All that really seemed the same were the old desk, the family books, and the small diamond-shaped windows at the back of the room.

Lenox and his brother had always been affectionate and spent a good deal of time together. But during this visit, sitting here together late at night, they had talked much more deeply than ever before. They discussed their family; they were the only people who remembered their parents as they did, and it was nice to talk about them together. They talked, at last, about Edmund's real role in Parliament, which his modesty had concealed for so long. Lenox told his brother about old cases, which he had never bothered to mention, and they conspired over small matters of the estate.

Now, when Charles knocked, Edmund was there and invited him to sit down.

"I've just been for a walk. I was wondering, do the Adamses still rent Darrow Farm?"

"Yes, indeed. Do you remember old Adams?"

"Remember him? He terrified us both for years."

The brothers laughed. "Yes," said Edmund. "I'm afraid he's dead, but his son keeps the farm up. He makes a very good living out of it, too."

"I'm glad to hear it. Do you remember—?"

They launched into a nostalgic conversation about the former tenants of the farms, which spread into a discussion of the masters at their grammar school, and it was nearly time for dinner when they had stopped.

"Are Molly and the boys coming back?" asked Lenox.

"I shouldn't think so. They're bound to go over to the Lenox Arms, which the boys think is the most thrilling thing they do. And Molly, truth be told, likes it herself. I'm afraid she's quite lenient about it. But old Jos. Turner runs it, and he's a good man. He's in charge of nearly all the politics down at Markethouse, these days."

This inaugurated another conversation, about Jos. Turner and his father, also called Jos. Turner.

They decided to eat in the library. It was dark by now, because the winter nights began early. Edmund lit some lamps and the

two ate in front of the warm fire, on small trays, while snow began to fall outside.

Sunday had been a quiet day, but by Monday the house was
again in full swing. Molly had invited a friend of hers to stay,
a rather pompous but good-natured old woman named Lady
Milton, and the boys went to school in the old wing of the
house with several of the local boys. Edmund rode out with the
land's steward to look at the fields he had taken for himself,
after an older childless tenant's death, and Charles, who kept
a three-year-old mare in the country, rode out with them.

The entire household had a lively lunch together with the local curate, who had just married a bashful young girl, and Lady
Milton, who acted as a sort of godmother to Molly.

After lunch Lenox retreated to his small study, where he sat
by the fire and read one of the books that his bookseller had
shipped out the other day, at his request that anything new be
forwarded to the country. It was a study of the Italian artists
with color plates, and he was enjoying it quite a lot.

But he laid it aside after a few moments, to write down several thoughts he had had about Barnard, and made a note to ask
McConnell for his opinion before picking the book up again.

He looked out the window. Yes, he thought, he was very
comfortable—very happy here, among his family. But he would
only stay for another ten days, not another three weeks as
planned. And though he smiled at the prospect of the ten days,
he smiled, too, at the prospect of being back on Hampden
Lane, where any ring at the door could mean a new case.

His thoughts were interrupted, though, when he saw a single
figure on the skyline. It occurred to him that he had been waiting
all day to see such a thing, for it was the day when Lady Jane had
said she would come up from the city to visit her brother, who
had only recently become the next earl, after their father's death.

He had been keeping an eye out for a carriage—but of

course, he realized, she would ride. She was an excellent rider, even in winter, and had been since they were children and rode all across the county together. It was typical of her, Lenox thought, his feet up on his desk and his back to the fire—a singular strand of strength, beyond most women, ran through her, even when she seemed weak. So very few women rode.

A few minutes later the reunion was complete. She had kissed Molly and Edmund, given the boys (who had been permitted to leave their schoolroom) a small present, and said hello to Lady Milton. And lastly, she had given Charles a kiss on the cheek and looked into his eyes happily, while her hat brushed against his hair, and said she was very glad to see him again, and London had been lonely without him.

Chance had it that it was nearly teatime, and all of the party consented, graciously, to stay, though Lady Milton said that she had really better be going afterward.

One thing Charles could say for Molly was that she served an excellent generous tea, almost as good as his mother's. There were hot muffins and biscuits, and there were a few sandwiches for the boys, who gulped them down as Charles and Edmund once had. Then there was a slice of cake all round, and after half an hour Lenox and Lady Jane had fallen into easy, happy conversation together while the group broke into smaller parts and everybody helped themselves to a third cup of tea.

Soon, unfortunately, Lady Milton would be obliged to go, and Sir Edmund returned to his office to look over a new report on the French alliance, and the boys went outside to play a complex ongoing game, which nobody but them could understand. Molly and her friend went upstairs to have a little time to themselves before Lady Milton's departure, and the two neighbors were left alone.

"I should be going, I'm afraid," said Lady Jane, "before it becomes dark."

Charles looked through the window. "It's started to already," he said. "May I ride back with you?"

"Oh, you needn't—it's awfully cold, you know."

"Ah, but I've been to get new boots, and I never get too cold, anyway."

"Well, then," she said, "yes, thank you," and they took their coats from the butler and walked out to the parkway, where they only had to wait a moment for their horses.

"You shall have to come over for supper tomorrow," said Lady Jane, while they waited. "Stephen"—her brother—"wanted me to ask."

"Of course," said Charles. "How long do you plan to stay?"

"Oh, two weeks or so."

"Well, we shall see a lot of each other, I daresay."

"Yes," she said, and smiled.

The air was cool, but it was a beautiful night, and they rode off in tandem, galloping out of the park and into the country-side. They rode briskly to the west, talking and laughing together, until some minutes later Edmund, glancing up by chance in his library, could only see their twinned figure against the pale darkness of early evening, blurred together into one, far off in the distance.

If you enjoyed A Beautiful Blue Death

read on for a preview of Charles Finch's upcoming novel

The September Society

to be published in August 2008

Visit www.minotaurbooks.com

for a chance to win free books and connect

with your favorite authors!

Prologue

The first murders were committed nineteen years before the second, on a dry and unremarkable day along the Sutlej Frontier in Punjab.

It was beastly hot weather, as Juniper remarked to Captain Lysander out on the veranda of the officers' mess, fit for little more than an odd gin and tonic, perhaps the lazy composition of a letter home. The flies, maddening creatures that had never learned to take no for an answer, crowded around the nets that blocked the porch, searching for a way in. "I would trade a hand to be back in London," Lysander said to Juniper after a long pause. "At least they have the decency to bar these flies from coming into the city there."

The battalion was on edge, because a recent retaliatory raid on a local village had turned bloody. Suspicion and rumor abounded. The officers, with a few exceptions, had long ceased to attend to their charges' morale. Though all the Englishmen in Punjab lived well, with villas and servants to themselves, every one of them at that uneasy moment would have made the trade Lysander proposed.

"Well," said Juniper. "I may go look around and have a bit of a shoot with Jim."

"Were you planning that?"

"Oh, yes."

"Where do you reckon you'll go?"

"That little patch of scrub east of here. Doubt we'll find anything worth a bullet. Maybe a darkie or two, looking for trouble."

Lysander smiled grimly. "Past that little grove of banyan trees, then?"

"Curious today, aren't you?"

In another place this might have sounded rude, but being white was a great equalizer in that country, and these men were too intimate to maintain entirely the ceremonies of respect and rank that defined the British.

"Always on the lookout for a decent bit of shooting, you know," responded Lysander, sipping his gin and tonic. He was a trim, forceful, savvy-looking man. "D'you know why they give us so much tonic, young pup?"

"No. Why?"

"Has quinine in it. Prevents malaria."

"I suppose I did know that, actually."

"They must've told you in training."

"Yes," said Juniper, nodding agreeably.

"Just past that grove of banyan trees, then?" There was a slight, casual persistence in Lysander's voice. "Ever shot anything edible there?"

"Not to speak of. There are a few birds, not much on the ground. It's poor sport."

"So's this whole country."

"Any more inspirational speech before I leave?"

"On your way."

Juniper stood up. "I'm sure I'll see you for cocktails."

But he wouldn't, and the other man knew it.

When Juniper had gone out of sight, Lysander leapt out of his chair and walked briskly up a small dirt path that led from the mess to his villa. The captain's batman, his assistant and a lance corporal, was on the porch, whittling an Indian charm to send back to his mother. He had been working on it for weeks.

"Best go do it now," Lysander said. "He's off with Juniper. Both of them, would you? They're hunting, out east, in that scrub."

"Yes, sir," said the batman, standing. Here rank still meant something.

"Do your best to make it look like an accident, obviously."

"Yes, sir."

Lysander paused. "By the way, that treasure?"

"Yes, sir?"

"There's talk of a society. Don't know what it's to be called yet, and it will be for officers alone."

"Sir?"

"But if you do right by us, we'll do right by you."

"Thank you, sir."

The batman ran off, and Lysander called to one of the servants, a fair Indian lad, swathed in brilliant pink and pale blue that contrasted with the dull beige of the landscape and the military man's uniform. The boy with some sullenness came forward.

"That box," Lysander barked. "Bring it to me. And it's worth your life to open it before it gets here."

A moment later he was holding the box, and, when certain he was alone, he opened it to reveal a massive, pristine, and beautiful sapphire.

As he snapped the box shut and had it taken away, Juniper and his friend Jim emerged from the latter's house, guns broken over their arms, both wearing beige broad-brimmed hats to keep the dying sun off their necks and faces. They had a bantering style of conversation that sounded as if it had been picked up from a thousand other conversations before. It was clear how much closer they were than Juniper and Lysander.

"A farthing says you'll never eat what you shoot," Juniper said with a laugh.

"A farthing? I've played higher stakes than that with women."

"That serving girl of mine you like, then."

"What do I have to eat?"

"First thing either of us shoots."

"What if it's the dirt?"

"Bet's a bet."

"How much dirt would I have to eat?"

"Nice haunch of it."

"Farthing for the first meat, let's go back to that. Don't shoot anything too horrible."

"I'm insulted you'd suggest it."

It was a little more than a mile outside of camp, away from Lahore—and that city's dangers, which these two men knew all too well—that they found a decent patch of land. It had a few bushes and trees scattered around it. They didn't have a dog, but Juniper shot into the undergrowth and drove a few birds out into the open, where the two men had a clear look at them.

They observed the birds fluttering, partially obscured, soon to be dead. Ruminatively, Juniper said, "What do you miss most? About England?"

His interlocutor thought it over. "I wish I hadn't left it so badly with my family, you know. I miss them."

"I do, too."

"Only six months, I suppose."

Then both men heard a scratching emerge from the undergrowth that lay off to their side.

A shot. The fall of a body. Another shot. The fall of a body. A lone figure, Lysander's batman, rose from his hidden

spot and ran off full bore back west. And then a long, long silence, in the empty land that stretched blank as far as the eye
could see, in every direction, forty-five hundred miles away
from Piccadilly Circus.

~ Chapter 1 ~

The only question left, he felt, was how to handle the matter—how it was to be done. Not if, for he had made his mind up entirely. Nor when; the moment would arise on its own.

But how?

Charles Lenox, noted amateur detective and scion of an ancient Sussex family, spent most of the morning of September 2, 1866, wandering around his study and pondering his few, daunting options. Normally imperturbable, he seemed during these long hours like a restless man. To begin he would sit heavily in one of the two armchairs by the low fire; then he would lean forward to tap the tobacco ash from his pipe into the embers; then he would stand up and walk across the room to shuffle the letters on his desk, or switch one book with another in the shelves along the wall, or straighten a picture that was to some imperceptible degree tilted; then he would return to his armchair, fill his pipe, and begin the entire dance again.

He was a lean man with a friendly face—even in the morning's preoccupation—hazel eyes, and a short brown beard. His carriage was upright, and as he paced he clasped his hands behind his back. It gave him a pensive air, the kind he had during the most difficult moments of his cases. But there was no case at hand this morning.

All of this pacing and worrying and sitting and standing took place in a handsome white house on Hampden Lane, just off Grosvenor Square. Fifteen paces down the front hall and to the right was this large library, a rectangular, high-ceilinged room with a desk near the door, a fireplace and chairs at the end of the room, a row of tall windows along the front wall, and books everywhere else. It was where he spent the great majority of his time at home, both anxious and happy alike. He pondered his cases there, and on wet, foggy days like this one, he pondered the world—or the part of it that Hampden Lane occupied—through his trickling windowpanes.

At ten he rang for coffee and at a quarter past he rang to have it taken away, cold and untouched. Graham, his butler, looked concerned but said nothing as he came to and fro. By eleven, however, he could no longer prevent himself from intervening, and presented himself unbidden in the dark oak doorway of the room.

At that moment Lenox had just taken up residence at his desk, where he was looking across the street at the bookshop.

"May I get you anything else, sir?" Graham said.

"No, no," said Lenox distractedly, still peering through the rain-touched window.

"If I may venture to say so, sir, you seem anxious."

In many of the aristocratic Mayfair households surrounding Hampden Lane, such a statement would have seemed like the highest impertinence. Lenox and Graham had a long and complex history, though, and in the end were friends more than master and man. While Graham, a sandy-haired man with perfectly arranged clothes and a strong, utterly honest face, always spoke and behaved respectfully, he never hesitated to disagree with Lenox, often helped the detective in his work, and even, on rare occasions, spoke with the frankness he just had.

"Eh?" said Lenox, at last looking up. "Oh, no, Graham— no, thank you, I'm quite all right."

"Will you take your lunch here in the library, sir?"

"No," said Lenox. "Thanks, I'm having lunch in the City, actually. I shall be glad to get on the other side of these four walls."

"Indeed, sir," said Graham. He paused before adding, "I am in the hall if you require anything."

"Thank you," said Lenox.

Graham withdrew then, and Lenox sighed. Well! he thought to himself. If Graham had noticed, it had gone too far. He would have to stop worrying and go to lunch with his brother. Standing with a decisive air, Lenox patted the pockets of his jacket and went through the double doors of the library out into the hallway.

"Graham, will you call out the carriage, please? I think I'll leave now."

"Of course, sir."

"I'll be waiting at Chaffanbrass's while they rub down the horses."

"Yes, sir," Graham said as he began to walk downstairs. "It shouldn't be longer than a quarter of an hour."

In the front hall, Lenox took his overcoat down from its peg and pulled his umbrella out of its stand. Then he took a breath, ducked outside into the rain, and crossed the street, dodging with no inconsiderable agility several hansom cabs and a landau to get to the bookshop. He pulled open the door and saw the proprietor.

"Mr. Chaffanbrass," he said with a smile. "How do you do?"

"Mr. Lenox!" said Mr. Chaffanbrass, beaming at him from behind a small counter. "Happy anniversary!"

"Oh?"

"The fire!"

"Ah, of course."

As it happened, that very day, September 2, was the two-hundredth anniversary of the Great Fire of 1666; what had started as a minor conflagration at the Pudding Lane bakery of Thomas Farriner, baker to Charles II, eventually consumed four-fifths of central London. By some miracle only a handful of people had died—the traditional count was reckoned at eight—but thirteen thousand buildings and nearly a hundred churches had vanished. Of the eighty thousand residents of the city, seventy thousand were left homeless. In a year that was already being heralded in some parts as the apocalypse because it contained the Number of the Beast, 666, few needed persuading in the first heady hours after the three-day blaze that the world was at an end.

"And yet," said Lenox, "my grandfather always said the fire did our city two great services."

"What do you mean?"

"For one thing, it allowed Wren to build his fifty churches, as well as St. Paul's Cathedral. The fire is the reason we live in such a beautiful city, Mr. Chaffanbrass."

"And the second reason?"

"Do you know how many people died of the plague in 1665?"

"How many?"

"About sixty-five thousand, and that despite two-thirds of Londoners leaving the city. The fire killed so many rats and fleas, leveled so many derelict buildings, that in the end it probably saved tens of thousands of lives."

Ruminatively, Mr. Chaffanbrass said, "Perhaps it's received a bad press, then."

"Perhaps," Lenox agreed. "Still, it would be better all around if it didn't happen again. Incidentally, has my copy of *Pickwick* come in yet?"

"It hasn't yet, I very much fear."

"Can't be helped," said Lenox.

"It will prove worth the wait, though! The finest red leather, with gold inlay!"

"And all the words inside?"

"Every last one!"

Ancient, homey, and comfortable, Calum's was one of the best bookshops around, small and a little dark with rows of crammed bookshelves along the walls. Mr. Chaffanbrass's squat counter stood in the middle of the room, just next to a freestanding oven that usually had a kettle on and a comfortable chair beside it. The owner himself was a very small, cheerful man, with red cheeks, tidy white hair, and a large belly. He wore perfectly round spectacles and a tweed suit, and the majority of his life was spent behind the counter and next to the warmth of the oven, reading. There was always a turned-down book on the arm of his chair.

"Anything else new?" asked Lenox.

"Nothing you haven't seen, no. Wait, though!" As Mr. Chaffanbrass skittered to the back of the store, Lenox looked idly through the books on the counter. Presently the gentleman came back with a small volume in his hand.

"What do you make of that, Mr. Lenox?" he said. "A new translation."

Lenox looked at the flyleaf. It was a thin, pebbled brown copy of *The Praise of Folly* by Erasmus, with an accompanying essay by one of the dons at Cambridge.

"Why not. May I take it?"

"Yes, of course. A poor bookseller I'd be if I said no," said Mr. Chaffanbrass, placing his hands on his stomach and chortling.

"Thanks. I'll be off, then."

"Wrapped?"

"No," said Lenox. "I need something to read straight away."

324 | Charles Finch

"As you please," said Mr. Chaffanbrass, taking a short stub of pencil from his breast pocket, opening a ledger, and making a small tick. "On your bill, then?"

"Graham will be around on the fifteenth."

"No doubt of it. I set my calendar by him!"

He said this with satisfaction and then shook Lenox's hand with great vigor, getting redder and redder and smiling furiously. After this brief ceremony he sat down again with a sigh and took his book up, groping with his other hand for a piece of toast on the stovetop. He would burn himself sooner or later. As far as Lenox could tell, the bookseller's diet consisted of dozens of pieces of toast a day, each followed by a cup of milky coffee. Not the regimen recommended by the best physicians, perhaps, but it suited him.

On the street again, wet smoke clouded the air. The drizzle continued. It had been a beautiful late summer until then, but perhaps they were in for a wet September, he thought. It would be too bad. He looked back across the street toward his brightly lit house and saw his carriage waiting, the horses occasionally stamping their feet and the driver huddled underneath a thick black coat to keep the rain off, with only a pipe protruding out of the coat's hood, its ember occasionally brightening to orange. Lenox dodged another cab and stepped into the carriage, and with a word to the driver he was on his way to meet his brother.

And while he was looking forward to lunch—and while he took pleasure in examining his new book—he could not rid himself of the question he had been asking himself for weeks, as well as that entire morning: How on God's green earth was he supposed to ask one of his oldest friends, Lady Jane Grey, to be his wife?